HAPPY Singles DAY

ANN MARIE WALKER

sourcebooks
casablanca

Published by Sourcebooks Casablanca, an imprint of Sourcebooks
P.O. Box 4410, Naperville, Illinois 60567-4410
(630) 961-3900
sourcebooks.com

Library of Congress Cataloging-in-Publication Data is on file with the publisher.

Printed and bound in the United States of America.
SB 10 9 8 7 6 5 4 3 2 1

For all those brave enough to try again

CHAPTER 1

PAIGE PARKER DID NOT NEED a man.

She'd just told her assistant as much, but that didn't stop him from swiping through the photos he'd prescreened for her on some app that promised to find a date for even the loneliest of spinsters. Okay, maybe they didn't word it *exactly* like that. But the home page featured a slightly overweight woman, typing on her computer while a cat sat perched on her lap. If Paige hadn't known better, she'd have thought they snuck into her apartment to take the photo. Even the woman's hair color was the same shade of auburn as hers. Of course, she would never have seen the site if it weren't for her assistant, let alone opened an account. One of the hazards of having an employee with access to your driver's license and credit card who also happened to be your meddling, though well-intentioned, best friend.

Speak of the devil...

He said nothing in reply to her proclamation. Instead, he merely pursed his lips into a frown.

"Present company excluded," she added. And it was true. If there was anything or anyone Paige couldn't live without, it was Samuel Lee, her assistant since the first day she'd opened Chaos Control. Although she hated to admit it, her dream of running a successful life-organization company would never have been possible without his hard work and dedication. If only he would stop trying to apply those same skills to resuscitating her long-dead social life.

Sammy sat a little taller in his chair.

"While I appreciate the exception, what if you wanted a man with more to offer than an uncanny ability to anticipate your every need? What if you wanted a little S-E-X?" He cocked his head to one side so dramatically, his jet-black hair would have fallen across his forehead had it not been gelled to perfection. "Come to think of it, that talent would be quite handy in the bedroom. But don't be getting any ideas." He waved his hand in the air as if to wipe the thought from her head. "This handsome exception plays for the other team." He tapped a few images, then swiped right. "Which leaves Mr. Rochester as the only other long-term relationship in your life, and last time I checked, dating your cat is frowned upon in most states."

"Thanks for clarifying." Paige rolled her eyes even though she knew he wouldn't see. He was far too busy humming over the next batch of men who had appeared on the screen.

"Well?" he said without looking up.

"I can have meaningless sex without being in a relationship. Men do it all the time." Except she wasn't. And she hadn't. Not for a long time.

He laughed a little too hard for her liking. "Right. And how's that working out for you?"

She straightened. "Fine."

"Fine?" Sammy knew the long hours she put in at the office, which didn't leave much time for life's more, um, carnal pleasures. Not unless she wanted a quickie at midnight, and to be honest, most nights she just wanted her fuzzy slippers and a glass of wine. Still, she didn't need him to shine a light on it.

Paige picked a nonexistent piece of lint off the sleeve of her ivory silk blouse. "Yes. Fine."

"What if you want more than fine? What if instead of a glass of wine and a tub of ice cream, you wanted a big O?"

She felt a warm flush creep across her cheeks. What in the world was wrong with her? It wasn't like she was a teenager. She was thirty flipping years old, and her assistant had made her blush just referencing an orgasm.

He grew serious, and all at once she knew what was coming.

"What if you wanted a family?"

"I don't," she said matter-of-factly. Why was it that people assumed every woman in her thirties was pining for kids? Was it so hard to believe that someone was happy with her work and her friends? Not that she had time for many of those, come to think of it. But she had her career and Mr. Rochester, and he was always happy to see her. Well, mostly. In fact, usually only if he was hungry, but still.

"Hypothetically, what if you did? Those eggs aren't getting any younger, you know."

She frowned. Lack of desire to trade in her pencil skirts for mom jeans aside, no woman liked to be reminded of her ticking clock. Ever since her birthday, it had rolled around in her brain like a grenade with the pin pulled out. Even if she felt no urge to use her ovaries, the thought of them shriveling up into prunes wasn't a pleasant one. There was still plenty of time to change her mind, and if she *was* suddenly hit with an inexplicable change of heart, she didn't need a man to procreate. Well, she did, but not in the way Sammy was implying. "Hypothetically," she said, leveling the full weight of her I'm-a-badass-businesswoman stare at him, "I could go to a sperm bank."

He raised one brow. "Uptight much?"

"I just don't need to be harassed into a dating life I neither want nor need." It wasn't like she didn't know what she was missing. She'd had all that and more. Hell, three years ago she'd even had a ring and a wedding date. But then she came home early one night to find her boss/best friend riding her betrothed like a bronco at the state fair. It was one of those moments in life where you can either wither up and die or come out swinging. Paige chose the latter. She tossed him out, quit her job, opened her own company, and never looked back. Problem was, she never slowed down either.

"What you *need* is a vacation. Someplace where you can let your hair down out of that supertight bun and cut loose a little."

Cutting loose was not in Paige's vocabulary. Order and control were the keys to happiness. They were the principles that had guided her through life and the ones that led her to becoming a certified organization professional.

"You do realize my entire existence is about the opposite?" She glanced around her immaculate office. From the bleached oak floors to the white, midcentury-modern sofa to the glossy white filing cabinets lining the wall beneath rows of glass shelves, every-thing was clean lines and clean space. Not that she didn't enjoy color and texture. Colorful blown glass dotted the shelves, and strategically placed throw pillows in various hues of red flanked both ends of the couch. But the overall look was simple. She had certainly worked with clients who preferred things a bit more shabby chic, but when it came to her own personal taste, the expression "Less is more" fit her to a T. Less clutter, less hoarding, less crap.

She reached for the mug of tea sitting on a coaster atop her desk. Like the rest of her furniture, the desk was minimalist in design, comprised only of a single piece of beveled-edge glass supported by polished chrome legs. Some might say it was imprac-tical, but it suited her just fine. Drawers served as a means to stash items that really didn't need to be that accessible. Her desk was a place for action items, not to stockpile Post-it notes and paper clips.

"Oh!" Sammy's exuberance should have served as a warning, but to be honest, nothing could have prepared Paige for what came out of his mouth next. "I once read this book where a woman went to a secret sex island."

Paige sputtered and coughed. "You're joking?" she said as she wiped tea from her chin. But even as she asked the question, she knew he wasn't. The glimmer in his eyes told her he absolutely had read a book about some erotic version of *Fantasy Island*, and what's more, he'd loved every minute of it.

"Total anonymity for three days." The tone of his voice was half that of someone revealing a dark secret and half of someone hatching a fabulous plan. "*Anything* goes." His fingers flew across the tablet screen. "I wonder if a place like that actually exists."

"Let me save you some time. No way."

His shoulders sagged. "How about Vegas then? It's a bit of a cliché—what happens there stays there and all that—but desperate times call for mediocre measures."

"You've lost your mind." Paige rounded the desk and tugged his shirtsleeve. "Now get out of my office so one of us can actually get some work done."

His sad-puppy eyes nearly broke through her resolve, but Paige held her ground, hitting him with a compliment she knew would ease the pain of being thrown out. "Nice scarf, by the way."

"Isn't it fabulous? I got it in France last year." His wide grin faded. "I know what you're up to, and don't think for a minute that you can distract me with flattery," he said as she herded him toward the door. "I'm not letting this go. You need a vacation, Boss Lady. I've worked for you for nearly three years, and you've never taken one. Time to take off those Jimmy Choos and walk barefoot in the sand."

Paige scowled at him as she shut the door, but her confident strut slowed with each step, and by the time she'd made it back to her desk, she could do nothing but collapse into a chair that was designed for anything but lounging. Sammy was right. She needed a vacation. The days and nights had started to blur together to the point that she was seriously considering an investment in day-of-the-week underpants if for no other reason than to keep track of her personal hygiene.

But there was work to be done: new clients to meet with,

existing clients to satisfy, and an entire file of new promotional ideas that had been on the back burner so long they were no doubt starting to congeal. Not that it mattered much. Business was good. Really good. So good, in fact, that she really didn't need to spend much time on marketing. Word of mouth was taking care of that just fine. Of course, that was only going to continue if she stopped thinking about vacations on sandy beaches where she'd have time to actually read a whole book and not just the Goodreads summary.

She shook her head to clear it of the thoughts that, thanks to her assistant, had begun taking root, and booted up her laptop. But when she launched the browser, a headline caught her eye that completely distracted her from the hunt for the perfect shoe cubes.

Couples Have Valentine's Day, Single People Have SAD

The unfortunate acronym was like her own personal catnip, eliciting a curiosity that was a mixture of defensive amusement, and before she knew it, Paige had read the entire article. In the end she'd learned this: Singles Appreciation Day began as a protest to a holiday many saw as nothing more than a nod to consumerism, raking in money for jewelry stores, candymakers, and greeting-card companies, while also serving as an affront to those who were alone, whether out of choice or circumstance. The article went on to say that millions of people have begun celebrating February 15th instead, opting for shopping sprees, spa days, and even solo getaways.

The author also noted that the number of divorced or

never-married adults in the United States now exceeded those in wedlock. Paige would have taken a moment to ponder that last bit of information—not to mention how the word *lock* came to be synonymous with eternal love—if it weren't for an ad promising to find her "the perfect Singles Day vacation destination" if she answered a mere three-question survey.

For the most part, Paige hated the targeted marketing that popped up whenever she was online, but she had to admit, this one intrigued her. And while she doubted a rental site would know what she needed more than she did, her curiosity about what questions they would ask outweighed her disdain for falling prey to clickbait. Besides, if she was going to take a vacation, emphasis on *if*, what better holiday to celebrate than Singles Day, which—she glanced at the date displayed on her desk phone—was only a week away.

She tapped the "Find your dream vacation now" button, which took her to the three-question survey. The first one nearly had her closing out the tab.

What is your astrological sign?

Paige never understood how the date of someone's birth was supposed to offer insight into their personality. She knew plenty of people who shared birthdays and yet couldn't be more different if they tried. And while she did have many of the characteristics of a Capricorn—practical, stable, loyal—her ex-fiancé had been born under the same earth sign and was none of the above, especially when it came to loyalty.

Still, *in for a penny, in for pound*, she thought, clicking the picture of the sea goat. She took a sip of her tea as the next question loaded.

Which Disney character do you most identify with?

Paige groaned, already wondering if this meant all quiz results led to Orlando, when she suddenly realized that all of the options were female. And more than that, all of them were princesses. And not even the complete set! She scrolled through the choices in search of the fierce, gender-defying Mulan, but when she couldn't find her on the list, had to settle for the Little Mermaid. At least she and Ariel both had red hair and loved the ocean, which was a lot more than she had in common with Snow White or Cinderella.

The final question was the most difficult to answer.

What annoys you the most?

The options were varied and yet, in Paige's opinion, each and every one deserved a click: waiting in line, slow internet, screaming children, crowds, group texts, traffic. She'd finally decided on traffic when she reached another conclusion as well: she was way too uptight. Sammy's words from not ten minutes before played through her head just as her "dream destination" loaded.

"The Copper Lantern Inn" was printed in intricate scroll across the top of the screen with a quote from a magazine she'd never heard of that described it as having "one of the best beaches on the Outer Banks."

She snorted quietly to herself. Must have been quite the algorithm, she thought, sending her to North Carolina in the middle of February. Not exactly prime beach weather. Then again, with her alabaster skin, she wasn't really much of a sun worshipper. Plus, the beaches would be quite empty this time of year. No crowds, no kids kicking sand or screaming because they didn't want to come out of the water to have more sunscreen applied. Maybe it would be the ideal place for her because, aside from chilly temperatures, the place looked absolutely perfect.

Cedar shingles covered what could only be described as a cross between a Victorian home and a European castle. The lawn in the front looked like something out of an old black-and-white TV show, impeccably manicured right down to the freshly painted white picket fence. But it was the photo of the rear of the house that took Paige's breath away. Rocking chairs faced tall seagrass that swelled and dipped atop dunes that stretched along white-capped waves for as far as the eye could see.

For a moment, she imagined herself wrapped up in a cashmere blanket, reading a book that had nothing to do with maximizing floor space and everything to do with escapism romance. Not that she believed in those types of happy endings, not anymore at least. But there was something about getting lost in a fictional world where love conquered all—and where the girl always came first—that she still found appealing if not a little comforting.

A barefoot paradise awaits you at the Copper Lantern Inn, a quaint, castle-like beach home fit for a queen. Featuring three unique guest rooms, a common room, and a porch overlooking a mile of secluded beach, the Inn offers one of the best views on Aurelia Island while still being only a short bike ride from town.

Normally, the mention of self-powered transportation would have given Paige a moment's pause, but she was far too focused on the name of the island to give much thought to the coordination it would take to maneuver a bicycle after a dinner that would undoubtedly be accompanied by a bottle of chardonnay.

Aurelia. Her grandmother's name. The woman who taught her how to play, and cheat, at Rummy 500, who reminded her to stand up straight and put her shoulders back because "If you got it, flaunt it," and who always told her that having no man was better than the wrong man.

It was a sign. It had to be. As if Granny was still looking out for her from the great, big kitchen in the sky.

Paige scrolled through the room options, settling on the one in the inn's turret, then clicked the tab that read "extras."

Champagne and roses

Nope.

Romantic beachfront fire

Nope.

Special occasion cake

She was about to scroll past that one as well, then paused, a devious smile curving her lips as she imagined placing an order for a cake that read "Happy Singles Day."

Paige hit a button on her desk phone, and a moment later Sammy was standing in the doorway. "You rang?"

"You could have just answered the intercom," she said.

"And miss out on a chance to add a few steps?" He held up his arm to reveal the ever-present Fitbit he wore wrapped around his left wrist. He was always on her to purchase one, telling her how they could have challenges. And while a part of her feared her competitive streak would have her walking laps around the office building, another part of her knew she spent far too much time in front of her computer. Maybe she would add one of the blasted devices to her packing list. Beaches were a great place to walk and think and kick your assistant's ass in a virtual race.

"Do me a favor and pick me up one of those tracking devices while you're at lunch today." She delighted in the look of utter shock that crossed Sammy's face, knowing full well that what she was about to say next would have his jaw hitting the floor.

Paige leaned back in her chair. "And clear my schedule for next week," she said as her assistant's mouth popped open. "I'm taking a vacation."

CHAPTER 2

LUCAS CROFT KNEW WHEN HE was being played, which was why he would have bet his last dollar on the fact that the woman sitting across from him was about to hit him with a whopper. Lucky for her, they shared the same DNA.

"Are you going to get to the point, or will there be more chitchat first?" he said.

His little sister's hazel eyes grew wide, but her feigned shock was no match for experience. Ever since they were kids, she'd been roping him into her crazy plans. He'd figured she would eventually outgrow it, but seeing as she'd just celebrated what she referred to as her twenty-ninth trip around the sun, that was looking less and less likely.

He leaned back in his chair and crossed his arms over his chest. "I know you're up to something, Smalls. Why don't you save us both the warm-up and just spit it out."

Her face scrunched up like she'd just sucked on the lemon dangling off the side of her herbal tea. "You know I hate that nickname."

"And you know I hate being dragged into your plans." Despite his best efforts to the contrary, Lucas couldn't help the smirk of amusement that tugged at the corner of his mouth. His sister might have been a complete pain in the ass, but her heart was always in the right place. Still, her ideas were usually a little eccentric and, if they involved him, often downright wacko. Like the time when she was seven and he was ten and she hatched a plan for them to run off to Antarctica to save some rare breed of penguin. He'd been grounded for a month over that one! Or when she convinced him to help her turn the old fire station into a used bookstore. The long nights painting the walls had been bad enough, but lugging all those books was worse than even the most punishing day in the gym. Although to be fair, that idea had actually turned out fairly well. After five years, Blazing Books was staying afloat, which was more than he could say for his own business venture.

Sophie lifted her chin in defiance. "Maybe I just wanted to see my big brother. Ever think of that, Mr. Smarty Pants?" Between her size—five foot two on a good day—and her pixie haircut, his sister was always being mistaken for a college student. Her insults, on the other hand, were one hundred percent middle school.

Lucas's smirk widened into a full-on grin. "You expect me to believe you closed the bookstore for an hour in the middle of the day just because you felt the overwhelming urge to buy your brother a blueberry muffin and a shot of espresso?"

She squirmed in her seat, a surefire tell if there ever was one. "I know they're your favorite. Besides, Maddie loves this place."

On instinct, Lucas's gaze shifted to where his four-year-old daughter was busy drawing rainbows on a pint-sized chalkboard.

As usual, she'd assembled the three stuffed animals that accompanied her most everywhere into a makeshift classroom. Lord only knew what she was teaching them today, but whatever it was had her smiling, and that was all that mattered despite the fact that they were a motley crew of fluff. There was Floppy, a long-eared rabbit from her very first Easter basket who was now missing his cotton tail; Stanley, half an avocado with a smiley face that was a gift from who else but the dork currently seated across from him; and a well-loved, pink-and-white teddy bear named Stinky. His name wasn't actually Stinky, but that's what Lucas had vowed to call him until Maddie relented and allowed the bear to take a bath in the "spinning machine."

"No fair using the kid to get you off the hot seat." He leaned forward and placed his elbows on the table. "Now spill. What are you up to?"

"Okay, fine." Sophie looked down, fiddling with the spoon, the napkin, the lemon—anything to keep from meeting his stare. "I *may* have reactivated the listing on the rental site."

Cute little sister or not, she had no right to reactivate the listing on his now-dormant bed-and-breakfast. It might have been his business, at least at one point, but it was also his home. This was crossing the line, even for her.

"Take it down."

She winced. "I already booked one of the rooms for next week."

If his daughter hadn't been within earshot, Lucas would have let Sophie have it. As it was, he was in danger of grinding his molars into dust.

"Look, I know you haven't hosted guests in a while, but it will be like riding a bike. Once you get going, it will all come back to you."

There was a litany of reasons why this was a bad idea, the most glaring of which was the fact that the place wasn't even close to being ready for guests, but he chose to focus on the most immediate one.

"Maddie won't like it."

"You don't know that."

"She was two the last time a guest stayed in the house. She doesn't even remember that lifestyle."

"She was almost three," Sophie corrected. "Your daughter is a lot more open to new experiences than you give her credit for, and unlike her dad, she actually likes meeting new people." Her words came quickly, no doubt an attempt to cut off his protests. "Besides, you don't have to worry about Maddie. She can stay with me."

"For a whole week?" He shook his head. "No way."

His sister looked genuinely hurt. "Maddie loves spending time with me."

"Yeah, for an afternoon, maybe a day here or there, but she's never been away from me that long." He tried to soften his objection with a little levity. "Plus, a whole week of glitter nail polish and ice cream before dinner?"

"It's not like you won't be seeing her every day. It's just so you can have the flexibility to get stuff done. And you should be thanking me. If it weren't for me, the poor thing wouldn't have even known what a skirt was, let alone tights."

"And that would have been a bad thing?" As far as he was

concerned, Maddie could stay a little girl in blue jeans and pigtails forever.

"I'm serious, Luc. I love spending time with my niece. Plus, it's good for her to have a female in her life, and since apparently the idea of actually asking a woman on a date is out of the question…"

He shot her a look he knew could freeze lava in hell. "Not this again." They'd been over the topic so many times he'd lost count. There weren't many women on the island to begin with, and by the time you weeded out the ones who were too old or too young, there wasn't much left. Not that he was in the market. *Love* was a four-letter word as far as he was concerned. "So help me, if you're about to tell me yet again how much Susan at the bank thinks I look like Ryan Reynolds—"

"Settle down, Cujo." Sophie held up her hands in innocence. "I wasn't even going to mention Susan." She stuck her tongue out. "Personally, I think you look more like Ryan Reynolds in *Deadpool*, but hey, to each their own. All I'm saying is that Maddie could benefit from a week of frills and glitter."

"She's fine. We both are." His voice lowered. "Plus, what if she has a nightmare?" It had been months since the last time Maddie had woken screaming his name, but the sound of her little voice quivering in fear was permanently ingrained in his mind, not to mention his heart. If she woke up looking for him and he wasn't there…

"Then you can FaceTime and sing that silly song she loves, and if that doesn't work, you could be at my place in less than ten."

Ten minutes away from a frightened four-year-old was ten minutes too long. The doctor said she would outgrow it, that as the memories of losing her mom faded, so would the night-mares she'd been having about losing her dad. It was a double-edged sword really. As much as he wanted his daughter to have a peaceful night's sleep, the thought of her mother fading from her memories was almost harder to bear than Maddie's screams.

"Or I could skip the late-night ride and she can just stay home and we can forget this whole thing." Lucas began to stand, but Sophie's next words stopped him in his tracks.

"I got double the summer rate."

"What did you just say?"

"You heard me."

"How the hell did you manage that?" No one paid double the summer rate in summer, let alone the dead of winter.

"I may have told her there was a man from Louisiana who came back every year to see the sea turtles."

"You spoke to her?" He wasn't sure what made him ask because at the moment, the fact that his sister was chatting with potential customers was the least of his concerns.

"We messaged through the site."

Lucas ran his hand through his hair. "Turtle season ends in August."

Her ears turned pink. Tell number two. "I may have fudged the dates a bit."

"And the place doesn't look at all like the website photos anymore." That was the understatement of the century. It wasn't like he'd meant for it to get so out of hand, but after the funeral, he'd focused all his attention on Maddie. Then one day slipped into the next, and before he knew it, even he had to admit it was a mess.

"Yeah, I may not have mentioned that either."

"What *did* you tell her?"

"That it was tranquil."

More like deserted.

"Good news is she booked the turret room," Sophie said as if reading his mind. Not that it mattered. There was only one guest room left. The others had been...repurposed.

"You know I haven't had a booking since..." A profound sadness crept into his heart like ink seeping into parchment.

"I know." Her voice had grown softer. "But the last thing she would want is for you to lose the inn. It meant so much to both of you. And with the taxes coming due..."

There it was, the truth he couldn't deny. Death and taxes, the two inevitabilities in life. One had rocked his world, and the other was threatening to clear away the rubble.

The cash from Jenny's life insurance policy had covered their mortgage and living expenses for the last two years, but that account was dwindling quickly. He had enough for about three more months—which, if he *was* going to reopen, would get him to the summer season—but not for the full tax bill as well. He and Jenny had poured their hearts and souls, not to mention every dime they had, into their little beachfront castle. The thought of running it without her brought the emotions he tried his best to bury right up to the surface. But the thought of selling it—or even worse, having it taken away by the county—would be like losing her all over again.

A week's rental at double the summer rate would certainly buy him the time he needed to figure out his next steps, not to mention get his little sister off his back.

Lucas pressed his lips into a thin line, then let out an exaggerated breath. "Fine. I'll take the booking."

Sophie clapped her hands together. "That's great!"

"What's great?" Maddie asked. Her dark-brown curls swayed as she skipped toward the table.

"Your dad just agreed to let you sleep over at my house for a few nights."

His little girl's eyes grew wide. "Like a slumber party?"

Sophie smiled. "Exactly like a slumber party." She cocked her head to one side. "Except it's not much of a party if it's only the two of us. Can you think of anyone else we can invite?"

"Stanley would love to come," Maddie said. "So would Floppy and Raymond," she added, referring to Stinky by his given name.

Shocker, Lucas thought. But there was no denying the warmth that spread through his chest at the sight of his daughter so happy.

"Then definitely bring them." Sophie pulled her niece into her lap, then turned her attention back to Lucas. "Want me to come by tonight to help you tidy the place up a bit?"

It would take a hell of a lot more than a little "tidying" to make the place presentable. For a moment, he almost felt guilty about that. But then he thought about the kind of uptight woman who would pay double just to beat out some imaginary schmuck looking for turtles in winter, and all thoughts of Southern hospitality left him. "No thanks," he said. "I am who I am. If my guest doesn't like it"—he narrowed his eyes at his sister—"she can message her host."

CHAPTER 3

PAIGE REALIZED SHE'D MADE A terrible mistake the moment she stepped off the ferry. The tiny hairs on the back of her neck stood at attention the way they always did when she was making the wrong move, but that wasn't even the most obvious sign that disaster loomed ahead of her. No, it was the enormous dark clouds that had suddenly shrouded the whole marina like a blanket of doom and gloom.

She should have hightailed it back to the mainland right then and there, but the room at the inn was prepaid and she'd flown all the way to North Carolina. Last thing she wanted was more time in an airport. Besides, snuggling up on a rocking chair, watching the storm move across the ocean while wrapped in a blanket and sipping herbal tea—or even better, a glass of chardonnay—might be just as nice as walking the beach. But first, she needed to get to the inn.

She pulled out her smartphone and opened the Uber app. Nothing. Not a single car anywhere on the digital grid.

What the...

She glanced around for a taxi stand. Again, nothing.

"Excuse me," she called out to a man loading the last of his fishing gear into a wagon-like device he had hitched to his bicycle. "Can you tell me where I can grab a cab?"

The man looked around and chuckled. "Raleigh maybe?"

Paige frowned, and the man's laugh grew deeper. "Just come in on the ferry?" he asked as he sauntered closer. He had a kind face, weathered from lack of sunscreen but in a way that made his eyes crinkle when he smiled.

She nodded toward the suitcase at her feet. "Pretty obvious, huh?"

"Not too many tourists this time of year." He took off his red cap and wiped his brow with the back of his hand before shoving the hat squarely back on his head. "But the ones we do get usually know there's no cars on the island."

Paige's mouth dropped open. "No cars?" Guess that's what she got for choosing traffic as the thing that annoyed her the most.

"Nope. That's the charm of Aurelia." His deep voice switched into a singsong. "Trade the hustle and bustle for the charm of a simpler time." No doubt he'd just recounted some sort of Department of Tourism slogan. Too bad Paige was only just now hearing it for the first time.

"In season, the bike rental shop is open," he continued. "They usually have a stand set up to greet the ferry. But in February..."

Good to know. Even her unspoken words were dripping with sarcasm because none of that information did anything to help her immediate predicament.

"Where ya headed?" the man asked.

"Copper Lantern Inn."

His brows shot up so high they were practically under his cap.

Paige was about to ask him about his reaction when he caught her off guard with an offer she wanted to refuse but couldn't.

"Tell you what," he said. "Load that bag of yours on top of my gear, and I'll drop you by on my way home."

For a moment, she thought he planned to pedal her to the inn on his handlebars like they were a couple of ten-year-olds, but then he wheeled the bike toward her, revealing a sidecar. On a bike. This day really couldn't get any worse, she thought as she used a bungee cord to strap her Louis Vuitton bag on top of a rusty tackle box.

But when she reached the inn, she knew her assessment had been premature. She also knew why her chauffeur had reacted the way he did when she told him where she was staying. To put it bluntly, the place was a dump.

From a distance, the outside of the inn looked pretty much the same as it had on the website. Aside from the fact that the bright-yellow shingles now looked a bit faded and two shutters hung slightly askew, it was still the epitome of beachfront charm. But as she drew closer, she noted that the manicured lawn was comprised of more weeds than grass and the white picket fence was now a shade of dingy beige, thanks to being weathered to nearly bare wood.

Paige took a deep breath. She wasn't planning to be out front much anyway. As long as the back porch still had rocking chairs and a view of the ocean, she'd be just fine.

Famous last words.

Determined, she made her way up the porch steps, careful to avoid a nearly rotted tread. But when she reached the front door, she hesitated. Do you knock at a bed-and-breakfast? Granted, it was a type of hotel, but it was also someone's home. What was the protocol?

"Go on in," her chauffeur called out as if reading her mind. "Lucas is probably out back."

She walked through the leaded-glass door and came to an abrupt halt. The website had used words like *quaint, charming,* and *picturesque,* but the adjectives ricocheting around Paige's head as she took in the sight of the front room were more along the lines of *cluttered, disgusting,* and *unsightly.*

Clothes were strewn about on every piece of upholstered furniture, while dirty plates and cups sat piled on the flat surfaces. And dear Lord, was that peanut butter on the banister? Her eyes were drawn to the back of the house, where a wall of French doors revealed the seagrass swells that led to the white-capped waves. At least the ocean was as advertised, because the rest of the place certainly wasn't. With the exception of being quiet, nothing was as she expected, but even that would have more appropriately been described as desolate.

"Can I help you?"

She turned around, ready to give her would-be host a piece of her mind, but at the sight of him, all thoughts of the pigpen left her because holy macaroni, the pig himself looked more like a freaking movie star than a swine. And there he stood, barely a foot in front of her, wearing nothing but a pair of faded jeans and a few days' worth of stubble. With his chiseled jaw, light-brown hair, and warm hazel eyes, he was a dead ringer for... What was that guy's name? Damn, she should have paid more attention to Sammy's screen savers because whoever this guy's doppelgänger was, he'd definitely been featured as Mr. October. But unlike the hot dude on Sammy's tablet, the man before her didn't have eyes that sparkled when he smiled. Well, maybe they did, but it was impossible to tell, because at the moment Mr. Look-Alike was sporting a brooding frown.

"I'm looking for Mr. Croft."

"I'm Lucas Croft."

Paige wasn't sure what she had been expecting an innkeeper to look like, but this guy wasn't it. He looked more like the hot-as-hell neighborhood handyman on some sort of *Desperate Housewives* reboot. Sammy was right. She really needed to watch less television and spend more time with actual humans.

"Paige Parker." She stuck out her hand. "From Chicago." When her introduction drew no reaction, let alone an extended hand, she added, "I have a reservation."

He yanked a T-shirt out of the back pocket of his jeans and pulled it over his head. "Guess that would explain why you just let yourself into my house," he said as his face poked through the neck hole.

"The man on the bike said..."

"It's fine." He let out a sigh that was about as far from welcoming as she could imagine. "You're paying enough to waltz in like you own the joint."

So much for Southern hospitality. Lucas Croft was crusty with a capital C.

"Your room is at the top of the stairs, first door on the right. Don't even think about going into any of the others. You're the only guest, but that doesn't mean you have the run of the whole place."

Forget crusty, this guy was downright rude. He sounded more like a drill sergeant giving her a tour of the barracks than the owner of a bed-and-breakfast greeting a guest. And not just any guest either, but the *only* guest apparently. *No surprise there*, she thought, nearly snorting out loud. She could hardly imagine people were beating down the door to get in. Well, not people who'd taken a minute to do their due diligence anyway.

"The bathroom is first come, first served, but keep the hot-water use to under ten minutes or I'll turn it off from down here."

She'd barely processed his threat when he motioned for her to follow him down the short hallway to the kitchen. "Dinner is served at six. If you miss it, you're on your own. Tonight will be pizza and salad." He opened the fridge door and pulled out a bag of what had once been mixed field greens, but was now more of a liquid, and wrinkled his nose. "Make that just pizza."

He launched the bag toward a trash can with a mildly impressive hook shot that would no doubt have been a three-pointer had the can not already been overflowing.

Frozen pizza served in a pigsty by a guy who made even her dirtbag ex-fiancé look like a pretty friendly guy? No thanks.

"You know, I think I'll pass. In fact, I'm going to take a hard pass on all of this." Her eyes darted around the room. "Nothing is the way it looked online."

"You're leaving?"

The hopeful lilt in his tone was impossible to miss. So was the satisfied smirk tugging at the corner of his mouth. *Jerk*. Well, he wasn't getting the better of her. No, sir.

Paige squared her shoulders. "I am."

Mr. Look-Alike leaned against the kitchen counter and folded his arms across his chest, which did crazy things to his already bulging biceps. *Don't stare*, Paige thought. She dropped her gaze in an attempt not to ogle but only ended up with her eyes locked on another impressive bulge. Holy hell, she needed to leave before she started drooling like some horny version of Pavlov's dog.

Her would-be host let out a condescending chuckle. "Good luck with that." He looked so damn smug and yet so unbelievably hot. It was an infuriating combination.

"I'll be fine." At the moment, even a night spent in the airport sounded like an upgrade. "And, rest assured, I will be filing a complaint with the booking website." Her tone matched the one she used with vendors when they didn't deliver on time, but unlike them, Lucas seemed totally unfazed. His only reaction was a casual shrug.

"Suit yourself."

Gah! She was so frustrated she nearly cried, and Paige Parker *never* cried. Not over sappy commercials, not when she broke her arm, and certainly not over this loser. The burning sensation she felt creeping over her cheeks was no doubt giving him a hint, but the last thing she wanted was for him to know how much he was affecting her. She had to get out of there. Fast.

Paige jerked up the handle of her bag and, with a sound meant to convey her disgust, turned toward the door. She was down the stairs and across the street before she remembered that this time she didn't have a ride. The distance to the harbor seemed a lot longer on foot, a fact that was made worse by the ever-increasing rumbles of thunder that grew closer with every clap. But the splattering of raindrops that pelted her face wasn't the worst thing to greet her as she arrived at the ferry office. That honor went to the CLOSED sign hanging from a nail on the office door.

Oh, hell no.

A light glowed from a window above the office. With any luck, it was the captain's residence. All she had to do was offer him enough money to make it worth his while, and she'd be on her way. She clomped up the wooden stairs and knocked, wiping water from her face while she waited for an answer. When the door opened, she breathed a sigh of relief. "Thank God you're home." A bolt of lightning zigzagged through the charcoal sky. "I need a ride back to the mainland."

The man shook his head. "We're closed, ma'am."

"Name your price."

He laughed. "Mother Nature doesn't care about money." He nodded to where the ferry was rocking against the dock. "We're closed until the storm passes."

A gust of wind blew up the edges of Paige's skirt. She was able to get her hands in front of her à la Marilyn Monroe on the subway grate, but had there been anyone behind her, they would no doubt have gotten an eyeful. "I thought hurricane season was in the fall," she said as she struggled to hold down her skirt.

"Not a hurricane, ma'am. It's a nor'easter. Turned our way at the last minute, and it's picking up steam. Won't be back up and running for a few days, I reckon."

He started to close the door. Paige reached out to keep it from closing, losing the battle with one half of her skirt.

"A few days?" she squeaked.

"Maybe day after tomorrow." He squinted at the sky. "Depends on the winds. If you give me your number, I can call you once we're back in business."

Her shoulders fell. "Great. Thanks." She handed him one of her business cards and turned to leave.

"You really shouldn't be out in this."

If the guy's name wasn't Captain Obvious, he really should have considered changing it.

"Tell you what," he said. She looked back to see him taking a key off a nail beside the door. "Take my bike. Lord knows I won't be needing it until this passes." He handed her a key chain that had the words *North Carolina* printed in scroll beneath a smiling sun. Talk about irony. "It's the blue one at the foot of the stairs. Has a rack for your case too."

"Thanks." It was a kind gesture, but it hardly made a difference. The rain was coming down in sheets by the time she started to pedal back to the inn, and when she stepped onto the stone porch, her reflection in the glass door confirmed her suspicions: she looked like a drowned rat.

Perfect, she thought. Not only did she need to ask for her room back, but she had to do it with her hair plastered to her head and her sweater plastered to her boobs.

She raised her hand to knock, then lowered it. Screw him and his snarky "let yourself in" comment. She was a paying guest—the only guest, as a matter of fact. Damn right she'd let herself in.

But when she did, she immediately felt more like an intruder than a guest. From the next room, she could hear the owner of the inn speaking to someone, presumably on the phone since there weren't any other voices. Guest or not, it felt wrong. She was turning to make her way back to the porch when the sound of her name stopped her dead in her tracks.

"I don't know what to tell you," he said. "Ms. Paige Parker from Chicago was a certified pain in the ass."

Pain in the ass? While under some circumstances that might have been an accurate description—although personally she preferred to think of herself as a dedicated perfectionist—people usually had to spend a lot more than five minutes with her to reach that conclusion. What the hell was he basing it on, the fact that she objected to accommodations with peanut butter on the banister?

As if on instinct, Paige stepped away from the stair railing. When she did, she nearly bumped into a tall curio cabinet. *Ugh.* Paige loathed curios. All that clutter on display in a glass case? Just the thought sent a shiver across her damp skin. But this one wasn't filled with the kinds of knickknacks she would normally have expected to find on display. No china cups or crystal statues. No thimbles or tiny silver spoons. Not even a pewter mug. Instead, the cabinet held a few dirty baseballs with illegible names scribbled above the seams, more seashells than you could collect in a month of beachcombing, and large chunks of driftwood.

Her scrutiny was interrupted by yet another derogatory declaration from her would-be host. "Good riddance to her and her overpriced luggage." The disdain in his voice was impossible to miss, and although she couldn't see him, Paige could picture the deep crease that was no doubt furrowing his brow. The image brought her a surprising amount of satisfaction. So did the thought of her plan to demand a refund from the booking agency based on false advertisement.

"Nice try, Soph," he said. "Need I remind you that this is all your fault?"

Soph...short for Sophie? Wasn't that the name of the woman Paige had been messaging on the rental site?

A beat of silence was followed by an exasperated noise that was half chuckle, half snort. "Oh no, no way I'm letting you pin this on me, Sis. You were the one who reactivated the listing, without bothering to ask my permission, I might add."

Well, that would certainly explain the fact that the place was far from "guest ready."

Paige eased forward, sliding her foot across the floorboard in an effort to keep the wood from creaking beneath her. She poked her head around the doorframe and stole a glance at Lucas Croft, reluctant innkeeper. He had his back to her, affording her a longer glimpse. With his broad shoulders and narrow waist, he was quite the sight for sore eyes, not to mention a waterlogged body. It had been months—okay, okay, more like years—since Paige had felt the press of warm skin against hers. Given her current state of near-hypothermia, climbing under a duvet with a hard, male body sounded like absolute heaven, and if there was one thing Lucas Croft had, it was a hard, male body. Every inch of him looked like an ad for a twenty-four-hour gym. Add to that the movie-star face and he was practically perfect.

Until he opened his mouth.

And what the hell was that actor's name anyway? It would come to her eventually, probably in the middle of the night if history was any indication, but until then, it would nag at the corners of her mind.

Paige tilted her head to one side. Despite the fact that part of her wanted to climb him like a tree, another part of her, the one that thought with her intuition instead of her lady parts, couldn't help but notice the tension that racked his frame. The tightness in his muscles was unmistakable—from the way he held the phone to how he shifted his weight—and when he spoke again, the same strain laced his words.

"Don't you think I know that?" His shoulders sagged in a resigned exhale. "Look, I'll figure something out. There's still a few weeks until the payment is due." He let out a quiet laugh, but there was an undeniable sadness in his voice. "If I don't, then I don't. Maybe it will be for the best. I'm not exactly the perfect host these days."

That was the understatement of the century. Still, as a small-business owner, she could definitely relate. She hated the thought of anyone losing their business, but even more so when that business was also where they lived. Even crusty jerks deserved a place to call home. And yet for some reason, the sorrow she heard seemed to be about a much greater loss. It was ridiculous, really. She knew nothing about this man, aside from the fact that he was a rude slob, yet somewhere inside her she felt a strange twinge of empathy.

Lucas pushed away from the counter. Paige nearly gasped aloud as she ducked back around the corner. Asking for her room back was going to be awkward enough, but it would be a lot worse if she had to do it after being busted for eavesdropping. She was inching her way back to the entryway when a frame in the curio cabinet caught her eye. It was tucked behind a piece of driftwood that had a heart shape carved into its rough, gray face. She peered around the side of the case for a better view of the photo. It was a picture of Lucas with his arm around a woman who was very clearly pregnant. They were standing in front of the inn, which looked even shabbier than it did now, smiling like fools and holding a real estate sign that had the word SOLD plastered across it in bright-red letters.

Dozens of questions popped into Paige's head, but before she had time to process a single one of them, she heard him ending the call.

Abandoning her inquisitive instincts for the time being, she hurried back to the front door and, after waiting a beat, opened and closed it before making her way into the kitchen.

"The ferry was closed," she said. Water still dripped from her hair. No doubt she'd left a puddle in the hallway. With any luck, he wouldn't think much of it.

Amusement lit his eyes as he looked her up and down, lingering a little longer than necessary where her soggy sweater hugged her curves. If she was honest with herself, she would have admitted she wasn't entirely displeased about that.

"So, you thought you'd come back here?" he asked.

She straightened in an attempt to muster what little pride she had left, but again, if she was really honest with herself, she would have admitted that wasn't the only reason. "Well, it *is* paid in full."

He stared at her, nonplussed. The bastard was actually going to make her ask. And just like that, his darkening stare lost its appeal. Okay, okay, not all of it, but still.

"I'm assuming you haven't rented the room?"

A smile tugged at the corner of his mouth, and for the first time, Paige noticed his lips. They were full and strong, and for a moment, she let herself imagine what they would feel like pressed against hers. Or maybe trailing down her neck, stopping to suck lightly on that spot just before her shoulder that never failed to make her knees go weak.

He cleared his throat, breaking the spell that had taken her out of his kitchen and into his bed. "As luck would have it, no."

"Great." Her cheeks felt hot again, but for an entirely different reason. Time to get the hell out of that kitchen. "I'll be out of your way in no time. Man at the dock said day after tomorrow."

Lucas laughed. "Guess you didn't check the weather while you were out?"

"Oddly enough, no." Her voice was laced with sarcasm. "Was too busy actually experiencing the weather to bother checking an app."

He moved a stack of bills to reveal a remote control. Paige tried not to gag as he wiped a bit of jelly off the edge before clicking on the television. A man was reporting from a beach in Wilmington. He was struggling to stand his ground against the raging winds, but his words came through loud and clear, and the news wasn't good. According to him, the National Weather Service had upgraded the storm, with bridges and ferries expected to be closed for most of the week.

Lucas turned his attention back to Paige, and a shiver racked her body. Problem was, she wasn't entirely sure if it had more to do with the temperature of her soaked skin or the intensity of his stare.

"Why don't you put some dry clothes on," he finally said. "And I'll whip us up some dinner." He yanked the freezer door open. "Pepperoni or sausage?"

"I'm a vegetarian."

"Sausage it is, then. Easier to pick off than pepperoni."

Paige said nothing. Instead she made her way up the stairs to the first room on the right, which thankfully looked like the room she'd booked. More or less. The carved wooden four-poster bed faced a turret of windows, just as it had in the photographs, and the overstuffed chair in the corner sat waiting with a cozy throw draped over one arm. The carefully arranged toss pillows were conspicuously absent, as was the vase of fresh flowers, but there was no sign of food remnants on any of the furniture, so all in all she considered it a win.

With a thud, Paige collapsed on the bed. As she did, a clap of thunder shook the house, which was the perfect punctuation to the realization that slammed into her head as it hit the pillow. She'd come to the island to celebrate the joys of being single, and yet for the foreseeable future she was stuck in a house that looked like the set of *Animal House* with a grumpy man who looked like he'd just walked off the cover of *Men's Fitness*.

And if that wasn't bad enough, there was always frozen pizza.

CHAPTER 4

LUCAS CROFT LIKED HIS LIFE exactly the way it was: simple and quiet. And if there was one surefire way to put an end to both of those, it was by having a woman in his home. He had his daughter and his sister, and that was all the estrogen he could handle. Because who needed a woman anyway? They nagged you to clean up your stuff, wanted the toilet seat put down, and expected the dishes to be done the same day the meal was cooked. No thanks.

And yet there he was, cleaning the dishes from the previous night's dinner. Granted, it wasn't technically the same day the meal was cooked, but it was within a twelve-hour window, which was bad enough. Reason number two hundred and twelve why playing host to the city lady was a terrible idea. Problem was, there were a few thousand reasons why it was a necessity, and they were all preceded by dollar signs.

He put the pizza pan in the rack to drain, and as he did, a satisfied grin crept over his face. At least he'd won the battle of the toilet seat. He'd just climbed into bed the night before when he'd heard her go into the hall bathroom. Moments later came the unmistakable cursing of a woman who'd just splashed into the bowl. Even now, the thought had him chuckling. It was her own damn fault, really. Why did women always assume the seat would be down? Maybe the default was up and they were being inconsiderate for always lowering it. Had they ever thought of that? Maybe it was his civic duty to men everywhere to start a new norm, leaving seats up all over town until the idea caught on. Then again, if he succeeded, a pain in the ass like his sister would probably organize some sort of protest march. He could only imagine the posters she'd have stapled to yardsticks. Hell, she'd probably knit some obnoxious toilet-seat hats for everyone to wear.

His phone vibrated against the kitchen counter, and he glanced at the screen. Speak of the devil. Lucas wiped his hands on a dish towel, then slung it over his shoulder. "Hey, Smalls."

"You know I hate that name," Sophie said after filling his ear with an exaggerated groan.

"And you know I hate it when you go behind my back." He paused to concede one small but significant point. "Even if it was because you were trying to save my ass."

"What's the penance?"

"Penance?" He couldn't help but smile. "Where did that come from?"

"What can I say? Some habits are hard to break."

"Twelve years of Catholic school, and the notion of penance is the only thing that stuck, huh?"

She made a sound that was more snort than laugh. "Well, that and the whole 'Thou shalt not kill.'"

"Sister Hildegarde would be so proud." He would have said his parents would have been proud, but bringing them up with Sophie was a bit of emotional roulette. It had been seven years since the accident, but sometimes she still had a hard time talking about them without tearing up. He had enough on his plate at the moment without wading into those uncertain waters. Luckily, his sister didn't miss a beat.

"Hey, at least I live by the Golden Rule, which is more than I can say for you."

"What did I do now?" He'd tried his best to convey genuine innocence, but he was a carpenter by trade, not an actor, so even he knew she wasn't going to buy it. Still, playing along was far more entertaining than cleaning the kitchen.

"Lost the only booking you've had in years," she said.

Lucas had to work to hide his amusement. "See, now that's where you're wrong."

"What?" Her voice was a few octaves too high. "I thought you said she left last night."

"She did."

"Then how am I wrong? Jeez, Luc, are you *trying* to be difficult?"

He was almost ashamed to admit how much he was enjoying this. And why shouldn't he? If his sister was going to insist on riding him for details, the least he could do was have a little fun with her while she did.

"She left last night." He paused for a beat, then added, "And came back."

Sophie growled into the phone. It was the reaction he'd been waiting for.

"Ferry was closed. Now she's stuck with me." His resolve cracked into a deep chuckle. Fun was fun, but if he didn't back off, Sophie was going to hit DEFCON 1. "At least until the storm clears."

"You're impossible. Do you know that?"

"Oh, okay, Pot. I'm Kettle," he said. "Nice to meet you."

"Can you be serious for five minutes?"

"Fine." Lucas leaned against the counter, crossing his legs at the ankle. As he did, his gaze fell on a cookie that was wedged between the refrigerator and the wall. At least he was fairly sure it was a cookie at one time anyway. At the moment it looked a bit more like a piece of corrugated cardboard. "Fire away."

"How did it go? What did she think of the place? Did she like her room? Did you clean up the kitchen? Were you rude? Please tell me you weren't rude."

"Whoa, when I said fire away, I was expecting a question or two, not an actual firing squad."

"Well?"

"I was my perfectly pleasant self." Even he was surprised he managed to say those words without laughing.

"Oh crap, that bad?" The teasing tone had left her voice.

"I was fine." And he was. He'd made her dinner. The sheets on the bed were clean. And he hadn't even turned off the hot water when she'd clearly violated the ten-minute rule. Women. How long did it take to wash one head of hair anyway?

"Fine isn't going to get you a five-star review."

Now it was his turn to snort into the phone. "No one would read it anyway." Admittedly, he hadn't paid much attention to the inn's website over the last two years. But thanks to the annoying updates the hosting site sent him every week, even he knew the traffic was about the same as it was on the streets of the island. In other words, nonexistent.

"That might be changing soon. Word is out that you're back in business."

"What? How?" Dammit. He'd agreed to this farce because, quite frankly, he was out of options. But he'd made it clear that this was a one-time deal, a temporary nuisance to buy some time, not permission to install a flashing neon OPEN sign in the front window. "I only agreed to one guest. One."

"Don't blame me," she said. "My contribution was limited to reactivating the listing." His sister waited a beat before adding, "Well, that and the porch."

He was half-afraid to ask. "What did you do to the porch?"

"Didn't you see?" It was impossible to miss the disappointment in her voice, but did she really think he'd been kicking back in a rocking chair watching the storm?

"Surprisingly, I haven't had much time to sit on the porch and read a book, Soph." In fact, it had been years since Lucas had had time to sit and do much of anything. Between caring for his daughter and dealing with repairs around the inn, he hardly had a free moment. He knew it didn't look like he spent much time on the place, but that was only the surface stuff. The nuts and bolts of the inn were always falling off, so to speak. It was all he could do to keep up, and that didn't even count the paperwork. So much paperwork.

Before Jenny died, Lucas had no idea how much administrative crap was involved in running a home, let alone a small business. Jenny had always taken care of it in a way that made it look so effortless. A sad smile tugged at the corner of his mouth as he pictured her sitting at the small table on the porch, tapping away on her calculator with a mug of green tea next to her laptop and a Carly Simon album playing on the turntable she'd found at a local flea market.

Lucas's chest tightened. "You didn't put the turntable out there, did you?" That, along with everything else of Jenny's, was in their old room, just as it had been on the day she died.

"Of course not," Sophie said. There was a tinge of sorrow in her voice, but then she cleared her throat and his upbeat sister was back. "I just figured if she needed to escape the clutter, she would appreciate a cozy blanket."

Lucas rounded the butcher-block island so as to have a clear view of the porch. Sure enough, the rocking chairs had not only been arranged in a perfect row, but each had a neatly folded blanket draped over the back. There were even pillows on the seats, but swear to God, if one of them had a picture of some smiling sea creature, he was pitching it right into the trash. "So first you list my place and then you decorate it?"

"Was that a thank-you?" She didn't bother waiting for a reply. "Guilty as charged, but I promise I haven't said a word to anyone about it."

"Well then, how—"

"After all this time, you still have to ask how news can make its way around the island in twenty-four hours or less?"

She had a point. The residents of Aurelia Island seemed to

know everything, from what a person ate for breakfast to what they streamed on Netflix before bed. But still, he'd have thought the storm might have dominated the local chitchat for at least a day or two.

"Mrs. Jones called to see if the bookstore was open," Sophie began, offering a level of detail he'd neither asked for nor wanted. It was like the woman was incapable of merely answering a question without first explaining the history. "And she said Mr. Adams told her that Mr. Lewis was down at the docks right when the storm started rolling in yesterday and that he gave a woman with some fancy luggage a ride in his sidecar. She said he said he could hardly believe it when she told him she was staying at the…"

She kept going, but Lucas tuned her out. He'd been doing that for a while now—not to be rude, but more as a matter of self-preservation. Ever since Jenny died, he'd been whispered about by the locals. Endlessly. At first, it was concern laced with a healthy side of pity. But as time went on, it started to take on a bit more of a bite. "What will he do?" turned into "Why isn't he doing anything?" and "Hopefully he will find someone new" turned into "Who would want to take on that mess?"

He knew deep down people meant well. They'd turned out in droves for the funeral, and it had been months before he'd even had to think about cooking for himself and Maddie. But surviving the loss of the woman he'd wanted by his side forever wasn't made easier by rampant speculation about why he seemed unable to move on. They didn't know anything about how it felt to live in his skin. How every night he fell asleep thinking about all the nights they'd never get to spend together or how every morning he would wake up, happy in that brief moment before full consciousness. But then reality would return as he wiped the sleep from his eyes and then it was all happening again, every last horrible moment relived like some sort of Nicholas Sparks version of *Groundhog Day.*

"Luc?" Sophie practically shouted into the phone, startling him back to a conversation that had apparently turned into a good old-fashioned scolding. Sometimes he wondered if his little sister remembered which one of them was the older sibling.

"What?"

"Did you hear what I said?"

"Of course I did," he lied. "You were saying how Mrs. Jackson was worried about her peonies coming back in the spring." Truth was, he had no idea what Sophie had said, but landscape was always a safe bet. If there's one thing people on the island liked to talk about more than the state of his personal life, it was their flowers. Either he'd hit the nail on the head, or his sister was just giving him a pass, because, without another word on the subject, she switched gears.

"What did you serve for dinner?"

"Pizza," he said matter-of-factly. It was a fine choice. Who didn't love pizza? Well, who aside from uptight chicks who didn't eat meat?

"You ordered a pizza?"

"No, I did not order a pizza. Who was going to deliver in that storm?"

"Tell me you did not serve the first guest you've had in years a frozen pizza?"

"Fine, I won't tell you."

"Luc!"

"Need I remind you that this inn is a bed-and-*breakfast*?" He really hadn't been obligated to feed her anything at all for dinner, and if it weren't for the storm, he wouldn't have.

"She's certainly paying enough for three meals a day."

Fair point, but still. "It's not like I had a lot of notice."

"And if you had, you'd have made her what, exactly?"

"Hey, I can cook," he said, suddenly feeling a bit defensive. Granted, his repertoire was a bit limited, but Maddie hadn't had any complaints. Then again, she was happy with chicken nuggets and mac and cheese. Speaking of which…

Lucas opened one of the cabinets in search of the trusty blue box of pasta only to find an empty shelf. So much for his lunch plans.

"Name one meal you can cook," Sophie insisted. But before he could respond, she added a qualifier. "That isn't from a kids' menu."

"Surely you haven't forgotten my famous lasagna?"

"You mean Mom's lasagna."

Lucas closed the cabinet. "Same difference."

"Well, either way, I suggest you use this second chance to win her over. What do you have planned for tonight?"

"Not sure. Need to run out to the store." If there was one thing Lucas could count on, it was that Mr. Jenkins would be open for business. The man was more reliable than the tides.

"In this storm?"

Lucas's gaze shifted to the window, where the view was all but obscured by the water splattering against the pane. "Well, it's that or feed her ramen noodles."

"Then get going," Sophie said with a laugh.

"Is Maddie close by?" It had only been twenty-four hours, but he already missed the sound of her voice.

"She's watching *Ryan's World*. And before you say anything, I told her only one video. Want me to get her?"

"Nah, I'll just swing by on my way into town." If there was one bright spot in the gloomy, wet day, it was his daughter's smile.

"Sounds good. Oh, and Luc?"

"Yeah?"

"You might say you don't care about online reviews, but you've got to think about the big picture." Her voice grew softer. "Ratings are public. If this lady leaves a scathing review, it's not just potential customers who will see it."

He knew what was coming next, but the words still cut.

"Jenny's parents might see it too."

As much as he hated to admit it, his sister was right. Again. So without any further debate, let alone smart-ass comments, he ended the call, scribbled a quick note to his guest, and reached for his coat. He stood at the door for a beat, watching the rain as it came down in what looked more like streams than drops, before yanking up his hood and heading for the store.

CHAPTER 5

PAIGE FORCED HERSELF TO STAY in bed because wasn't that
what people did on vacation? And it wasn't like she had much
on her agenda anyway. Even from her pillow perch, she could see
the rain pelting the windows in the turret. So much for long walks
on the beach. She straightened the covers, folding the sheet over
the top of the duvet before letting her hands come to rest beside
her. A minute later, she realized she was tapping what sounded
like some sort of marching-band drill against her thighs. This was
ridiculous, she thought. There was only so much lying about a
person could take, and besides, she had to have been there for at
least an hour by now. That was a respectable amount of vacation
laziness.

She reached for her phone. Fifteen minutes? She rubbed her
eyes and looked at the screen again, but the situation remained
the same. After fighting the urge to get up for what had seemed
like an eternity, she'd only managed fifteen minutes of lounging,
and even that was if she rounded up. Still, for her it was a bit of
an achievement. On a normal Monday, she would have been at

the office by now, reading through emails with a second cup of coffee in hand. So in a way, she was totally winning at this whole vacation thing.

Sammy's voice popped into her head as clearly as if he'd been in the room. *If you say so, Boss Lady.* Turned out imaginary Sammy's sarcasm was just as impossible to miss as the real-life version. Speaking of her assistant...

She glanced back at her phone. He'd definitely be at the office by now.

She considered calling him for all of two seconds before pressing the button on the phone.

It rang once.

"No" was all he said.

The line went dead.

Paige pulled the phone away from her ear to look at the screen. Still three bars. That little...

She called back, but this time, she spoke before he had the chance to. "What do you mean 'no'? And before you hang up on me again, remember who signs your paycheck."

There was a heavy sigh. "No means no. No work. Period. No calling about work. No thinking about work. No, no, no, no, no."

"I can't call my friend while I'm on vacation?"

"You're just calling because I'm your friend?" The way his voice rose at the end of the sentence painted the perfect visual of his eyebrows raising at the same time.

"Don't be so skeptical. Of course you're my friend." And he was. Heck, these days it seemed like he was her only friend. Not that she was without blame in that department. But one long day ran into another, and before she knew it, all those promises to "get together soon" fell to the bottom of her to-do lists.

"And you're not calling to ask me if I went over the invoices, or if I sent out the two new proposals?"

"No, absolutely not because that would be work and I promised not to work this entire week." Although she *may* have had her fingers crossed behind her back when she made that pledge because yeah, that was totally something a normal thirty-year-old woman would do.

"And because you know I'm your outrageously reliable and talented assistant who would never forget to place the order for the Juarez master closet."

"That too. But since you brought it up…"

"Nice try but no way, Boss Lady. Oh sorry, guess I can't call you Boss Lady now that we're friends." He hummed into the phone. "Lady Friend? No," he said, answering his own question. "That sounds like something your generation called that 'time of the month.'"

"I'll have you know that was my mom's generation, maybe even my grandmother's, but certainly not mine. And it's *our* generation. Exactly how old do you think I am?" Not really wanting to hear the answer to that question, she quickly added, "And besides, it wasn't Lady Friend; it was Special Friend." Paige cringed as she added, "Or Aunt Flo."

"I know you didn't call me on the first morning of your vacation to talk about menstrual slang."

"I told you, I just wanted to chat."

"As your friend?"

"Right."

"Out of curiosity, are we *Friends* friends or *Seinfeld* friends?"

Paige frowned. "What's the difference?"

"Well, on *Friends* they were true friends. Like, you just know that after Monica and Chandler moved to the burbs, they all still hung out."

"I'm pretty sure they said Joey was going to have his own room." She tried her best to act nonchalant about knowing this nugget of *Friends* trivia, but truth was, Paige was a bit of an expert when it came to the iconic sitcom, just one more example of the useless knowledge her brain seemed to catalog and store. But hey, if Heads Up! ever became a TV game show, she could probably triple her IRA.

"Exactly. But Jerry and Kramer were friends by situation, in their case geography."

Most people might have found the turn in their conversation a bit odd, but for Paige and Sammy, a quick tangent to analyze nineties television was just par for the course. Sometimes it amazed her that they ever got any work done at all. Then again, perhaps that's why they were so successful.

"So, am I your Joey or your Kramer? And for the love of Central Perk, please do not say I'm your Ross."

Paige laughed. "Samuel, my friend, you are most definitely my Phoebe."

He clicked his tongue against the roof of his mouth. "I can live with that."

"Good, now that we have that settled…"

"If you're about to slip some work in, don't. You're there to relax." There was a pause during which the proverbial light bulb turned on. "Oh my God, it's killing you, isn't it?"

"Little bit."

He laughed. "You just have to get through the detox phase."

"Detox? I'm on vacation, not in rehab."

"For you, Boss Lady—I mean, Bestie—they are one and the same. You're strung so tightly, it's going to take more than a few in-flight cocktails to bring you down to cruising altitude."

She sighed. "It's just so…quiet."

"Well, you *are* there to celebrate Singles Day."

Paige had known she would eventually regret filling him in on that little nugget. But still, enjoying being single didn't mean she wanted to be alone. Not all the time anyway. "Yes, but not in solitary confinement."

He laughed again, but this time when he spoke, his tone had softened. "Tell you what, we can chat as friends as long as there's no mention of work."

Considering her options were either that or going downstairs for more nonexistent conversation with her host, she decided to take the deal. "Agreed."

"Oooh, this will be fun." There was a rustling followed by the unmistakable sound of her office door creaking open. "Let me get a libation," Sammy said. "It's a smidge early for a martini, but since the boss is away, what the hell. I'll even throw in some cranberry juice to make it feel more like breakfast."

"Samuel."

"Chill. You know I've got shit under control."

He was right. She never had to worry about the office when

she left it in Sammy's hands. Although until now that had never been for more than a few hours, and even that was when she was so sick she couldn't stand up.

Bottles clanked. "So how was your first night?"

She waited until he'd finished shaking the ice before giving him all the gory details.

"Dear Lord," he said between sips. "Sounds like your worst nightmare. And you're trapped there on an island." He gasped. "It's your personal Alcatraz."

"Very funny," she said over the laughter that had erupted over his own joke. "Are you almost done?"

"With my drink? Just started." Somehow she knew he'd made himself at home on her white sofa. Probably had his feet on the coffee table, if she had to guess.

"You know that's not what I meant."

"Sorry," he said, not sounding the least bit contrite. "Is there any redemption? Is the view nice at least?"

"More than nice." She paused for a beat before adding a bit of a tease. "Outside and in."

"In? I thought you said the place was a pigpen."

"It is." She smiled in anticipation of the reaction the next bit of info was going to get. "But the swine looks like one of your calendar men."

"*Whaaat*? Which one? Is it a Hemsworth? Please, let it be a Hemsworth."

"No, it wasn't Thor or his brother."

"Real-life brother or movie brother? Because I could totally be down for some Tom Hiddleston action."

"I think it was Mr. October. Ryan something…"

"Ryan Gosling?"

"Is he the one married to Blake Lively?"

"No, that's Ryan Reynolds." There was another gasp, but this one held a completely different meaning. "Holy Green Lantern, Batman. You have a Ryan Reynolds look-alike hosting you in his den of rubbish, and you're wasting time talking to me? I mean, I know that I'm your new best friend and all, but still…go get you some of that."

"I'm not here for romance, Sammy. I'm here to celebrate the joy in being single. And to relax."

"Yeah, and how'd you say that's going?"

"I have to detox, remember?"

"Forget detoxing. Just let your hunky host turn you inside out. A big ole O will do the trick a lot faster than curling up with a mug of chamomile."

"Thanks, but I think I will settle for the tea and an hour with a book."

"Good idea. Nothing like a little swoon reading to get the juices flowing." He took a loud slurp of his cocktail. "Oh, and I'm definitely going to need a picture of this doppelgänger ASAP. Preferably shirtless."

Not that she would ever do that, but even if she were the type of woman to snap surreptitious shots of a hot guy working shirtless, say in the rain maybe…

An image of Lucas Croft all slick and bare popped uninvited into her mind, sending a warm flush to her cheeks. "No way," she said, half to herself and half to her assistant.

"Fine." He sighed. "With clothes then, but a tight T-shirt would be appreciated."

"Still no." Shirtless or not, the last thing Paige needed was to return to her office to find Lucas Croft was next month's screen saver. What she really needed was the aforementioned cold shower because honestly, that little fantasy came out of nowhere. *Sammy.* She nodded to herself. It was all his fault, really, and she'd tell him so as soon as she was back in Chicago. But for now, it was time to end the call.

"Goodbye, Samuel."

She was halfway to the door before she realized she had no idea what the dress code protocol was for the breakfast portion of a bed-and-breakfast. Obviously at a hotel you would get dressed before going down to eat, but wasn't this sort of establishment meant to be more like a home away from home? Did that mean a robe was sufficient? Her eyes darted to where her suitcase stood open on a luggage stand, and her gaze fell to her powder-blue chenille robe. When she'd packed for the trip, she'd envisioned herself curled up by a fireplace in that ultra-cozy bathrobe. Of course that's when she also pictured the innkeepers as an elderly couple who rented rooms at their beachfront Victorian home as a way of re-creating the happy times when their kids all lived at home. But now schlepping downstairs in a fuzzy robe covered with bright yellow and white daisies wasn't quite the image she wanted to project. She had more pride than that.

Maybe Sammy was right. Maybe she really did turn everything into a competition, even breakfast attire. Oh, who was she kidding? Paige's desire to look better than she did for Mr.

Rochester had nothing to do with winning some sort of breakfast beauty pageant and everything to do with Lucas Croft. Because as much as she would have liked to, Paige Parker couldn't deny the attraction she felt for her host, no matter how unappealing he might have seemed below the surface.

She needed a shower—and definitely a toothbrush—but decided that, given the circumstances, she'd dress for trips to the bathroom. So instead of grabbing her robe and fuzzy slippers, Paige changed into a pair of jeans and her favorite green cashmere sweater, the one she knew darn well was the exact color of her eyes. She looked at herself in the small mirror above the dresser. *Not too bad*, she thought as she ran her fingers through her hair.

She reached for the knob but caught herself before she threw open the door. What if her handsome host was on his way to the bathroom? And what if he took the more at-home approach since, after all, this *was* his home? These were all issues she wouldn't even have to consider at a Marriott. Which is exactly why Paige had never booked a room at a B and B before this one. Even those home rental apps, while all the rage, held little appeal for her. She couldn't understand why that would be preferable to a nice suite at a hotel where you knew exactly what you were getting before you arrived and your bathroom was in your room. No risk of false advertisements using out-of-date pictures or half-naked innkeepers with killer abs causing you to spend a ridiculous amount of time overthinking a trip to the bathroom.

And just like that, thoughts of him sauntering shirtless down the hall popped into Paige's mind. She took a deep breath, letting herself enjoy the images from head to toe. He'd no doubt be sporting bedhead, but on him it would probably be that casually disheveled look guys work so hard to achieve, even though they'd like you to believe they don't try at all. His eyes would be sleepy but in that sexy, come-hither way, and his chest would absolutely be bare. She nearly hummed out loud as she pictured the way his abs would ripple as he sauntered down the hallway, drawing her eyes lower and lower until her gaze found the trail of brown hair that led right beneath the waistband of his...*hmm...boxers or briefs?* Her host was probably more of a boxer guy, but for this particular fantasy, Paige decided to envision him in a pair of boxer briefs, the kind made out of soft brushed cotton that clung to every hard inch of his...

Paige jolted. Holy moly, Samuel was right. She needed to get laid. But even if she could muster some of that sex-island mojo her assistant had described—which was a big *If* with a capital I—the odds that Lucas Croft could make it through one night without offending her on about twelve different levels were slim to none. Plus, it would be a tad bit awkward doing the walk of shame down the hallway of his house. Nope, a cold shower would have to suffice. Which shouldn't be a problem given the likelihood of the Crusty Crab turning off the hot water anyway.

Paige opened the door an inch or so and listened for the sound of running water, or footsteps in the hallway, or even the clang of a pot or two from downstairs. But all she heard was a blissful silence interrupted only by the sound of the raindrops pattering against the leaded-glass windows that ran the length of the staircase.

With the coast clear, she scampered to the bathroom, and after she'd made herself sufficiently presentable for breakfast—and returned the items Lucas had left on the pedestal sink to the medicine cabinet where they belonged—headed downstairs. But instead of finding a continental breakfast, let alone a hot one, all Paige found waiting for her was a note that looked like it had been written by a monkey.

The jagged scrap of paper was stuck to the top of a box of Froot Loops. "Gone to town. Help yourself" was all it said. At least that's what she thought it said. Could have just as easily read "Game tour. Hop Yahtzee."

Paige picked up the cereal box and shook it. From the sounds of it, her generous host had left her a box of fruit-flavored dust. Just as well. She hadn't had Froot Loops since she was a kid and really didn't have a desire to revisit that culinary experience now. Still, nice of him to abandon her like that, all alone in a strange town with nothing but a raging storm to keep her company.

All alone.

The words practically lit up in her brain like a neon sign. She had no idea how long Lucas would be gone, but she was fairly certain she had enough time to check out the place.

If Sammy had been there, he would no doubt have chimed in with a snarky "Don't you mean enough time to snoop around?" But he wasn't there. No one was. Which meant Paige was free to take a self-guided tour of the place that brazenly referred to itself as "the hidden jewel of the Carolina coast." Yeah, right. If the internet was a library, that website would undoubtedly have been filed under fiction. And not on the romance shelf either. She smiled at her own joke as she began exploring the first floor. She'd seen the kitchen and the living room the night before—and she'd definitely spent enough time lurking in the hallway—which left only the back of the house.

There was a small area off the kitchen that served as a pantry and laundry room, although it seemed to be failing on both fronts as the shelves were mostly bare and the laundry was piled nearly as high as the machine. What food *was* in stock looked like a cross between what you'd find in a dorm room and a day-care center: six bottles of Gatorade, two boxes of Scooby-Doo fruit snacks, a few bags of pretzels, a case of beer, a box of graham crackers, individual servings of applesauce, and a haphazard pile of ramen.

Without thinking, Paige lined the Gatorade up by color and arranged the dehydrated squares of noodles into an orderly stack. When she realized what she was doing, she stopped. Her host's mess wasn't her problem, and if she didn't get out of there soon, she'd end up sorting his laundry into darks and lights.

She turned to leave, but not before moving the Gatorade to the same shelf as the beer. Pigsty or not, it just made sense to keep the beverages together.

As sad as the pantry situation was, she could almost look past it once she saw the true gem of the house: the back porch. Spanning the entire rear of the building, the now-glass-enclosed three-season room was the one thing about the inn that was exactly as advertised: wooden rocking chairs stretched the length of the porch, each accented with a small pillow on the seat and a cozy throw draped over the back. Honestly, it was the only part of the house that looked as though a woman was in charge. She hated how sexist that sounded, but seeing as how her host himself was such a walking, talking stereotype, she felt her assessment of the room was more than a little justified.

Without the glass, Paige was sure the ocean breeze would only serve to make the setting all the more perfect. But since it was February and said ocean breeze carried more than a bit of a nip, not to mention monsoon-level rains, she was grateful that her host had replaced the screens with glass. At least he kept up with some household chores. Then again, for all she knew, the glass had been in place all summer too.

As welcoming as the porch itself was—right down to the potbelly stove in the far corner—it paled in comparison to the main attraction on display through the windows that accounted for three of the four walls. Paige stepped toward the glass for a better view of the Carolina coast that seemed to stretch indefinitely in both directions. Tall seagrass swayed and bowed to the raging storm, but she knew on a sunny day it would stand in welcome to the guests who ventured down the wooden planks that lead to the ocean. At the moment, the water looked gray and daunting, its white-capped waves more like the teeth of an angry growl than the foam of an enticing bath, but somehow it seemed to set just the right tone. All she needed was a hot drink and a good book.

Paige turned toward one of the chairs. When she did, she couldn't help but smile at the pillow propped on the seat. It was the ideal shape for lumbar support, but its functionality wasn't what made her smile, despite the gloom of the day. It was the very happy-looking sea turtle woven into the tapestry. Again, not at all what she was expecting. If it weren't for the fact that she didn't know how much time she had on her own, Paige would have curled up with the little turtle and enjoyed a much-needed cup of coffee under the cozy throw. But for now, a quick survey of the room would have to do. She still had the second floor to explore.

She took the stairs slowly and methodically, although she had no idea why. No one was going to hear the creak of the treads beneath her feet. No one was around to raise so much as an eyebrow at her blatant disregard for her host's rules, although truth be told, her conscience wasn't exactly keeping her mouth shut. Neither was her assistant. Even a thousand miles away, the sound of Sammy's all-too-familiar tsking was impossible to miss. Not that it stopped her from opening the first closed door she came upon.

It was another guest room, or at least that's what she assumed. Because unlike the one she was staying in, this one was more of a work in progress, and that was putting it nicely. The only furniture in the room was a mattress, and even that was on the floor. There was a stack of books beside it with a small lamp resting on top and a few piles of haphazardly folded clothing leaning against the far wall. For a moment, Paige wondered if someone else *was* staying in the house after all, but then she realized that the T-shirt at the bottom of the unmade bed was the one Lucas had been wearing the night before. He slept there? It seemed a bit odd to her that the owner of such a large inn would sleep in such a small room. It had to be less than half the size of the one Paige had rented. Then again, maybe he left the best accommodations for guests since those would fetch the highest rates.

She closed the door and turned to the one on the opposite side of the hall. As surprising as it was to discover that her host slept on the floor as though he lived in a hostel, that was nothing compared to what she saw behind door number two. It was a child's room—a girl's, if the pink gingham comforter was any indication—and while it wasn't as bad as the rest of the house, this room could still have benefited from a few days of her company's services. There were toys and dolls everywhere. So much so that you could barely see the pink-and-green tufted rug for all the Legos and Barbies. And books. Stacks and stacks of books. Paige followed the trail of picture books that stretched across the hardwood floor to a window seat flanked by bookcases. She remembered the charming nook room from one of the photos on the website, but while the bookcases and cushioned window seat looked the same, the rest of the room was much different and certainly not ready for guests.

For a moment, Paige wondered what would've happened had she selected that room for the week. Would the Barbies and Legos have remained? She nearly laughed out loud for even wondering if her host would've cleaned up before her arrival. But then a more sobering question popped into her head. Whose room was this?

Paige pulled the door closed and made her way to the far end of the hallway. Judging by the double-door entry, she assumed this was the master bedroom. Who stayed there? Certainly not the master of the house. He was too busy living like a squatter in the smallest room.

She lowered the brass lever and pushed the door open a few inches. From the hallway, she could see a queen-sized bed with wrought-iron posts and a ruffled comforter, a cluster of candles on top of what looked to be an antique dresser, and a vase of dried-up flowers on a small nightstand next to the bed. As she stepped inside, she saw a rocking chair in the far corner and, beside it, a small marble-top table covered with framed photos. As she moved closer, she could see that each silver frame contained a picture of Lucas and the woman from the photo she'd seen in the curio downstairs, but in these there was also a baby. A girl. That would explain the pink, toy-filled room, Paige thought. But where was that child now?

Paige glanced around the room. Unlike the rest of the house, this space was immaculate. Well, aside from the dust, and judging by the amount that covered the furniture, it had been ages since anyone had even been in this room, let alone slept there. She turned back to the arrangement of frames on the table. There'd been a woman in Lucas's life, and a baby girl, but now there was no sign of either one. What happened to them?

Paige was about to pick up one of the photos when a noise from downstairs stopped her dead in her tracks.

CHAPTER 6

LUCAS SHIFTED THE TWO BROWN-PAPER grocery bags to one arm so he could reach the latch, then pushed the front door open with his foot. He assumed his uptight guest was still asleep, which was why he was surprised to see her bounding down the stairs, all bright eyes and smiles and already dressed for the day.

"Good morning," she said in a tone that was far too cheery for such a dreary morning. "Still raining, I see." She squinted toward the bay window in the front room. "It's so dark. You can hardly tell it's daytime. Guess it will have to be an indoor day."

So many words in such a small amount of time.

He kicked the door closed behind him. "You've got a lot of energy for someone who hasn't had a cup of coffee yet." He wasn't sure which prospect sounded worse, a day trapped inside with the uptight city chick of last night or a day trapped inside with this bouncy, cheerful version.

"How do you know I haven't had coffee?" she asked. Still far too happy.

He nodded to the bag in his right arm, sending water from the hood of his coat streaming into the already soggy paper. "Because it's in here."

She reached for the bag. "Let me help."

That was the last straw. "Okay, what gives?" he asked as she relieved him of one of the bags.

"What gives?" Her eyes were wide and innocent, and all at once Lucas noticed how green they were. So green they looked like they weren't even real but had been colored with of one of Maddie's markers. Had her eyes looked like that last night?

"What gives with the attitude?"

"What do you mean?" She turned and started down the hallway toward the kitchen. As she walked, his gaze instinctively shifted to the sway of her hips. He might have been on a "chick fast," as his college buddies now referred to his life whenever they called, but he was still a man with a pulse walking behind a very sexy woman, uptight pain in the ass or not. He knew it made him a bit of a jerk to be such a dick to her one night and then get a semi the next day just from watching her walk down the hall, but he couldn't help it. There was something about her that got his blood pumping, and not just in anger.

He'd barely slept the night before, alternating between being pissed at his sister for going behind his back, pissed at the city woman for being so damned annoying, and pissed at himself for thinking she was so smoking hot.

When she'd shown up in his house the first time, he'd been what his grandfather called "spittin' mad." So mad, in fact, that he'd hardly given her a second glance. But then she came back. Every inch of her had been soaking wet, from her auburn hair to her overpriced shoes. But it was the way her sweater clung to every luscious curve that was permanently seared into his mind.

"Lucas?"

His head snapped up to meet her raised brows. "Huh?"

"You asked what gives. With what?"

"Um, with you." He slid behind the island in an attempt to hide the evidence while he tried to get his dick under control and set the remaining grocery bag on the counter.

"Me?" she asked. Her voice was a few octaves too high, which meant either she was nervous or hiding something. Unless... For a moment, he wondered if maybe it was because he was having the same effect on her. Her cheeks were a bit flushed, after all, and in his experience that usually meant one of two things: either a woman was working out or turned on. But then he remembered the way she'd looked at him last night. Like he was some naughty schoolboy who should be sent to his room to clean it up. Hmm, naughty schoolboy. Now there's a fantasy he hadn't thought of since college. Christ, what was wrong with him? Two years without sex, that's what.

"Yeah, last night I was the bane of your existence and now today you're all"—he waved his hand back and forth while he searched for the right word—"perky."

Her eyes grew wide. "Perky?" The way she looked, you'd have thought he'd said she had perky tits. Which she did by the way, but that wasn't what he'd meant. Dammit, now it was all he could do not to stare at her boobs. Forget college, he'd gone clear back to high school.

"Nice, cheerful," he said, trying to dig himself out. "You even offered to help me."

She softened. "Look, I think we got off on the wrong foot last night—probably because of the storm, I don't know—but either way, here we are, stuck with each other." The tone of disgust those words would have conveyed the night before was conspicuously missing. "At least until the storm passes," she quickly added. "I figure there's no sense in making it worse by fighting the entire time."

"A truce?"

"An uneasy one, I'm sure." She let out a nervous laugh. "But yeah."

"Deal," he said.

She stuck out her hand.

"You want to actually shake on it?" This was possibly one of the strangest women he'd ever met. And that was saying something, considering his sister. But to go from an uptight bitch one night to a cheerful sweetheart the next morning was nearly Jekyll-Hyde territory. Then again, maybe she was nuts. He'd heard stories about crazy people on the hosting site's owners' blog, but he'd never really considered the possibility that he'd end up with a nutjob in his house. Leave it to his sister to book him a woman who was cuckoo for Cocoa Puffs.

She stood there, expectantly, during his entire internal debate, her hand stuck out and her lips curved into what seemed like a genuine smile. Fine. He could play Hyde, too, if that's what she wanted.

Lucas took her hand. Her grip was firm, not timid like some

girls, especially the ones who liked to play all delicate, but like a woman who was confident in who she was and what she was doing. A woman who shook hands over business deals on a regular basis. A woman who would give one hell of a hand job.

Jesus.

Lucas dropped her hand, then headed to the pantry with one of the bags of food, which also gave him an opportunity to adjust his fly because that semi was now full blown.

"Need any more help?" she asked, interrupting his attempts to run through the Braves' starting lineup while his dick headed to the locker room for a cold shower.

"Nah, all good." He emerged from the pantry to find her perched atop one of the kitchen stools. "Did you eat?"

Her eyes darted to the box of cereal he'd left on the counter. "No, not yet."

No dig on the Loops? She must have been serious about the truce, because even Maddie would have had something to say about the end-of-the-box crumbs.

"Gotta admit, I was a bit stumped over what to get a vegetarian for breakfast. I mean, are eggs okay? If not, I have oatmeal." At the store, he'd been mainly concerned about getting a few items that weren't most commonly found on a kids' menu, but now he found himself wanting to make her something she might actually enjoy.

"Eggs are fine. I'm not a vegan."

"So just a run-of-the-mill veg head?"

Her head fell back on a laugh that was not at all what he expected. Based on their first meeting, he would have expected her laugh to be a harsh, shrill sound. Not something so delicate and joyful. "Sorry," she said when she caught her breath. "I've just never heard that slang before. But if you want to be specific, I'm a pescatarian."

The look on his face must have been as blank as his brain was at the moment because she offered more of an explanation.

"It means I eat fish but not meat, and that I also eat dairy and eggs."

He clapped his hands together. "Then a veggie omelet it is." Omelets were one of the few items Lucas cooked with complete confidence. It was like the meat loaf of breakfast, if you really thought about it. Just throw everything in a bowl, mix it up, and cook it. "But first, coffee." He cringed as he heard the words coming out of his mouth. Sophie had a light-up sign on the counter in her kitchen that said exactly that. *But first, coffee.* It even had a motion sensor that caused it to blink when she walked into the room in the morning. Needless to say, it was annoying as hell. He'd ridiculed her when she set it up, and nearly every day since then, but now there he was quoting the damn thing. Judging by the smile on his guest's face, she'd seen a similar sign or meme or T-shirt and knew exactly what he'd done.

To his surprise, she didn't bust his balls. Instead she complimented his coffee choice.

"Nice blend," she said, picking up the silver pouch.

"You don't have to seem so shocked."

"What can I say? I half expected instant."

Not too much of a stretch, given the hospitality level to date. "I may eat frozen pizza," he said, feigning offense. "But I'm not an animal."

They both laughed—and not in a forced polite way, but a genuine laugh shared between two people who'd found a common ground. No coffee pun intended.

Lucas reached into the cabinet above the stove and pulled out a chrome-and-glass French press.

"Wow, now I'm really impressed. Most guys would just use a Mr. Coffee."

Lucas stilled. The French press had been Jenny's idea. She thought it would give their little inn a more sophisticated vibe. She'd intended to buy something to grind her own beans, too, but she never had the chance. There was so much she never had the chance to do...

"You okay?"

He looked up to meet his guest's gaze and was surprised to find it filled with genuine concern. "Yeah, why?" he asked, trying to shake off the fog that encased him far too often.

"You just looked really serious all of a sudden."

"Well, coffee is serious business." He opened the silver pouch and began to scoop grounds into the glass carafe. "I got this," he said. "Why don't you go relax—rain or not, it's still your vacation—and I'll let you know when the coffee and eggs are ready."

Go relax.

The words felt more like a dismissal than hospitality, and for the life of her, Paige couldn't figure out why. Sure, they'd had a horrible first meeting, but this morning things had seemed better. Friendly even. She'd even go so far as to say her host had been a little flirty. She'd definitely caught him looking at her boobs. Then again, most guys looked at Paige's boobs. She'd spent her teenage years hunched over in an attempt to minimize them. But in college all that had changed. She decided to embrace her curves, and by the time she was in her midtwenties, she was actively dressing to accentuate her ta-tas. Not at work though. Never at work. But this wasn't a business situation, and Lucas Croft was definitely not a client, although he could certainly use the benefit of services like hers. But truth be told, even the compulsively organized clean-freak side of her could look the other way for an afternoon with her handsome host in her four-poster bed. Hell, she'd even get down and dirty with him on that mattress on the floor.

Mattress on the floor.

What was she thinking?

The whole reason she'd come downstairs ready to propose a truce was because of what she'd seen in the bedrooms upstairs. Whatever had happened to the woman and child in the photographs, one thing was certain: Lucas Croft was a man in pain. One, who from the sounds of it, hadn't even wanted to be back in the innkeeper business. Given all that, she could hardly hold his rude behavior against him. Nope. Instead there she was, thinking about him holding *her* against him.

It was official: she was a horrible person.

Maybe he hadn't noticed the way her nipples hardened when he stared at her chest. Or the way her cheeks flushed when his hazel eyes locked on hers. Of course some of that flush was due to nearly being caught snooping around his house. She was lucky she hadn't sprained her ankle hightailing it out of that bedroom.

Lusting after her heartbroken host *and* snooping through his house? Yeah, she was making the folks on *Big Brother Island*, or whatever that show was called, look like upstanding citizens.

Her phone vibrated in her pocket. It was her mother, which made perfect sense seeing as how the woman was the Beetlejuice of bad decisions. Without fail, every time Paige had so much as a questionable thought, let alone action, her mother would call or text. She swore the woman had some sort of sixth sense. At least Paige didn't have to say her mother's name three times. That, and the fact that her head didn't spin in a three-sixty on her shoulders.

Are you really on vacation?

Leave it to her mom to get right to the point. No "How are you, darling?" or "Have you been sleeping okay?" Not even the quintessential mother question: "Have you been eating?" Then again, Paige's mother wasn't like most moms. She didn't fill her days worrying about whether her kids got a good night's sleep or if they ate three square meals. She was far too busy worrying about her own life to spend much time worrying about the lives of her two adult children. Except of course when her Beetlejuice/Spidey senses started to tingle. Then she was laser-focused.

Paige's mother had been the first woman in her family to go to college, let alone law school. But she'd no sooner accepted a job with a big New York firm than she met the love of her life, a man who thought the Chicago suburbs would be a far better place to raise a family than the Big Apple. So Janice Parker said no to her dream job and followed the man she loved to a sleepy commuter town where he rode the train to work and she stayed home with the kids. The decision had been mutual, yet Paige always had the feeling that her mother was haunted by the life not lived. So much so that she was nearly manic about making the most of the path she'd chosen instead.

At first, that mania was focused on Paige and her brother. But as she and Martin grew older and there was less for her mom to do, she became almost obsessed with making sure her two children were happy, independently functioning adults. Marty was married and living in California, where he owned his own home and had two kids and a dog, so Janice had been able to check the proverbial box next to his name. She'd nearly been able to mark Paige "sorted" as well. Until her fiancé decide to sleep with her boss, messing up Janice's motherhood completion timeline.

It was as though marriage was the ultimate graduation from childhood, although whether it was Paige graduating or her mother, she was never fully sure. Either way, her mom's plan to join her father in early retirement had been derailed by a loser who couldn't keep it in his pants. Her mother had been so upset, you'd have thought she was the one who'd been cheated on, not Paige. But not in the way you'd expect. *"Don't you think you could give him another chance?"* Most moms would have wanted to claw the guy's eyes out, but not Janice Parker. Not when she'd been *this* close to having both of her kids married off, happily or not.

That was when Paige made two important decisions. First, when it came to her mom, everything in life was going to be absolutely fine. At least on the surface. The woman had given her and Marty the prime of her life. If she needed the second act to herself, then far be it from Paige to stand in the way of that. It was ridiculous, really. Having a husband wasn't some magical fix-all for life, but to Janice it meant that she didn't have to worry about her daughter. And while it was doubtful a walk down the aisle would be happening for Paige anytime soon, she could still give her mom the peace of mind that everything was right in her world.

The second decision Paige made was more of a promise to herself. She would never change her life plans over a man. Ever.

Her phone vibrated in her hand. This time all that was sent was a question mark. It was her mother's not-so-subtle way of nudging her for a reply.

Yes, Paige replied. Then added, How did you know that?

She knew the answer even before the little bubbles of her mother's typing filled the screen. "Sammy," Paige said out loud just as his name popped up on the screen. Two seconds later, her phone rang in her hand.

"I just hate texting," her mom said. "I can talk so much faster."

"Everything is fine, Mom." They were the same words she said every Monday when her mom called for her weekly check-in.

"Well, you hadn't mentioned anything about a trip last week, so when Samuel picked up your office line…"

"Sorry, it was all so last minute." Paige kicked herself for not thinking to text her mom over the weekend, which would have avoided all this. "But like I said, everything is fine. I just decided to treat myself to some R and R."

Her mother sighed in relief. "Thank goodness. For a moment, I was worried maybe you'd gone to rehab and your assistant was covering for you."

Paige's jaw fell open. Rehab? Her mother might have tried

to bury her head in the sand for life's day-to-day stresses, but when she surfaced, she took the art of worrying to a new high. "I promise, everything is absolutely perfect. I will even send you a photo of the adorable little inn I'm staying at."

"Great. Have fun."

And then she was gone.

Paige opened her phone's browser to grab a photo from the inn's website to send to her mother. An actual picture would have revealed a pigsty engulfed in a monsoon, and that would have given her poor mother a coronary. Just like Paige's life, everything about the inn had to be absolutely fine as well.

She paced the length of the porch. There really wasn't much to do indoors when you weren't allowed to work.

She thought about calling Sammy back, but if she did, she would no doubt end up spilling her guts about everything she'd seen on her house tour—okay, okay, snoop fest—and everything that had been said (and unsaid) during her morning conversation with Lucas, who was well within earshot. Plus, it had barely been an hour since her last call. She didn't want to seem totally inept at this whole vacation thing. So instead of calling her assistant, she shoved her phone back in her pocket and stared at the gray horizon through rain-splattered windows.

A few moments later, Lucas served her a quite respectable omelet and a more-than-respectable cup of coffee. She ate her breakfast alone on the glass porch, which was also where she spent the better part of the day. Her host had told her to help herself to any of the books stored inside the wicker cabinet. So after rearranging the inn's small library by the color of the books' spines, she did exactly what she told Sammy she was going to do: curled up in a rocking chair with a comfy pillow and a cozy throw and read a steamy novel. She couldn't help but wonder if the woman who'd slept in the now-dusty bedroom had selected the reading material for the inn, or if maybe it had come with the house when they bought it. Either way, she doubted Lucas had selected a book called *Scoundrel of the Manor*.

Unlike breakfast, dinner was served in the formal dining room. It was a surprisingly delicious lasagna made with zucchini and mushrooms, which Paige scarfed down in record time since breakfast had apparently been lunch as well. Lucas ate his meal in the kitchen, or so she presumed, which meant Paige once again dined alone. It shouldn't have felt so odd really. She dined alone nearly every night at home. But there she had her cat—who, while not much of a conversationalist, was at least a warm body in the room—and a constant stream of HGTV. At the inn, there was nothing but an eerie silence, broken only by the sound of the storm or the occasional clank of pots and pans. Plus, at her apartment there wasn't another person who was also eating alone in the next room. The whole thing was beyond strange.

After dinner she was back to the porch, this time with a mug of hot cocoa to accompany the Scoundrel's tales. Turned out even a scoundrel had the capacity to love, which was no surprise given the genre's requisite happy ending, but what did surprise her was that it was nearly midnight when she finished reading. She took great pride in the fact that she'd made it through a whole day and night of self-imposed relaxation, but was dreading the thought of doing it all again the next day. With any luck, the rain would ease up enough for her to at least explore a little bit of the island.

Paige put the book in the cabinet and was about to head up the back staircase when she heard a noise from the front room. She made her way down the narrow hallway, past the curio cabinet and the banister, noting that the latter was now peanut butter free. *Thank God for small victories*, she thought.

She paused before rounding the wooden casement that marked the entry to the room, choosing instead to steal a quick peek. The room was dark except for the light of one small Tiffany-style lamp that sat perched atop an ornate cabinet. Lucas sat in a tufted chair with only his profile visible to her. He held a photo album in his hands, with two more stacked on the floor beside his feet. Under normal circumstances, she'd have gone on in and made a bit of small talk by asking about the photos. But something about the way Lucas sat, his shoulders tense and his head down, told her that this was not a situation that called for chitchat. It was as though he was engrossed and anguished at the same time. Over what, she couldn't say for sure, although she suspected it had something to do with the woman in the photo that sat behind her in the curio. She turned, her gaze falling on the frame tucked behind the driftwood. Clearly that was the woman who had lived in the room upstairs. But Lucas didn't wear a wedding ring anymore. Did she leave him or, worse, was she…

Paige stopped herself. There was absolutely no reason for her to go all Nancy Drew. Lucas Croft was her host, not her friend and certainly not her date. What may or may not have happened in his personal life was none of her business. So instead of joining him in the living room, she merely watched him for a few moments more, then turned and went up to bed.

CHAPTER 7

ANOTHER SLEEPLESS NIGHT.

But this time, instead of tossing and turning with seething anger, Lucas spent the night racked with guilt.

He and Jenny had dreamed not only of earning a living running the Copper Lantern Inn, but of raising their family and growing old together there. That dream had vanished like morning fog. He'd never intended to continue the business without her, but now there he was, hosting a guest on his own for the first time— and what did he do? Ogled her boobs like a horny teenager while making a few lame attempts at... What was that shit even? Hell, he'd had better moves when he actually *was* a teenager. To be fair, he was more than a little rusty. And Paige Parker was more than a little hot. Not that it justified his behavior. Paige—Ms. Parker— was a guest at the Copper Lantern Inn. Not a contestant on some sad reality show. Like *The Bachelor*, only worse. *The Widower: Come for the view, stay for the sexual harassment.*

Of course he'd sealed the fate of his sleepless night when he'd broken his own cardinal rule. It had been just over a year since he'd let himself look at even one of the albums Jenny had made documenting their life together, let alone the complete set. It was amazing really. They'd had such a short amount of time together, but you'd never know it by the number of photographs she'd crammed into those books. And who did that anyway? The rest of the world had thousands of photos on their phones or misplaced flash drives. But not Jenny. She would print them, write on the backs, and then arrange them on colorful pages. Sometimes Lucas wondered if deep down she somehow knew they wouldn't have forever. If maybe she had created an archive for their daughter so when she was older, she would know about the love they had shared.

Lucas scrubbed a hand down his face. Nothing he could do about either of the screwups from the day before. All he could do was move forward.

Move forward.

If he had a dollar for every time he'd heard those two words, well, let's just say he wouldn't have had to accept the booking. It had started as a little trickle. A prod here and there from his sister, a few comments about "getting back in the game" from his college buddies, or the less-than-subtle request from a few of the island's older residents to show a visiting niece or granddaughter around the island. Like he didn't know a blind date when he heard it. But lately that trickle had turned into a steady stream.

In his heart, he knew that Jenny would want him to move on, to make a life for himself and Maddie with a woman who would never take her place, but rather fill a gaping void. Sometimes he wondered if that's why the dreams had stopped. In the month after her death, Jenny had come to him nearly every night. It was always the same, just different scenarios: he and Jenny in a scene from their lives that felt so vivid, so real, that when he woke to his reality, it was like hearing the news of her death all over again.

But those dreams became fewer and farther between until about nine months ago when they stopped altogether. In a way, it made her loss feel all the more permanent. Like somehow as long as he'd been dreaming of her every night, she wasn't really gone. But now that nocturnal comfort had vanished. Was it his subconscious's way of telling him it was time to move on? Maybe. Didn't mean he had to listen to that advice, even if it was coming from his own brain. He pushed the thoughts to the recesses of his mind, just like he always did, focusing instead on whatever task lay directly at hand. For now, that meant cooking breakfast.

He showered quickly—had he put his toothbrush and deodorant in the medicine cabinet?—then listened for any signs of life from his one and only guest. Satisfied she was still sleeping, he went downstairs for a quick video call with Maddie. He'd seen her the day before when he'd popped out to go to the grocery store, but judging by the way the wind was rattling the windows, he might not be able to make it to the other side of the island until tomorrow. The thought of going a day without seeing his daughter made his heart ache nearly as much as the damn albums had the night before. But the tightness in his chest dissolved into a familiar warmth the moment her little face filled the screen.

"Hi, Daddy."

"Hey, Peanut."

Her lips twisted in the most adorable pout. "You know I'm

not a peanut anymore." He'd started calling her that the first time he held her in his arms. She was so tiny, it was the first word that popped into his mind. A few months ago, she had insisted that he come up with a new nickname. One more befitting a woman about to turn five years old. He'd merely smiled, knowing full well he'd still be calling her Peanut on her wedding day.

"Yes, you are. Always will be to me."

She smiled, and all was well in his world.

"What are you and Aunt Sophie doing today?"

Maddie twirled one of her dark curls around her finger. "We are going to make cookies and then have a tea party with..." She wandered off-screen and returned a minute later with an armload of stuffed animals that she began holding in front of the camera one by one. As if Lucas wasn't already well acquainted with the motley band of characters who accompanied her everywhere she went. "But don't worry, my cup will only have milk," she said, once all the tea party's guests had been introduced.

Sophie appeared behind her. "Hey, how did it go last night? Still have a guest?"

"Of course." He smiled. "She's trapped, remember?"

Sophie laughed. "I wouldn't be so sure about that. Speaking from experience, you could be enough to drive a woman to sleep outside in the rain."

Maddie giggled, even though she hadn't bothered to look up from her toys.

"Very funny, Smalls," he said, knowing full well it would irritate her. "I made an omelet, coffee, and lasagna. I even had salad."

Her brows shot up. She was obviously impressed, maybe even

a little shocked, by this news, but leave it to his sister not to cut him any slack. "And today?"

"Another omelet for starters." And why not? She'd enjoyed the first one, and it was really all he knew how to make aside from smiley-face pancakes. Maddie claimed his pancakes were the best she'd ever had, but to be fair, she was only four years old. Her pancake consumption was limited to whatever he or his sister made for her, and he was pretty sure he could top Sophie's cooking with the frozen kind that are heated in the microwave.

The floorboards above the kitchen creaked. His guest was awake.

"Gotta run, Soph. Call you later."

He'd no sooner flipped the omelet when Paige appeared at the bottom of the stairs. She was wearing the same clothes as the night before, which was surprising given the size of her suitcase. Then again, he thought, as he glanced down at the jeans he'd worn the last five days, who was he to talk?

"I was going to shower, but I didn't see any towels."

That would explain the repeated outfit. Because as much as Paige Parker struck him as the type never to wear the same clothes two days in a row, she also struck him as the type who wouldn't put clean clothes on a dirty body. Women. Scratch that. Uptight women.

"There should be some in the wardrobe in the bedroom."

"Cool, thanks. I'll eat first if that's okay." She glanced at the plate of food sitting on the counter. "Don't want it to get cold."

"Sure, yeah, absolutely."

Three ways of saying yes? Holy hell, forget college or high

school, he was acting like he was back in seventh grade when his mom let him invite Mary Margaret O'Connell over to study. He'd hoped that was code for make out, but unfortunately for him, Miss A+ really just wanted to cram for the history test. He'd stuttered and stammered his way through the whole afternoon, which might have been one of the reasons for her utter lack of interest, and he was doing the same thing now. Only this time it wasn't a potential middle-school girlfriend but an actual paying customer. *Get it together, Croft.*

He wiped the palms of his hands on his jeans and handed her the china plate. She took it from him, then hesitated. For a moment, he thought she might pull up one of the island stools and dine with him, but then she turned and headed out to the glass porch. Only problem was, Lucas wasn't ready to let her go. It had been ages since he'd spent any quality time with a woman over the age of four. Except for his sister, which didn't really count. Usually Lucas was just fine with peace and quiet. He seemed to have so little of it as the parent of a toddler. Maybe that was the problem. Maybe he was so used to the nonstop chatter of a four-year-old that he forgot how to just enjoy the silence. Whatever the reason, he found himself actually wanting to make conversation with his houseguest. Go figure.

"Oh," he said as he followed her out onto the porch, "and I should have told you this last night, but feel free to make yourself at home."

She placed her plate on the small glass table and pulled out a chair. "I'm staying in your house," she said on a delicate laugh. "Doesn't get much more at home than that."

"I mean if you need a drawer or something when you unpack. Unless you did already, which is totally cool." Why did he sound so nervous? It wasn't like he was offering a drawer to a semi-moved-in girlfriend or anything.

"A drawer?"

"In the bedroom. Or in the bathroom. Although I know you ladies like to spread out all those lotions."

"Us ladies?" She flashed him a playful grin. "I know plenty of guys who use more products than I do."

"Gay guys?" he asked.

"Not necessarily," she said.

"All I'm trying to say is that it's cool if you want to unpack. That's all."

"Thanks, but I wasn't really planning to unpack."

"Ready for a quick getaway?" No doubt that had been her plan. As soon as the call came, she'd be only one zipped bag away from a hasty exit. But that had been before "the truce." Maybe a speedy exit wasn't such a high priority anymore, which would be fine with him. She'd paid for the whole week. But more than that, much to his surprise, Lucas realized he wasn't in a rush to see her leave.

She met his amused grin with one of her own. "Well, the harbormaster did say the service could resume any day. Plus, I'm not really one for spreading my stuff all over the room, especially not in a shared bathroom."

A loud clap of thunder rattled the windows.

"That sounded close," Paige said.

Lucas looked toward the charcoal horizon. "Maybe we should

move into the main house." It was a more of a statement than a suggestion. The sky was even darker than it had been the day before.

By silent agreement, the two of them turned toward the kitchen. But as they did, they heard what sounded like a muffled scream from behind the back door.

"What was that?" Paige asked.

Lucas had no idea. But before he'd had a chance to answer, there was another sound. This one was a loud thud.

Paige jumped. "This house wasn't used for one of those Stephen King books, was it?"

He knew she was joking, but Lucas had to admit, at the moment it seemed like a legitimate question.

That was when the barking began. High-pitched, frantic yelps accompanied by claws scratching at the door.

"It's a dog," she said, opening the door before Lucas could stop her. Not that he didn't love animals, but they had no idea what was waiting on the other side of that door. The animal could have been hurt or, worse, rabid. Either way, throwing the door open to invite Cujo in without at least first taking a look through the window wasn't exactly the smartest move.

His fears were unwarranted because Paige had no sooner swung the door open when the rain-soaked dog barked and ran away. Odd. But then again, so was the fact that he was temporarily back in business. These days, nothing really should have surprised him.

Rain splattered their faces as the two of them peered out into the storm. "Do you think she's someone's lost pet?" Paige asked.

"Maybe. But she spooked so easily, I doubt she's been around many people. My guess is she's a stray," Lucas said. Best he could tell, the copper-colored dog was some kind of pit bull/boxer mix. Probably a few other breeds as well, but those were the most obvious.

"Poor thing. She's probably so scared."

Lucas stepped back. "Shut the door before we are as wet as she was."

Paige closed the door. It wasn't more than a few seconds before the barking and scratching started again.

She eased the door open. "Maybe I scared her off last time."

The dog waited until the door was fully open, then turned toward the beach. She didn't run as far this time, only to the wooden-planked walkway that led to the shore.

"I don't understand," Paige said. "She clearly wants our attention, and yet every time I open the door, she runs back."

It was then that Lucas noticed the dog's teats were engorged. "She's had a litter recently."

"What? How do you know that?"

He nodded toward the dog. "Look at her nipples."

"Leave it to a guy to notice tits," Paige said more to herself than him. "Even on a dog."

Lucas ignored her jab, partly because he wasn't entirely sure she realized she'd said it out loud, and partly because she was sort of right. He'd certainly spent enough time over the last two days checking out her tits to deserve that one. "From the looks of it, she needs to nurse the pups."

Paige wiped her face with the back of her hand, then leaned forward for a closer look. The dog took a step toward them and barked. "She wants us to follow her."

"So now you speak dog?" She had to be kidding.

Paige shook her head. "Think about it. She's scratching for help but then backs away when we open the door. She wants us to follow her."

Lucas watched as a small crease formed between Paige's brows. Then she looked up at him with wide eyes, and he knew the next thing to come out of her mouth was going to be nothing but trouble. It had to be. The look on her face was like the one cartoon characters make when a light bulb glows above their head.

"Oh shit! The puppies are in danger."

"Did your mom make you watch *Lassie* reruns when you were a kid? Because there is no way you got all that from one bark."

"This isn't a joke, Lucas. With all this rain, they could be drowning somewhere."

"You don't know that."

"Well, I'm not going to stand here and do nothing." She grabbed a blanket off one of the chairs. "I'm going to see where she takes me."

Lucas watched as Paige pulled the blanket over her shoulders and headed out into the storm. Crazy woman. She could at least have taken a minute to grab her coat. He reached for the windbreaker he always left hanging by the back door and dashed out into the rain. The cold air hit him hard, and yet Paige hadn't so much as flinched as she'd taken off down the stairs and across the dunes. He squinted against the steady stream of rain. At the rate she and the momma stray were moving, he'd have to break into a jog just to catch up.

They followed the stray for about a quarter mile, first on the beach, then up into the dunes, where a bank of sand and seagrass all but obscured the opening of a large storm drain. The dog stopped in front of the metal bars that covered the opening and began to bark.

"They must be in there," Paige said.

"We don't even know if that's what she's trying to tell us." Good Lord, now even he was acting like the dog could speak.

Water poured through the grate in a steady flow, but aside from that, all he could see was darkness.

"Do you have a flashlight?"

Now that would have been a good idea. "Maybe if you'd waited a second before charging out into the storm…"

A clap of thunder shook the sand dune, and the dog howled.

Paige dug into the front pocket of her jeans and pulled out her phone. A moment later a weak beam of light shone into the drain. Sure enough, huddled on a piece of broken concrete lodged against one wall of the pipe were what looked to be at least three newborn pups.

"We have to get in there," she said. The opening was certainly large enough. It reached well past waist high, but it was covered with prison-like bars. Lucas yanked on two of them. "I don't think I can get these off, not without my tools."

"We don't have that kind of time." She was right. The rain was coming down harder than it had all day. Judging by the flow of the water, it wouldn't be long before the pups were covered.

The mother dog whimpered, and that time no crazy doggie translator was needed to make out her plea.

"Here, take this," Paige said. She handed him the now soggy blanket. "I'm going in."

Her words took a moment to register. "You're what?"

"I'm going in."

Lucas looked down to where Paige was already wedging one leg through the bars, but before he could tell her to stop, an arm and boob had followed.

She looked up at him. "I might be stuck."

The whole thing had been a horrible idea, but she couldn't stop now. Not with half her body inside the pipe and half out. "You can do this," he said. "Close your eyes and take a deep breath."

She narrowed her gaze. "You mean 'suck it in'?"

He rolled his eyes. "Focus, Paige." Lightning zigzagged through the sky. They needed to get out of there. Fast. "If you made it halfway in, then you can make it halfway out."

"*Out?*" She shook her head as much as the bar would allow. "No way. I'm not coming back out without those pups."

Steeled with a new determination, or maybe just pissed off at him, Paige closed her eyes, took a deep breath, and wriggled herself into the opening of the drain.

"Hold this so I can see," she said, passing him her phone. "I'm going to need both hands free." The water was up to her chest as she waded through it in some sort of squatting duck-walk, and judging by the expletives he heard echoing through the pipe, it was filled with less-than-desirable debris.

"How many are there?" Lucas shouted to her over the rain hammering the top of the metal drain.

She didn't answer until she'd made it back to him, a puppy in each arm. Their short fur was slick from the water, and their eyes were barely open. "Four," she said, passing the two pups through the bars. The mother dog leapt against him, her tail wagging like a propeller.

"Okay, little momma," he said to her, holding them low enough for her to nuzzle and lick them.

Paige pushed back the hair that was plastered to her face. "Let me grab the other two."

"Hurry."

"Nah," she said. "I was thinking I would splash around a bit in this sludge. Maybe do the backstroke."

"Very funny," he said as she started waddle-walking back through the pipe. But it wasn't funny. Nothing about this was. He glanced over his shoulder at the raging surf behind them. Tide was coming in, which wasn't going to make this any easier. His gaze shifted to the sky. Another crack of lightning zigzagged through the clouds just as Paige let out a bone-chilling scream.

CHAPTER 8

PAIGE'S ASS HIT THE BOTTOM of the drainpipe. Hard. She knew it would leave a bruise on her tailbone, but neither that nor the considerable bruise to her ego mattered at the moment. Because even though Mr. Hot-As-Crap had no doubt seen her less-than-graceful tumble into the vat of disgust, all she cared about at the moment was rescuing the two remaining pups.

Once she had them, she somehow managed to shimmy her way back through the bars with a pup in each hand, although she knew for certain her ass wasn't the only thing that would be black and blue come morning. Her boobs were going to look pretty rough from the smooshing they'd received. And she'd thought her first mammogram was bad! That nurse at the hospital with her cold hands and her X-ray vise had nothing on a drainpipe jail break.

But the important thing was that the mother and all four pups were safe.

Back at the Inn, Lucas gathered as many towels as he could find. "Let's bring them into the living room, and I'll start a fire."

"Shouldn't we stay out here on the porch?" She was a mess. Dripping wet and covered with mud. At least she was telling herself it was mud. Judging by the smell, it was probably a whole lot more than that. Surely he didn't want her and the five dogs in his living room.

Apparently he did.

"That old potbelly won't give off enough heat." He gathered the puppies into his arms in one scoop and led Paige and the momma stray through the house. Once the canine family was all settled in front of the hearth, he began piling logs onto an iron grate.

"That was a crazy thing to do," he said.

It was. But in the moment Paige hadn't been thinking logically. All she knew was that she needed to get to those dogs. "They looked so helpless." Her gaze shifted to the momma, who was now nursing her pups. "And she was so sad." A lump formed in the back of Paige's throat. What was it about this island? First, she almost cried in front of Lucas, and now she was about to turn into a puddle over a canine reunion. At the rate things were going, she'd be a snotty mess when holiday commercials rolled around again.

Lucas lit a match and held it to the kindling he'd arranged under the logs. Once it caught, he turned to Paige. "You're shaking." He stood and started for the stairs. "Let me run and grab some more blankets."

"Actually, do you mind if I take that shower now?" she asked. Her teeth actually chattered as she spoke.

"Of course." Then after a flash of lightning he added, "But isn't there something about not showering during a storm?"

She laughed, but the stuttering sound was more shiver than

joy. "I'll take my chances. It's either that or death from my own smell. Besides, it's a lot less dangerous than being in that pipe."

"True." He smiled, and damn if he didn't look perfect. Certainly not like a man who'd just participated in a daring animal rescue. Even his hair had that sexy, rumpled, wet look some guys tried to get by using products they would later deny they ever bought. Sure, his coat and jeans were soaked, but at least they were clean. Then again, he hadn't gone for a swim in sludge. "There's a laundry chute in the bathroom. Toss the dirty stuff down, and we can throw it in the washer after dinner."

Paige couldn't imagine a detergent that was strong enough to clean her clothes. Not to mention the fact that her sweater was dry-clean only. She sniffed her shoulder and winced. "Might just throw them away." Or burn them. "But thanks."

When she walked into the bathroom, the sight of her own reflection nearly made her scream. Unlike her host, Paige's "wet look" was far from that of a model. She pried a lock of hair from her temple. More like plaster. If plaster was made from mud.

She dumped her clothes down the chute and turned on the tap. As soon as the water was warm, she stepped into the claw-foot tub and pulled the curtain around the circular rod. A soak would have felt like heaven to her aching muscles, but she didn't want to be away from the pups that long. So for now a shower would have to suffice. It took two rounds of shampoo to get her hair clean—marking the first time in her life she actually followed the bottle's directions to lather, rinse, repeat—and when she was finally satisfied that the water flowing to the drain was actually clear, she turned off the tap. As she did, the room went dark.

What the...

Paige slid the shower curtain open and groped along the wall in search of a towel, but when she found the hook, it was empty. *There should be some in the wardrobe in the bedroom.* A lot of good it did her to remember that now. She tried to picture the layout of the room. She was certain she'd seen at least a hand towel on a small rack next to the pedestal sink. She stepped out of the tub and slid her hand along the wall. Sink, faucet. She dropped to her knees...trash can...toilet...and then finally... bingo! Towel rack. She ran her hands along each shelf. Empty.

She thought about trying to take the shower curtain off the hooks, but that would take forever in the dark, and she was already freezing. Again.

There was only one choice: make a run for it. Paige opened the door and peeked out into the hall. Everything was dark except for the intermittent flashes of lightning illuminating the windows on the stairs. If she timed it just right, she would have enough light to make it to the door.

A bolt of lightning zigzagged through the sky. Paige stepped out into the hallway, and sure enough, the lightning did allow her to see. It was more what she saw that was the problem. Standing in front of her was Lucas Croft. Holding a flashlight. With the beam of light pointed directly at her chest.

Shit.

For a moment, neither of them said a word. Paige was far too shocked to form a coherent thought, let alone move. Lucas just stood there, his jaw slack, his eyes wide, and—her gaze dropped lower—his dick hard.

Holy hell.

He blinked, and the trance was broken. "Oh, shit. Sorry," he blurted out.

Paige tried to cover herself, one hand low and one hand high, although a lot of good one hand did on her boobs. "What are you doing up here?"

Lucas spun around. "Bringing you a flashlight." He waved the device in the air as proof. "What are you doing walking down the hall naked?"

She scurried toward her bedroom. "There weren't any towels in the bathroom." She closed the door behind her, not bothering to wait for his reply. A bolt of lightning lit the room, allowing her to see the bed. Perfect, she thought, as she dove under the covers. First time a man has seen her naked in what, three years? And then it only happened by accident. A slow smile curved her lips. Then again, from the looks of what was going on behind that button fly, Lucas Croft definitely liked what he saw.

....

Their awkward moment wasn't mentioned when she came downstairs. Lucas had left the flashlight outside her bedroom door. While she was appreciative, since without it she would probably have fallen and broken at least one body part, she didn't dare thank him, as doing so would acknowledge that he'd been upstairs at all, and that was one degree of conversation too close to that-which-shall-not-be-discussed.

He'd been busy while she was in the shower, serving the momma stray not only a bowl of water, but judging by the nearly licked-clean plate, a helping of leftover lasagna as well. He'd changed clothes, too, looking devastatingly handsome in a pair of faded jeans and a long-sleeved, hunter-green T-shirt that made his hazel eyes look the same color. Paige had chosen a pair of supersoft gray drawstring pants and a white T-shirt. She knew her white lace bra was visible through the thin fabric—a subtle reminder of what he'd had a not-so-subtle glimpse of in the hallway—but it served him right. He'd left that beam of light shining on her boobs a lot longer than necessary. Then again, maybe he was in shock. She smiled. Or maybe her boobs had secret powers. Stun-gun ta-tas. Her lame joke almost had her laughing out loud. Maybe she was the one who was in shock.

"What's so funny?" Lucas asked. He reached for the iron poker and jabbed at a few embers. The fire he'd started before "the incident" was nearing bonfire status, yet he still kept tending to it. Paige assumed it was his way of ignoring the elephant in the room.

"Just thinking about that tumble I took in the pipe," she said. "Not my finest moment. Then again, my mom did always tease that she should have named me Grace." A little self-deprecation was way better than admitting the truth: that she was imagining her breasts would qualify her to join the Avengers. Right, time to change the subject before her overactive, sex-deprived imagination started conjuring images of her alongside Thor that had nothing to do with saving the world.

She came to sit on the floor next to the litter of pups. They'd all nursed until their little bellies were full, then fallen asleep right where they were. Paige could relate. Not that she would ever eat in bed—crumbs and sheets were a horrible combination, second only to sand on sheets—but she could certainly see the advantage to having her food ready and waiting the moment she woke up. "How old do you suppose they are?"

Lucas looked over his shoulder at them. "Not sure." He stoked the logs one more time, then came to sit on the floor across from Paige. "They're small, but their eyes are open. So two, maybe three weeks?" He leaned back against the sofa. "They're cute though. In a naked-mole-rat kind of way."

Paige's mouth dropped open. "They do *not* look like naked mole rats."

Lucas raised a brow.

"Okay, maybe a little." She laughed. "But just at first. Now that their fur is dry..." She reached for one of the pups who had wriggled way from its mother. "They look adorable." She picked up the tiny brown puppy and nuzzled him against her chest. "Yes, don't you?" she asked the small dog and, to her absolute horror, realized she'd spoken to the animal in baby talk. Paige *never* spoke baby talk. Granted, she had zero experience around actual babies, but she hadn't spoken that way to her cat when he was a kitten. Then again, it's somewhat hard to treat a cat named Mr. Rochester like a baby, no matter what his age or size.

Fortunately, Lucas didn't seem to notice. That or he didn't care. Either way, Paige needed to change the subject. Her stomach growled, reminding her of the uneaten omelet and offering her the perfect means to switch topics. "Now that the pups are all fed..." She put the puppy back next to his mother and picked at a small piece of fuzz on one of the blankets. "I was thinking maybe we could eat lunch in here." She paused to gauge his reaction but saw nothing. "Or dinner, whatever meal is next." She shrugged. "But you know, together."

Lucas looked up to meet her gaze, which she quickly shifted back to the dogs. Dogs were safe. No complications. No mysterious women from their past and no chance of a broken heart. "To keep an eye on the puppies," she quickly added. But truth be told, hot-as-hell innkeeper aside, Paige didn't think she could stand to eat another meal alone. If she had to spend one more night listening to the grandfather clock tick off each passing minute, she was going to lose her mind.

"I have a confession to make."

This was it. He was going to tell her that although they were living under the same roof and had just battled the elements to save a canine family, he had absolutely no interest in dining with a guest. Nice breasts or not. Paige swallowed. "What's that?"

He took a deep breath. "I know the website talks about gourmet meals, but omelets and lasagna are sort of the limit to my culinary skills."

She couldn't hold back the laugh that bubbled up inside her. Of all the false advertising on the inn's website, that's what he was worried about?

"To be fair, you didn't indicate vegetarian on the reservation."

"And if I had?"

Now he laughed with her. "Touché."

"At this point, I would settle for mac and cheese." Paige hadn't eaten the powdery concoction since she was a girl, but the adrenaline shot of their adventure, not to mention the hallway incident, had worn off. If she didn't eat something soon, she thought she might actually faint. And with her luck, it wouldn't be a graceful swoon into her host's arms. No, she would undoubtedly fall ass over tits and end up sprawled all over the floor.

"Now that I can handle. One problem though." He glanced around the room lit only by flames. "No power."

"Oh yeah." *Smooth one, Parker.*

"I bought some meatless burgers," he said, glancing up at the rain-soaked window. "I could try firing up the grill."

"Absolutely not. Bad enough to have been out in that mess for these little guys. No way you're going out to cook."

Lucas pushed to his feet. "Let me see what I can find."

He went to the kitchen and, after opening what sounded like every one of the cabinets, returned with a wooden tray. Whatever was on it was covered by a dish towel.

"Do you know what the best part of being an adult is?" There was an unmistakable gleam in his eye.

"What?" She had to admit, her curiosity was piqued.

He sat down next to her and pulled the towel away with an exaggerated flourish. "You can eat dessert for dinner."

On the tray in front of her were chocolate bars, graham crackers, and a bag of marshmallows.

"S'mores?"

"Yep. I also have some cheese and an apple. But what fun would that be?"

His enthusiasm was contagious and Paige found herself playing along. "So an indoor camp-out?"

"Exactly."

She half expected his next idea to be building a pillow fort out of the couch cushions.

"I figured you'd want to keep an eye on these guys, so I thought we could get some blankets and pillows and just make a night of it."

Not quite a pillow fort, but close enough.

"Unless you think it's a bad idea," he quickly added. "But you might get cold upstairs without—"

"No, no," she interrupted. "I think camping *in* sounds great." She knew the grin on her face was far from playing it cool, but she didn't care. In front of her were a hot guy, puppies, and chocolate. Life didn't get much better than that.

They took turns roasting marshmallows on a straightened wire hanger Lucas dug out of the front closet. Paige couldn't remember the last time she made s'mores. Girl Scouts, maybe? When they were done, she was sure she'd exceeded her sugar intake for the next month if not two. "Those were…"

"Fattening? I know. But sometimes you've got to live a little."

"I was going to say delicious. And I couldn't agree more."

Lucas leaned closer, and his gaze dropped to her mouth, and all at once her insides felt as gooey as the marshmallows. "You've got…"

"Yes?" The word was more breath than sound.

He reached up, cupping her cheek with his hand while his thumb stroked her bottom lip "…a bit of chocolate."

"Oh." Her hand flew to her mouth.

"Don't worry." He held up his now chocolate-streaked thumb as proof. "I got it."

"Thanks." Usually her radar was a lot more accurate than that. Although to be fair, this guy was a hard one to read. One minute he's telling someone on the phone what a pain in the ass she is, and the next he's flirting with her. Then he's got a raging boner for her, then he's acting like they are in grade school. And not the age where you play spin the bottle either. More the age where you're all buddies and actually sleep at a sleepover.

"I can keep an eye on them if you have anything you need to do."

Whoa, talk about a change in direction. Paige wasn't sure if Lucas was suddenly trying to get rid of her or just double-checking that she really wanted to be there. Either way, she decided to go with honest and direct. "As it just so happens, my calendar is pretty clear," she said. And it was. She hadn't had so much as a text, let alone a call. That either meant the office had burned to the ground and Sammy was afraid to tell her or he was handling everything just fine. Something told her it was the latter. She'd bet her business on it. And in a way, she had. "Plus with the power and internet out…"

"Ah, good point." An awkward beat passed before he asked, "Is there anything you'd like to do?"

Nothing came to mind. "It's your house. What would you usually do about now?"

He shrugged. "Watch TV. Play video games."

She rolled her eyes. "What is it with men and video games?"

He raised a brow. "That was rather sexist." While she knew he was teasing, he was also correct.

"Touché," she said, echoing his earlier response.

"So you're telling me you've never played Xbox or PS4?"

"Let's just say eye-hand coordination isn't my strong suit." She'd failed at most sports and sucked at playing piano. "But I am pretty good at Wii, if you've got one of those." Who was she kidding, she was pro level when it came to bowling. Pro at electronic bowling. Was there a more pathetic declaration ever made? Thank God she hadn't said that out loud.

He smiled. "Afraid not."

Right, because that was popular like what, ten years ago? *Smooth, Parker. Might as well have asked him if he had a Nintendo 64. Or even better, Atari.* "Cards?"

"I don't think I have a full deck."

Now she was the one who raised a brow. "You do realize you left yourself wide open for a serious burn."

"Serious burn? Are we back in high school?"

"No, because then we would be playing Wii."

He laughed. It was a deep, warm sound, and all at once Paige knew she'd do just about anything to hear it again.

"It's just as well you don't have a deck."

"Why, are you a sore loser?"

Her face flushed. "And an even worse winner." Maybe it was years of playing cards with her grandmother and her older brother, but she and Marty had taken gloating to a new level.

"Why does that not surprise me?"

"I may or may not have a fairly obnoxious celebration dance."

"Spared by the missing jack of diamonds," he teased. A moment of silence passed between them, and once again, Paige thought Lucas might kiss her. It was a perfect moment—the fireplace bathing them in a warm glow, the rain tapping a hypnotic rhythm against the windows. Lucas leaned closer, but when his lips parted, all he did was speak. "We could just talk?"

"Talk?" Was this guy for real? Since when did a man suggest talking as a way to spend an evening? And what the hell was wrong with her radar? Had it been so long since a man made a move on her that she had forgotten how to read the signs?

Lucas nodded. "Seems like we've been doing that just fine for the past ten minutes. Maybe we could try to keep the streak going."

"Like tossing a ball back and forth as many times as we can without dropping it?"

"As long as your competitive nature doesn't apply to conversation as well."

"Do I strike you as the type who would make everything a competition?" She was, but how could he have already figured that out about her? So far they'd mostly spoken about food, dogs, and rain.

"Well, the ball analogy was very Monica Geller."

Sweet Jesus. The man had abs to die for, didn't mind spending the evening talking, *and* he got *Friends* references? Maybe the storm had taken her through some wormhole into another dimension. This guy was too good to be true. Unless the whole "let's talk" thing was just a ruse for getting her naked. Not that she thought that was a terrible idea; it would just be a sneaky way of going about it.

Yeah right, she thought. *He already had you naked today, and now here you are "just talking."*

She leaned back against the front of the couch so they were sitting side by side. "What do you want to talk about?"

"I don't know, whatever." Barely a beat passed before he had an idea. "Why don't you tell me what it is you do in Chicago."

Paige stiffened. Why was it that everyone assumed a single woman's life was lacking in some way? "I have a very full life, as a matter of fact. I have friends," who she never spent time with, "and hobbies," although for the life of her she couldn't really think of one, but if pressed she could find a way to pass a few hours. "And I have Mr. Rochester."

"Is that your boyfriend?"

"My boyfriend? Who I call Mr. Rochester?" She had to cover her mouth to keep from laughing.

He shrugged. "After all that *Fifty Shades* stuff, I don't presume to know what people do in their private lives."

"Mr. Rochester is my cat." She winced. "Okay, maybe not the best example of having a full life." And certainly boring compared to the images his reference conjured. "He's a four-year-old tabby."

"That's great and all." His smile softened. "But what I meant was what do you do for a living?"

"Oh." She felt a bit foolish but also relieved because *that* was a question she was more than happy to answer. "I'm a certified professional organizer." She said the words with pride, but they went over like the proverbial lead balloon.

He frowned. "That's a real profession?"

She sat up a little taller. "It most certainly is."

Lucas considered that for a moment, then asked, "Why do people hire you?"

"Because I'm good at what I do." She wasn't being cocky—okay, maybe a little—but she had the profits to back it up.

He smiled. "Obviously, given your ability to pay the rates here."

"I'll admit, it was a bit steep, but the woman I messaged led me to believe the place was in very high demand." She glanced over her shoulder at the empty parlor.

"Yeah, about that..." He shifted in his seat. "That was my sister. Her heart was in the right place, but her head? Not so much. She's also a bit of a con artist apparently."

"I don't know about that, but she did"—Paige searched for the right word—"embellish a bit."

Lucas snorted. "She embellished a *lot*." There was an awkward silence before he added, "I'm sorry she tricked you into thinking this place was open for business, let alone in high demand." He hesitated, then said, "If you want, I can issue you a full refund."

"No, that won't be necessary." The place wasn't exactly as advertised, but in some ways, it was exactly what she needed. "I've enjoyed my time here." She grinned. "You should consider adding animal rescue adventures to the website offerings."

"Lightning and storm waste available for an extra charge, of course."

"Of course."

They smiled at each other, and then a beat passed. And then another. Until they were just two people sitting in front of a romantic fire, close enough to...

"Does your sister live on the island too?" Paige asked. *Gah!*

Why the hell did she ask that? It was like she had some sort of disease that required her to fill every moment with conversation.

"Yeah, she runs a bookstore in the old fire station." He'd no sooner offered the tidbit of information than he abruptly changed the subject.

"Back to your...professional organization," he said. "No offense to your career and all, but why don't people just clean out their own mess?"

Paige looked around the room. Piles of books, old magazines, empty Amazon boxes. Had the guy ever heard of recycling? There were a bunch of free weights in one corner, a stack of electronic equipment that at some point had probably been a very nice surround-sound system, and six or seven Rubbermaid bins. She could see that a few were filled with paperwork, but the rest were a hodgepodge of who knows what.

"Hey, I like my stuff just the way it is," he said.

"That may very well be the case, but you are most definitely living in a 'before.'"

"Before?"

"As in 'before and after.'"

He stared at her nonplussed before the facade gave way to another genuine laugh. "Okay, okay, I may have a few items out of place."

She leveled her stare.

He held his hands up, palms facing her. "Okay, more than a few. But people really hire someone to clean out their house?"

"Not just clean it out, but organize it so hopefully they can manage to keep it that way on their own." Judging by the number of repeat customers, Paige knew that wasn't always the case, but it was always the goal. "Basically, I get rid of clutter. Most people are far too attached to make the cuts they need to simplify their life. That's where I come in."

He turned so he was facing her. "How can you make decisions about what other people should throw away?"

"I start with the keeps," she said. "That's how the first wave of sorting begins. I bring them into a room and I say, 'Your house is on fire and you can only keep as much as you can carry in one armload. What will you take?'"

"And that works?"

"It's how we start. But most of what survives the final cut ends up being the items they took out of the room that very first day."

He didn't look convinced.

"Like this," she said, sitting up straighter. "If your house was on fire and you knew all humans"—she glanced at the dogs—"and animals were safe, what would you take?"

Lucas stared into the flames. "Nothing. It can all burn to the ground."

"You don't mean that."

"Of course I do. It's only stuff. None of it matters." He turned back to look at her. There was a sadness in his eyes that took her breath away.

Her gaze shifted to the ornate cabinet next to the chair where Lucas had been sitting the night before. "What about that album you were looking at last night?"

"How do you know about that?"

"I came down for some water and—"

"And figured you'd spy on me?"

"No, it wasn't like that," she sputtered. "I...I just... When I saw—"

"It's none of your business what you saw." Lucas pushed to his feet. "You've got a lot of nerve, lady, coming into my home and invading my privacy like that." A vein pulsed in his neck. "And now you're going to try and tell me what I should do with all the crap in my life? Go to hell."

Paige wanted to explain. To start over. To go back in time. But he was gone before she could even utter an apology, taking the front stairs two at a time as he stormed up to bed.

She slumped back against the couch. He wasn't wrong; he was just venting about the wrong situation. Because while she hadn't been spying on him the night before, she *had* invaded his privacy when she'd snooped around the bedrooms he'd specifically told her were off-limits.

She deserved everything he'd said and more.

Paige stroked the momma dog's head. She'd come to the island to celebrate being single, and yet for some reason, the lifestyle she'd come to cherish suddenly rang hollow. "Looks like it's just you and me." The dog licked Paige's palm. At least someone in the house didn't hate her. She tossed another log on the fire, then arranged a blanket and one of the toss pillows into a makeshift bed on the floor before curling next to the litter of pups. "Goodnight, guys," she whispered. "Happy Valentine's Day."

CHAPTER 9

LUCAS STORMED UP THE STAIRS, and when he reached the tiny room he now called his, he slammed the door. Not because he was mad at Paige—she really hadn't done anything wrong by coming downstairs for a glass of water—but because he was mad at himself. Partly for being such a horse's ass and biting her head off and partly for the fact that he'd nearly kissed her. Twice.

He wasn't entirely sure he was going back into the B and B business, but either way, his sister was right. He didn't need his bad behavior documented online for all the world to read. If Sophie thought a review that mentioned limits on hot water usage would be bad, she'd really flip over one about an innkeeper who couldn't keep his hands to himself.

But Paige had looked so beautiful in the firelight, and in the quiet moments, it was all he could do not to take her in his arms. There were times he could have sworn she felt the same way. Like when he'd put his hand on her cheek and her lips parted in invitation. It was the perfect opportunity, but instead of kissing her senseless, he'd merely wiped a bit of chocolate off her lower lip. *Smooth, Croft.* Forget striking out; he hadn't even bothered to take a swing.

Lucas groaned. He was doing it again, acting like Paige was a potential hookup, when, in fact, she was a paying guest. Of course, it didn't help matters that he'd come upstairs to find her standing buck-ass naked in the hallway. The sight of her, all slick and soft feminine curves, had been like a shot of adrenaline right to his dick. He didn't think he'd ever been so hard in his life, something that wasn't lost on his houseguest. He wasn't sure if she even realized what she was doing, but in that moment, the one before the hasty covering and the fumbled apology, her gaze had dropped and her eyes had flared. And then her teeth had sunk ever so slightly into her bottom lip, and all he could think about was having those lips wrapped around…

Holy hell.

Lucas ran a hand through his hair. It didn't matter how much he'd wanted to press her against that wall, or how later he'd wanted to lay her out in front of the fire, taking his time to explore every inch of her until neither of them could wait one second longer. He needed to get a grip. And not just on how he was acting around Paige, but on his life in general. He owed it not only to Maddie, but to Jenny's memory as well.

He climbed into his makeshift bed. Lucas knew it was ridiculous that he still slept on the floor in the spare room. But that first night alone, he couldn't bring himself to sleep in their bed. He was too afraid he would reach across the mattress in the middle of the night to find nothing but emptiness. The small twin bed didn't leave much room for false hope or expectations, and somehow that made it easier to sleep.

But not tonight.

He didn't remember falling asleep, but when he did, he dreamed of Jenny for the first time in months. The other times his late wife had visited his subconscious had been truly dream-like. Soft-focused and ethereal, they were as delicate as the early-morning mist. But this time it was different. This time her image was so vivid, her presence so lifelike, Lucas could have sworn that it was real.

She came to him like she always did, wearing the pale-yellow sundress she'd had on the day he proposed. He'd brought her a bouquet of daffodils, which she swore were her favorite though he suspected she'd told him that because at the time, stealing a few from his neighbor's garden was all he could afford. Years later, she'd planted daffodil bulbs in front of the inn so whether they'd been her favorite all along or not, they'd certainly taken on a special meaning after that day, which was why Lucas wasn't at all surprised to see this dream version of her holding a bouquet of the bright-yellow flowers.

Jenny sat on the porch in one of the rockers. As he drew closer, she looked up at him and smiled. "She has your eyes."

"Maybe, but the rest of her is all you," Lucas replied.

Jenny laughed. The delicate sound was the sweetest torture to his ears. "She does have my crazy curls."

That he knew. Lucas had spent countless mornings trying to tame Maddie's dark mane into submission, but he never complained because running a brush through his daughter's hair felt like a tangible connection to a past she was slowly forgetting. Most days he pulled it all back into pigtails, but on the rare occasion that she wanted to leave it down, she was the spitting image of her mother, something he was quick to point out.

"I miss you" was all he said. Three simple words that held so much truth.

Jenny grew more serious. "I'm okay, Luc." She was suddenly in front of him. No standing, no walking. She was just...there. "And you will be too." Then she leaned forward and kissed him on the cheek. Even asleep, part of him knew it wasn't real, but that's not how it felt. Unlike the movies, where ghosts were cold and had no touch, he could feel Jenny's lips on his cheek, her warm breath on his face, and when he reached for her, he wasn't grasping thin air, but rather soft skin.

"How..."

She pressed a finger to his lips, and he felt that too. He wanted to believe she was real, to open his eyes and know that Jenny was back in his arms and in his life, but even asleep he knew it wasn't true. All he could do was enjoy the moment before it vanished.

He flexed his fingers against her waist. "Don't go." The words fell from his lips like a prayer, but he'd no sooner said them than she was suddenly by the rocking chair again. She set the daffodils on the table, then turned toward the ocean. Lucas followed her gaze out to the dark beach, but saw nothing. When he looked back to Jenny, she was gone.

Lucas opened his eyes to find he was alone in the dark. But unlike the countless other times he'd woken from a dream where

Jenny had visited him in his sleep, he didn't feel the overwhelming sense of loss. In fact, as he stared at the plaster ceiling, he felt unusually calm.

He'd once told Sophie about the dreams he'd had of Jenny. According to her, dreams were an important part of the grieving process. She'd even brought him a book on the subject. He'd balked at the idea, claiming he had too much to do to read about wacky dream theories, but one night a few months ago, he'd finally cracked it open. He'd never admit as much to his sister, but some of it made sense.

According to the book, there were two types of dreams. The most common were memory dreams. Those were scenes from the lives of the deceased, or memories that came to life, bringing the lost loved one with them. The second type was called a visitation dream. That was when the deceased loved one supposedly crossed over to visit someone left behind. These were meant to provide reassurance and peace.

Lucas wasn't sure what he'd just experienced, but before he could give it too much thought, he drifted back to sleep. When he woke again, he felt more rested than he had in years. When he checked his watch, Lucas's eyes grew wide. Ten o'clock? He hadn't slept that late since college.

He rolled off the mattress and pulled on his jeans. He picked up the T-shirt he'd worn the night before and gave it a sniff. Nope. After tossing it into the overflowing hamper, he settled on the black V-neck sweater Sophie had given him for his birthday. Seemed a bit dressy for a day around the house, but it was soft and it was clean, so it worked.

The electricity must have come back on at some point, because when he got to the kitchen, there was a carafe of coffee waiting on the counter. He touched the glass. Still hot. Excellent. There was a lot he needed to say to his guest, but words came easier after caffeine. So instead of heading straight to the living room, Lucas reached for a mug so he could pour himself a cup of courage. There were usually at least one or two on the counter, but for some reason none were in sight. Weird. But then he opened the cabinet, and it all made sense. Inside were rows of mugs, organized from left to right in descending size. Occupational hazard? He'd certainly bring that up later, but for now he was more concerned about apologizing to Paige than he was with questioning her compulsive need to organize his cabinets.

"Morning," she said from behind him.

Lucas turned to find her standing in the doorway, an empty coffee mug in one hand and a sleeping puppy held against her chest with the other.

"I needed a refill," she said. "But this guy was so content, I didn't have the heart to put him down." She made her way closer to the French press, then paused.

"Here, let me," Lucas offered, refilling her mug. He took a large swig of coffee, followed by a deep breath. "I'm sorry for the way I acted last night." He meant the apology in more ways than one, but Paige only seemed aware of the most obvious.

"I swear I wasn't spying on you. I just came down for a glass of water, and then I heard a noise so I went to see what it was, and then I saw you sitting by the fireplace and—" She was talking so quickly, even the pup opened one eye.

"It's okay," he said, cutting her off so she could take a breath. "You didn't do anything wrong. I totally overreacted."

She exhaled in relief, then smiled. "I honestly didn't intend to lurk in the shadows. I would have come in and probably annoyed you by asking a bunch of questions." The smile slipped from her face. "But I thought it best to leave you alone." She hesitated, like she wanted to say more but wasn't sure if she should. Clearly she'd chosen the latter because when she spoke again, it was on an entirely different subject.

"The power is back on." She rolled her eyes at herself. "Which I guess you already know."

Lucas's gaze shifted to the unlit router on top of the refrigerator. "No internet though."

"I'll survive." From the look on Paige's face, Lucas wasn't the only one surprised by her statement.

"Listen," he began, "I know that not much about this place is as advertised. And I've been possibly the worst host ever..." He took a deep breath. "Anyway, there's this small hotel down by the harbor. I'm sure they have rooms. If you want, I can move your stuff over there until the ferry opens."

Paige smiled. "Thanks, but I'm just fine here."

"Really?" Lucas cleared his throat. "I mean, that's great." Talk about the understatement of the century. The money from the booking had already been applied to the balance of the tax bill. Moving Paige to the hotel would have had to go on his credit card, which was already busting at the seams. Still, the relief he felt had less to do with his budget and more to do with the woman currently nuzzling a puppy in his kitchen. He couldn't explain it, but he wasn't ready for Paige Parker to walk out of his life just yet.

"What do you say we start over?"

A tiny furrow formed between her brows. "Didn't we already do that?"

"And what, you've never heard of a double do-over?" Lucas knew his reference was a bit immature, the side effect of spending the majority of his time with a four-year-old. With any luck, Paige would see it as less dork and more charm.

Her mouth curved into an amused grin that could have gone either way, but then she bit her lip ever so subtly, which definitely tipped the scales in charm's favor. "Um, no, can't say I have," she said. "Does it require some supersecret handshake?"

Lucas wanted to say that it was customary to seal such deals with a kiss, but instead he merely stuck out his hand. She placed her free hand in his just as she had the first time they'd started over, only this time she didn't grasp his hand like she'd just negotiated the deal of a lifetime. This time her touch was gentle and soft, and all at once Lucas wanted to feel those fingers strumming leisurely down his back. Preferably in bed with their naked bodies entwined in a postorgasmic embrace. *Whoa. Way to be oddly specific, Croft.*

"Shall I whip us up some eggs?"

"Actually," she said, lifting the tiny puppy so she and the dog were nose to nose, "Leonardo and I already ate. He had some milk from his momma, and I found a granola bar in a cabinet." Her eyes darted to his. "Hope it's okay that I scrounged around."

He should have been down in time to offer his guest a proper breakfast. Bad enough she had to fend for herself, but even worse

that his behavior had her feeling unsure if she should. "Of course."
He raised a brow. "Leonardo, eh?"

"I couldn't very well call them puppies one through four."

"After DiCaprio, I presume. Let me guess… Your favorite
movie when you were young was *Titanic*?"

Paige rolled her eyes. "*Please.*"

"Da Vinci?" he asked. Not quite as clichéd but still fairly
"extra," as his sister might say.

Paige surprised him by shaking her head. "Da Turtle."

Now that one he didn't see coming. He was fairly certain he
knew the answer to his next question, but he still asked, "And the
other three?"

She grinned. "Michelangelo, Raphael, and Donatella."

"You've named the puppies after the Teenage Mutant Ninja
Turtles?" This woman was turning out to be quite the enigma.

"Well, they *were* living in a sewer."

"Fair point. But don't you mean Donatello?"

"Nope. One is a girl."

"I stand corrected."

She turned toward the living room, then looked back over her
shoulder. "Come on. I'll introduce you to the rest of the pack."

"Does this mean you're their—"

"Don't you dare say rat sensei."

Lucas chuckled as he watched her walk out of the room.
Smoking hot and a knowledge of his favorite comic-book heroes?
Paige Parker might have been a certified pain in the ass, but in the
back of his mind, part of him already knew she had the potential
to be his perfect match.

....

Paige made her way down the hall and into the living room. When she'd turned around, she could have sworn Lucas was checking out her ass. And it wasn't the first time. Even now she could practically feel the heat of his stare following each sway of her hips. On one level, she knew she should have been offended. Eyes up here, buddy, and all that. But on another level, she was shamelessly flattered. Not to mention completely fascinated with Lucas Croft's apparent obsession with her backside. Guys had always checked out her breasts. But her butt? Let's just say it was a lot to look at.

When she reached the fireplace, she knelt on the floor next to the pups. Their mother lifted her head for a moment before going back to sleep. Poor thing. Couldn't have been easy to endure that storm all day and then have four rug rats feeding on her all night. She cringed at the thought of having one hungry mouth munching on her nipples. But four?

Speaking of breasts...

She looked down at the puppy she still held in her arms. He was snuggled quite contently against her chest and let out a squeak of protest as she passed him to Lucas. "You've already met Leo," she said. "And this is Raphael." She reached for the pup trying to nudge his brother out of the way for what was apparently a more desirable teat on which to feed. "He's a bit of a bully." She lifted the tan-colored dog to look him in the eyes. "Aren't you?" The pup wiggled his rear end in an attempt to break free. "No matter where the others are feeding, that's where he wants to be."

Raphael yelped. The sound was far stronger than the noises his siblings made.

"I see he's got the New York accent down," Lucas said as he sat on the floor beside her.

Paige smiled. "All he needs is a little red mask." She kissed the pup on the head and placed him back with his mother.

"That is Michelangelo," she said. "But I just call him Mikey." The black-and-white pup was tugging on his sister's tail. "Fitting, as he seems to be the most playful." She moved him to the other side of the pack. "Jury is still out on whether or not he likes pizza."

Lucas nodded. "Or if he can surf."

Paige was impressed. Not everyone she met was so well versed in TMNT trivia, and if she was honest, it was more than a little bit of a turn-on. *Wow, couldn't get much nerdier than that*, she thought. Sammy was always on her to let him list her on whatever dating app was trending hottest that week. For a moment, she imagined the look on his face if she finally agreed, but only if the listing said she was looking for a nonsmoker who did his own laundry, knew how to cook, believed "ladies first" applied to more than just doorways, and had a working knowledge of all things Ninja Turtle.

"And this little sweetie," she said, picking up the smallest pup, an all-black female, "is Donatella."

"And are you calling her Donna?"

Paige considered the option for a moment, then decided against it. "No. She's delicate and, though small, has a personality large enough to justify the name."

"I can see you've given these a lot of thought."

She shrugged. "I had a lot of time on my hands," she said. "These guys are cute, but they're not big on conversation." She left out the part about not having much else to do once he'd huffed out of the room, leaving her alone for the night with nothing but canine companions.

Lucas stroked the head of the pup snuggled in his lap, tracing the white zigzag that stretched between his eyes. "What made you name this little guy Leonardo?"

"Well, Leonardo is the courageous leader and also the most devoted to Splinter," she explained. "And this one was always trying to wiggle over to me last night."

Lucas smiled. "So you *are* their rat leader."

She wrinkled her nose at him. "Sensei. Not rat."

Paige had to fight back a grin. She might have feigned outrage over being called a rat, but deep down she was secretly pleased Lucas referred to her as the leader of the pack—vermin or not—versus typecasting her as April, their plucky human companion.

"What about the momma?"

Paige considered her answer. "I'm not sure. Will have to get back to you on that."

"Fair enough." Lucas looked up from the litter to meet her gaze. "I have to admit, I'm more than a bit impressed by your comic-book knowledge."

She laughed. "Well, don't be. My expertise in the area is limited to turtles and Power Rangers."

"Power Rangers?"

"Oh yeah. Begged my mom to let me be the green one for Halloween, but she thought the mask would obstruct my vision."

"Now see, I would have totally guessed Pink Ranger," Lucas said.

"Guess there's a lot you don't know about me," Paige said.

There was a lot she didn't know about Lucas Croft, either, something she would very much like to correct. "We could change that," she blurted out.

Lucas cocked his head to one side. "What did you have in mind?"

Talk about a loaded question. If this had been some X-rated version of a nineties Disney Channel show, a tiny animated version of Paige would have appeared on her shoulder to whisper all manner of depraved suggestions. Scratch that, she thought. A tiny animated version of Sammy would have appeared, no doubt holding a martini glass and wearing his favorite Elton John bedazzled sunglasses. But this wasn't *Lizzie McGuire: The Sex-Drought Years*, this was her very real, very boring life. So instead of suggesting any of the dirty thoughts that immediately came to mind—all of which involved far less clothing—she went with her original idea. "How about Twenty Questions: The Paige Parker Edition."

He grinned. "I'm not familiar with that version."

"It's quite simple really. I ask you twenty questions."

His head fell back on a laugh. "That's not even close to the point of the game."

He was right, but what fun would that be? "My version, remember?"

Lucas narrowed his eyes. "Okay, deal. On one condition. We each get ten questions."

"You're a tough negotiator, Mr. Croft, but you have a deal."

"Ladies first."

Not quite the "ladies first doesn't only apply to doors" exception she'd been hoping for, but it was a good start.

She took a moment to consider her first question. There was so much she wanted to know about her mysterious host and his even more mysterious house, but she needed to tread lightly. This wasn't a prospective client or vendor, and it certainly wasn't someone she was interviewing for a job. If it were any of those, she'd have had no problem. But real life, personal interactions? Paige was more than a little rusty with those, and even if she wasn't, the expression *bull in a china shop* came to mind. Last thing she wanted was to scare him away.

"So, what made you decide to live here?" she asked. It seemed like the perfect place to start, somewhat general but still on topic.

"You mean a sleepy little island with no cars?"

Paige nodded. Aurelia Island wasn't exactly a hotbed of social activity.

"My parents bought a place here years ago."

"Oh, so you grew up here?"

"No. I grew up in Pennsylvania. The home they bought here was meant to be for their retirement." There was an unmistakable sadness in his voice.

"I take it that plan changed?" Paige didn't want to pry, but the way he looked at her made her want to comfort him. It was a sorrow that made him look like a very young boy. Then again, Paige had once read that no matter how old you were when you lost your parents, you all at once felt like a vulnerable child. It was hard to imagine Lucas Croft feeling like that, but if the look in his eyes was any indication, the article she'd read was absolutely right.

Lucas nodded. "They were killed by a drunk driver." He

exhaled a heavy breath. "Classic story. Asshole has one too many, no one takes his keys, and he ends up crossing the line into oncoming traffic." He drew one leg up to rest his elbow on his knee. "The officer on the scene said they didn't suffer. The head-on collision killed them instantly." His gaze was locked, unseeing, on the empty hearth in front of him. "I guess I should be grateful for that."

"I'm so sorry." The words alone seemed trite and inadequate, but she meant them. Hopefully that came across.

His eyes met hers, and in that moment, she knew he felt her sincerity. "Thank you." He mustered half a smile. "Ironic, really. They buy a retirement dream home on an island without cars and end up killed by one before they could even move in."

"Is that why you live here now?"

"Sort of." Lucas reached for Michelangelo and began stroking his back. The tiny pup's eyes closed almost instantly. "Soph had just graduated from college. She came down for a few weeks to clean the place out and ended up staying."

"She was young to lose her parents. You both were."

"She took it really hard," he said, totally deflecting the second part of what Paige had said. "At first, I thought maybe she was hiding out here, you know? Like clinging to their memory or maybe avoiding drunk drivers by avoiding cars." He gave a weak smile. "Maybe both, who knows? But she just sort of clicked here. The people, the pace. It was all perfect for her."

"And you?"

He grimaced. "If you'd have told me when I was in college that I'd be living here now, I would have said you were crazy. But when Sophie called to tell us about this place... Well, it seemed like the perfect spot to raise a family."

The use of the plural pronoun wasn't lost on Paige, and her thoughts went immediately to the photograph of Lucas and his pregnant wife. Should she ask what happened to her, or was that too personal? She'd barely had a chance to consider the options before Lucas changed the subject.

"I'm starving." He glanced at the grandfather clock as it struck noon in the hallway behind him.

"But what about my ten questions?" Paige asked.

"By my count, you have five left." He stood up. "Four, if I count the one you just asked."

Her mouth popped open. "That doesn't count. I was only asking if we were going to finish."

Lucas reached for Paige's hand and pulled her to her feet. "Relax, I'll credit you back the point...I mean the question."

She smiled to herself. Seemed she wasn't the only one with a competitive streak.

"But first, I'm going to run and borrow some dog food from my neighbor. Then we'll see about cashing in that rain check for mac and cheese."

CHAPTER 10

ADMITTEDLY, LUCAS WASN'T MUCH OF a cook, but he considered himself an expert when it came to mac and cheese. Sure, it was the powdered kind that could probably survive the apocalypse, but it was warm and tasty, and for a few months when she was two years old, it was all Maddie would eat. That, and these little baby-food chicken hot dogs, and even those were only acceptable if piled into some sort of modern-art display.

Paige seemed to enjoy it. In fact, she said it brought her back to her childhood. Although to be fair, that didn't necessarily mean it was a positive memory. Either way, he was sure it hit the spot when all she'd had to eat in the past twenty-four hours was a granola bar and s'mores.

After lunch, Lucas washed the dishes while Paige dried them. He felt guilty about a guest doing household chores, but the more time they spent together, the less Paige Parker seemed like a paying guest and the more she felt like a—the word *date* came to mind, but he quickly dismissed it—friend? Yes, that's it. And why wouldn't she? Her stay had been far from customary, what with the storm and the puppies and then the power outage. It was normal for her to feel more like a friend than a customer after all they'd been through.

"I believe there is still the matter of my five questions," Paige said when they were done. The tone of her voice made it seem like they were in a boardroom, not the kitchen of what his sister referred to as a "shabby chic" inn, whatever that meant. Perhaps that was just how Paige operated—all business, all the time. Then again, she certainly had a softer side when it came to the dogs. She was downright mushy with them at times, which was directly at odds with almost everything else he knew about her, although admittedly that wasn't much. But that was all about to change, since he still had all ten of his questions.

Paige, on the other hand, did not. He noticed that she conveniently ignored the controversial sixth-question debate, but Lucas didn't mind. Partly because he'd only been teasing her and partly because, much to his surprise, he didn't mind answering her questions. He'd never been an open book, as they say, preferring to listen rather than speak, and after losing both his parents and later his wife, that inclination had only grown stronger. But for some reason, telling Paige about the loss of his parents felt cathartic, even after so many years.

Lucas took a seat on one of the iron barstools. "Shoot."

Paige joined him at the island, but rather than diving right in, she took her time. Lucas assumed she was weighing her options. She was already halfway through her ten questions. If she was as competitive about Twenty Questions: The Paige Parker Edition as she was about cards and video games, she was probably strategizing how to turn five into seven.

"Just so you know," he teased. "Two-part questions count twice."

"I'll keep that in mind." She smiled, but the expression didn't reach her eyes. "I was actually just trying to decide…"

Her tone had changed. Lucas knew exactly what was coming next.

"When you were talking about moving here," she said, "you said your sister called 'us'…"

"Me and my late wife," he offered. It was a fair question for her to ask. To be honest, he was surprised it hadn't come up sooner. He'd been dreading it, of course, the moment when the look on her face would turn to one of pity. It was an inevitable reaction when people heard the news. But as he searched Paige Parker's expression, he didn't find pity, but rather genuine concern.

"What was her name?" she asked. The question took him by surprise. Most people blurted out "I'm sorry" or "How terrible." But not Paige. She didn't belittle his loss with some generic response. Instead, she asked her name. It was a simple question, but it meant so much, because his late wife wasn't a statistic or a tragic story. She was a person who had a name and loved ones who missed her.

"Jenny." Lucas's gaze shifted to the hallway. "I was looking at photos of her the other night when you saw me in the living room."

"I figured they had to have been of someone you'd lost," Paige said. "You seemed so sad, but there was also something almost peaceful in your expression. At least from what I could tell."

Lucas knew exactly what she was talking about. He felt it, although he never quite understood it. How he could be so filled with anguish, yet at the same time feel like there was no place in the world he'd rather be. Looking at those images made him long for happier days, but at the same time brought him comfort like nothing else in his life. In the end, the pain far outweighed the comfort, which was why he'd forced himself to keep those albums locked in the cabinet. Until that night.

"She died two years ago," he said. She hadn't asked, but it was the next logical question.

"Will you tell me about her? Or is that too painful?"

Lucas considered his answer. "No, I think it actually might help." In the early days, Jenny was never far from his thoughts. She was with him every day, from the moment he opened his eyes and reality seeped through the sleepy edges of his consciousness until he lay down in the bed at night. But lately thoughts of her seemed fewer and farther between. It wasn't something he could control. It just...happened. "Lately, my memories of her are starting to feel like those old 8mm movies, sort of grainy and fuzzy around the edges." He hated that. Hated it even more that Maddie was starting to forget her mother entirely. "Most everyone in my life tries to avoid the topic." He smirked. "Probably because I bit their heads off when they tried to bring it up before, but now..."

"You feel ready?"

He nodded, but it was more complicated than that. He wasn't ready to talk about Jenny to just anyone. He was ready to talk about her with Paige.

"How did you two meet?" she asked, offering him a place to start.

Lucas smiled. "In a completely boring way," he said. "Wish I had a better story for you—like we were high-school sweethearts or we met at the top of the Empire State Building or something—but fact is we met while waiting in line at a Starbucks."

"I guess if it's meant to be, it will be. No drama necessary," she said. "Nice *Sleepless in Seattle* reference, by the way. Didn't peg you for a rom-com fan."

"I'm not," he said. "But what man hasn't been subjected to watching that film?"

Paige nodded. "Or *When Harry Met Sally*. Or *Notting Hill*. Or *The Proposal*."

Lucas held up his hands. "I get your point."

Paige blushed. "Sorry. Favorite genre."

"I can tell," he said.

"How long were you married?"

Not long enough, he wanted to answer. But instead he stuck to the facts. "Five years."

"And did you live here the whole time?"

Lucas appreciated the fact that Paige was asking him questions about Jenny's life, as opposed to her death. People were usually so focused on the tragedy, they forgot that before the loss, there'd been a life.

"Only two years," he said. "The place was a real mess when we bought it. Personally, I thought it was a lost cause and that the sellers should have been looking for a developer to tear it down, not some poor saps to spend their life savings trying to restore it." He smiled. "But the Realtor was no fool. She framed this big black-and-white photo of the place in its heyday. Jenny took one look at it, and she was sold."

"And you?"

"Not so much." He chuckled. "But I was never very good at saying no to her, so here we are." He looked around the room. "The place has gotten away from me a bit lately, but you should have seen it when we were done." He felt a sense of pride that was quickly dashed by the disappointment he felt over letting their hard work slip so far away.

"It still looks great. Just needs a little TLC."

Lucas laughed. "You're a horrible liar."

"Okay, maybe a little more than that," Paige admitted. "But I can still tell how much work it must have been."

"Took forever." Lucas drew a deep breath. He'd reached the point of the story where things would take a dark turn. He wasn't quite sure what to say. *And then my wife died at the ripe old age of twenty-nine* would be a surefire conversation killer.

Paige seemed to sense his uncertainty. Her expression softened. "How long has she been gone?"

"Just over two years," he said. "She went to the store and..." He paused to regroup. No matter how many times he told the story, this part still ripped him apart. "The doctor said it was a cerebral aneurysm. Didn't make sense. She didn't smoke, didn't have high blood pressure. And no one in her family had any history. Not that logic mattered. She collapsed in the store and was gone in minutes." He focused his gaze on a grain pattern that stretched the length of the wooden countertop. "Paramedics said there was nothing they could do."

Lucas paused to swallow the lump that had formed in his throat. But when he tried to speak again, he found he had no words. He looked up at Paige and their eyes met, and for the first time he felt as though someone understood him. And not just in a way that expressed condolences or concern, but someone who really understood how it felt to have found love and lost it.

Neither of them spoke for several minutes. It was Paige who finally broke the silence. "I can't imagine having to pick up the pieces after that," she whispered.

"Believe me," he said. "There were days I didn't even want to try." When he got the call that Jenny had died, his first thought was that he wanted to go with her. After all, they'd stood before God and their families and promised to spend their lives together, and lives were supposed to be a hell of a lot longer. Their marriage was meant to be a hell of a lot longer. It wasn't the deal he'd signed up for, so why should he honor the lines about till death do us part? Why did death have to mean the end of their love?

But then he'd had his second thought: Maddie. That sweet girl was the manifestation of everything he and Jenny had meant to each other. Now she was left with only one parent to keep the promise they'd both made to her the morning she was born. *We'll always take care of you.* Jenny couldn't hold up her end of that promise, so it all fell on Lucas's shoulders. He'd never felt so unprepared for a job in his entire life, but he kept going, dragging himself out of bed each morning not only for Maddie, but for Jenny. He couldn't bring his wife back to her daughter, but he vowed he was damn well going to try to fill the void.

"How did you get through it?"

"My sister was a huge help," he said, knowing full well that was the understatement of the century. Sophie had been by his side every step of the way the last two years. She'd come with him to the hospital when he had to do the unthinkable and claim his young wife's body, and she'd stayed with him while he made all of the necessary arrangements. "To be honest, I barely even remember those first few days. She took care of everything." Aside from caring for Maddie, which he was somehow able to do without fail, he was barely able to function. But thanks to Sophie, the necessary decisions were made, the flowers were ordered, and the church was booked. Not that different from their wedding but for the color of the clothing and the fact that Jenny was alone on the altar. Funny how some of life's biggest moments had some of the same rituals.

"You're lucky to have her so close," Paige said.

Not trusting his voice, Lucas merely nodded. Although he often complained about just how close, the truth was he owed his sister more than he could ever repay. She'd seen him through his grief-filled fog and every horrible night after. And don't even get him started on what a help she'd been with Maddie. He gave her shit for all the sparkles and glitter she introduced into his daughter's life, but if it weren't for Sophie, Maddie would probably be sporting a crew cut by now. No way he could have dealt with those curls on his own. At least not right away. Which brought him to the other truth he needed to share…

"I have a daughter," he said. "Her name is Maddie." The thought of his life with her brought a smile to his face. She'd not only gotten him through that dark time, but she was still pulling him through the memories.

"How old is she?" Paige asked. Lucas hadn't given much

thought to dating, so he'd certainly never considered how a woman might react to the news that he came as part of a package deal. But Paige seemed unfazed by this information and, if anything, genuinely interested.

"Four." He gave a small laugh. "She'll be five in a few weeks, which, as she is constantly reminding me, means she won't be a baby anymore."

Paige smiled. "Five going on fifteen?"

He nodded. "I blame her Aunt Sophie. Maddie is perfectly content to fish and skip rocks when she's with me, but then she spends the day with her aunt and it's all glitter nail polish and," Lucas cringed, "boy-band music."

"Hey, don't be knocking boy bands." Paige sat up a little taller on her stool. "I'll have you know I had a Backstreet Boys poster on my wall when I wasn't much older than she is."

Lucas groaned. "Guess I should be grateful she hasn't redecorated her room."

"Oh, but she will. I hate to break it to you, but what you're seeing now is just the tip of the iceberg. Pretty soon there will be YouTubers in your life."

"Already happened." He grimaced. "Her favorite show is some kid opening toys." He shook his head. "Guess I'm the dinosaur for thinking Barney was still a thing."

Then they both laughed. Was he really smiling and even laughing after reliving the events of the last two years? Sophie would no doubt tell him that was progress. Lucas didn't know about that. What he did know was that it felt good to be able to speak of the past without feeling the crushing weight of overwhelming grief.

"You'll be fine," Paige said. She was talking about navigating Maddie's teenage years, but Lucas knew she meant it in the broader sense as well. And for the first time, Lucas agreed. He would be fine. So would Maddie. Still didn't mean he wanted a teenager anytime soon.

"I don't want her to grow up too quickly. It's already flying by." A friend of his mom's had given him some advice at Maddie's christening. She'd told him to enjoy every moment because "while the days will feel long, the years will be short." At the time, he didn't fully understand what she meant, but he was starting to.

"What about you?"

"Me?" She stiffened. The movement was subtle, but not lost on Lucas. "Oh, I don't have any kids." That wasn't what he meant, but now that he realized the miscommunication, he could understand her reaction. No doubt she was regularly inundated with questions on the topic. It never ceased to amaze him how people could be so pushy when it came to something so personal. He and Jenny had experienced it pretty much from the moment they walked down the aisle. "When are you going to start a family?" "You're not getting any younger," and his favorite, "Time to get a bun in that oven."

"No," he said. "I mean, what made you come here?"

"You mean to a sleepy little island with no cars?" she asked, echoing his earlier line.

"In winter no less." Lucas leaned forward, placing one elbow on the counter and resting his chin in the palm of his hand. "You know my story, Paige Parker. Now tell me yours. And you can start with why in the world a beautiful woman like you is spending a week alone at the beach."

Her face flushed and a warmth spread through his chest. Complimenting her was an attempt to put her at ease, but her response pleased him far more than he'd expected.

She shifted in her chair, and the red in her cheeks became more noticeable. "I'm celebrating Singles Day."

For a moment, Lucas drew a blank. But then he remembered the special request that had accompanied the booking. "Ah, that would explain the cake." He'd thought a request for a cake inscribed with the words "Happy Singles Day" was a mistake, or maybe even a joke. Either way, he had ignored it.

Paige raised a brow. "Yeah, where is that, by the way?"

"Afraid you'll have to add that to the grievances you'll be filing with the booking site."

She shook her head. "It's becoming quite a list."

"Ah yes, but on the other hand, there are unadvertised perks."

"Like what?"

"Not every day you get to play with a litter of adorable puppies."

Paige nodded. "So we'll call it even on the cake."

He was half-afraid to ask, but curiosity got the better of him. After all, whatever she was about to tell him had brought her to the point of booking a last-minute vacation. Surely he would find it amusing if nothing else. "What is Singles Day anyway?"

Her eyes lit up. "Actually, it's called Singles Appreciation Day or, in some places, Singles Awareness Day."

He cocked his head to one side. "Sad."

She pursed her lips, then let him have it with both barrels. "It's not sad. There's nothing *sad* about loving yourself and being content with who you are. The latest census showed that nearly half the country is single."

That wasn't what he meant, but the exasperated look on her face was so adorable, Lucas couldn't help but laugh. And once he started, he couldn't stop. Paige glared at him, which only made him laugh harder, and when she crossed her arms indignantly over her chest, he nearly doubled over. He hadn't laughed this hard in ages. It was like he was back in grade school with a serious case of giggles. "No, no, I mean the acronym." He struggled to catch his breath and, when he finally did, explained. "Singles Appreciation Day," he said, saying the words slowly so as to separate them. "S-A-D. Sad. Rather unfortunate acronym, don't you think?" He'd no sooner finished when the laughter returned. Hell, his abs actually hurt.

Paige's resolve cracked, and her frown melted into an amused grin. "Yeah, I noticed that as well. But for some reason when you said it—"

"You figured I was just being an asshole?"

"Let's just say you're lucky I don't have that cake," she said, shaking her head. "Or you would be wearing some of it right now."

"Sorry," he said, trying his best to act contrite and failing miserably. "Let me make it up to you."

She narrowed her eyes. "How?"

"By celebrating Singles Day with you."

She snorted. "I think you're missing the point of the holiday."

"Not at all. We can celebrate being alone." He winked. "Together."

"You seriously want to celebrate Singles Day with me?"

He'd have thought she was being intentionally obtuse if it weren't for the genuine look of surprise on her face. "Yes. When is it?"

"Today actually. The day after Valentine's Day. The day also known as Half-Price Chocolate Day, but that is beside the point."

Lucas clapped his hands together. "Perfect." He started for the front door.

"Where are you going?" she asked.

"To the store." He shrugged into his coat. "A special occasion calls for a special meal."

CHAPTER 11

PAIGE COULDN'T SAY FOR SURE, because as far as she knew there weren't any guidelines or rules when it came to celebrating Singles Day. But she was fairly certain that it wasn't customary to mark the occasion by going on a first date. Then again, she wasn't entirely sure if that's what Lucas had suggested. He'd merely left for the store, promising to return with the ingredients for a suitable celebratory meal and hopefully a bottle of wine to go with it.

She hurried upstairs to grab a quick shower before he returned. As she stood under the pulsing water, she ran through the scenario in her head: food, wine, candles. Granted, the candles were there in case of another power outage, but still. Add to that an impossibly hot man who just so happened to also be single. On paper it certainly sounded like a date. But in reality? Maybe they were just hanging out as friends. And maybe they wouldn't even be that if it weren't for the circumstances.

Of course, that didn't stop her from shaving her legs. All the way up. None of that to-the-knee crap she was sometimes guilty of when she knew darn well no man was going to have a peek any higher. She even found herself wishing she'd had a wax before she left town. But what woman in her right mind would subject herself to that pain when she was going away to protest romance?

Stop, she thought. She was so far ahead of herself that she wasn't even visible in the rearview mirror. Lucas was just trying to make the best of a lousy situation. And while it seemed like he was attracted to her—hello, hallway boner!— even that could have been an involuntary reaction to a seeing a naked woman. It didn't mean he was truly into her. The man was still grieving the loss of his wife. He didn't need Paige throwing herself at him just so she would have her own sex island story to tell Sammy next week.

Of course, that didn't stop her from wearing her favorite jeans, the ones that hugged her in all the right places and made her ass look pretty fine, if she did say so herself. She paired them with a navy-blue cardigan, then spent far too much time debating how many buttons to leave undone. One for "just friends," two for "maybe more," or three for "forget dinner, just do me on the table." In the end, she erred on the side of "just friends." Thanks to "the incident," as she now thought of it, Lucas had already had an eyeful of what was under that sweater. If he was interested in her as more than friends, his imagination, not to mention his memory, could certainly fill in the blanks.

When she was satisfied she'd struck a balance between temptress and storm buddy, she made her way down to the kitchen. Lucas wasn't back yet, but the Wi-Fi was. The router on top of the refrigerator was glowing bright green. *Excellent*, she thought. Because while she was proud of herself for surviving over twenty-four hours without internet access, there were a few pressing items she needed to investigate.

Paige grabbed her laptop from her suitcase—even though technically the device was considered vacation contraband—and set up at the kitchen island. She was deep into her research when Lucas walked through the door. Every inch of him was wet.

"You really didn't need to go to all this trouble," she said as he set a rain-soaked bag of groceries on the counter along with a rather hefty bag of dog food.

"Yes, I did." He looked at her and winked. "It's Singles Day." She would have thought he was mocking her if it weren't for the wink and the fact that he seemed genuinely excited about their celebration. "Although don't get your hopes too high. The market was a bit picked over so..." He winced. "I had to get creative."

Paige lifted a brow. "Can't be worse than pizza with the sausage picked off."

Lucas laughed. "Might want to reserve judgment until after you taste it."

Paige watched as he shrugged out of his wet coat and began unloading the bags. She didn't think something as mundane as unpacking produce could be sexy, but damn if watching him wasn't the hottest thing she'd seen in months. She particularly enjoyed the way his sweater rode up ever so slightly when he reached into one of the taller cabinets, revealing a smattering of dark hair that disappeared just below the waist of his jeans. Sure beat the hell out of watching Mr. Rochester lick his paws.

"Thirsty?" he asked when he was done.

She nodded, not sure if she could trust her voice not to sound as hot and bothered as she felt.

Lucas snapped ice cubes out of a plastic tray before plopping them into a pair of mismatched glasses, which was perfectly in keeping with the eclectic style of the inn. To put it bluntly, nothing in the entire place matched, sort of the way that nothing in Monica's apartment matched on *Friends*, something Paige had always thought was a significant error on the part of the producers. Honestly, if Monica was half as neurotic as Paige, there was no way in hell she would have been able to deal with all those mismatched kitchen chairs!

He filled both glasses with iced sweet tea and handed one to her. It was such a Southern thing to do. She certainly couldn't picture any of her friends in Chicago having a pitcher of iced tea on hand. In fact, Paige was fairly certain the last time she'd had iced tea, it was of the Long Island variety.

"The internet is working," she said after taking a sip.

"So I see." Lucas nodded to the paper towel that was now covered with her scribbled notes. "Getting some work done?"

"Actually, I was doing some research on caring for puppies."

"Really?"

"Yes, really." She would have given him a hard time for being so surprised, but truth be told, no one was more shocked than she was that she used her first opportunity to get online for puppy research rather than checking emails. Then again, she would have had to go back and mark them all as unread anyway for fear of incurring the wrath of Samuel.

"I wish we knew how old they are." She began to read from

the site she'd discovered just before Lucas had arrived. "It says here that larger breeds can start eating soggy kibble between three and four weeks, but if they get it too soon they can just play in it and get really dirty or..." She gasped. "One lady said she had two puppies suffocate when they inhaled mush they weren't ready to eat." Holy shit, how did parents survive the first year, let alone a lifetime? Paige's heart was racing, and she was only trying to figure out how to feed a few puppies. "And should we be introducing water?"

"I think they had enough water yesterday," he teased.

"I'm being serious, Lucas. Should they be starting to wean? Should we bathe them?" Her thoughts were racing as fast as her heart. "It says that if you give them a bath too early, they can shake from cold or fear and it can actually kill them."

"Those little guys already conquered cold and fear, not to mention water, and they came out swinging."

Paige took a deep breath. "I'm being ridiculous, aren't I?" Lucas had a point. Up until last night, they'd lived outside. Too bad that logic did nothing to stop her from worrying about them, a sentiment that must have been written all over her face.

His tone softened. "I think it's very sweet that you're so concerned." He reached across the counter and placed his hand on hers, sending a tingling shiver down her spine. It was a simple enough gesture, and yet at the same time unbelievably intimate. They stayed like that for a moment, their eyes locked in what felt like anticipation, until the clock in the hallway chimed.

Lucas straightened. "Tell you what," he said, back to the business at hand. "As soon as the storm clears, I'll have the vet come out from the mainland to give them a good once-over. In the meantime, they seem very content on their mom's milk."

Paige tried her best to focus on her laptop, her notes, the countertop. Anything but the fact that all she could think about at the moment was Lucas and how badly she wanted his hands back on her skin. And not just holding her hand, but everywhere... exploring, enticing, satisfying. *Whoa, baby*. Maybe she needed to just pour the iced tea straight into her lap. Instead she began to read from the computer screen, which, while less effective, was a lot less messy. "According to the websites," she said, "Puppies in this age range need to eat every four to six hours." She looked up to discover Lucas watching her with an intensity that did nothing to calm her overheated libido.

"Those little guys are certainly bellying up to the table that often," he said.

She rolled her eyes. "In the case of Raphael, even more than that."

"I'd say they are thriving just fine," he said.

Were they really just going to carrying on chatting about the dogs while undressing each other with their eyes? Yes, yes, they were.

"Well, they're more active, that's for sure. I had to roll the edge of one of the towels to keep Leo from wiggling under the couch," she said. "Do you maybe have some cardboard or something that we could use to keep them in one place?"

"I can do you one better than that," he said. "Be right back."

Paige watched as he ducked through the laundry room and into the garage. She had no idea what he was looking for, but he sure was making a lot of noise. A few minutes later, he returned, carrying what looked like an armload of plastic gates.

"This ought to do the trick," he said.

She followed him into the living room, where she watched him assemble the panels into an octagon-shaped pen. Paige suspected it had once been used for a youngster of the human variety, but it worked nicely for canines as well.

"That should hold them," Lucas said as they placed the last pup next to his mother. "Looks like their dinner is ready. I better get started on ours."

"Can I help?" Paige asked.

"You're the guest," he said. "I might be far from a website superhost..." Even he couldn't keep a straight face as he said those words. "Okay, I might be the worst in the site's history. But I draw the line at having a guest cook her own dinner."

"At least let me set the table." She glanced at her laptop. "Otherwise I might be tempted to log into my work email, and then I really can't be held responsible for my assistant's actions."

He shook his head. "Can take the girl out of the office, but can't take the office out of the girl?"

"Hey, I'll have you know that I haven't checked my email once this trip."

"Which has nothing to do with the fact that the Wi-Fi was down."

"Aaand," she added to her defense, "I read an entire book the other night."

"Well, then I'd say you're totally winning at this whole vacation thing."

"That's exactly what I said!" The words were barely out of her mouth when she noticed the corner of his mouth quirk up. "You're mocking me, aren't you?"

"Not mocking." His smirk turned into a full-on grin. "Only teasing."

Paige narrowed her eyes. "Just for that, I'm absolutely setting the table."

"You're a tough negotiator, Paige Parker." He was still smiling. "But you have a deal."

This time she didn't extend her hand. Instead she turned, giving him the middle finger over her shoulder as she made her way to the kitchen, a response that elicited an outburst of robust laughter. Mission accomplished.

When he finally stopped laughing, Lucas told her she could find most anything she needed in the two built-in cabinets that sat in opposite corners of the dining room. She popped the doors open to find china that looked as though it had once belonged to someone's great-grandparents. *Oooh, fancy dishes!* Seemed as though Lucas was taking this whole "special celebration" thing seriously, a realization that made her far happier than she would ever admit.

After organizing the shelves so all the bowls were on one and the plates on another, Paige set to work, laying out china and stemware. As she was arranging the napkins and flatware, she heard a cell phone ring in the kitchen.

"Hey, Peanut, what's up?" she heard Lucas say. Then a

moment later, "No, I will not stop calling you Peanut. And yes, I will sing the special song."

Special song? Paige had to admit, she was more than a little curious. She listened intently, but Lucas had lowered his voice to barely a whisper.

Casually, she inched backward until she was next to the door that led to the kitchen. It wasn't technically eavesdropping. He knew she was in the next room. She was just...adjusting the volume.

"'Skidamarink a dink a dink, skidamarink a doo,'" he began to sing. Paige's mouth dropped open and she quickly covered it with a napkin. "'I love you in the morning, and in the afternoon,'" he went on. It was simultaneously the sweetest and most ridiculous song she'd ever heard, and all at once her heart clenched at the thought of Lucas trying to find his way as an unexpectedly single parent. It couldn't have been easy, but from what she was hearing, he'd more than mastered it.

His voice grew closer. "'I love you in the evening, and—'"

Not wanting to be discovered, Paige scurried through the living room and onto the back porch. As she passed the canine family, she could have sworn she saw the momma stray shoot her some serious side-eye. "Don't judge me," she whispered. Great. If imagining a dog was giving her a dirty look wasn't bad enough, now she was talking to her as though she were Sammy. *Oh! That's it*, she thought. Samantha would be the perfect name for the sweet, if not slightly disapproving, canine.

The rain had slowed to nothing more than a drizzle, giving the porch a much more serene feeling than when the water pelting the windows had made Paige feel like she was in a drive-through car wash. She watched the light-gray clouds moving across the horizon until she assumed enough time had gone by for her to return to the dining room and finish setting the table. As she passed by the living room windows, she noticed a cluster of bright-yellow daffodils blooming in the front yard. Were those there yesterday? Perhaps they were and it had been raining too hard to notice. Either way, they were just the finishing touch the table needed.

Paige slipped outside to grab a few of the blooms and, after rooting around the cabinets for a vase, headed to the kitchen to fill it with water. Lucas had finished his call, and from the looks of it, had finished cooking dinner too. As she rounded the island, she could see he was spooning the last of a vegetable stir fry into a serving bowl.

"Food is ready," he said, scraping some very sticky rice into the next bowl.

"And the table is all set." She turned on the faucet and filled the crystal vase. "Well, except for the flowers."

Lucas froze with a bowl in each hand. "What flowers?" He didn't wait for an answer. Instead he headed to the dining room, with Paige not far behind. When he saw the pile of blooms on the table, he stopped short, nearly sending her colliding into him. "Where did you get those?"

"The front yard."

He turned to looked at her. Paige couldn't figure out what was happening. Surely he wasn't this upset over her picking a few flowers from the garden?

"I hope it's okay that I snipped a few? I know it makes me

rather basic," she said in an attempt to lighten the mood. "But daffodils have always been my favorite—maybe because they remind me of sunshine?—and I thought after all this rain, we could both use a little brightening up."

For a moment, he just stared at her, unseeing, but then something happened and he relaxed. It was as though every muscle in his body had been released from a vise. He closed his eyes, and when he opened them, it felt like he was seeing her for the first time. Even in her head, it sounded ridiculous, but she felt the shift. It was palpable.

"It was a great idea." He smiled as he lifted the bowls higher. "Now let's eat before my masterpiece gets cold."

The two of them sat across from each other at the table, spooning rice and vegetables onto their respective plates.

"It's delicious," Paige said, after taking a bite.

"You don't have to sound so surprised," he said, playfully feigning insult. Then he laughed. "Actually, I'm a bit shocked myself."

The conversation flowed easily from talk of Maddie and her desire to ride without training wheels before her fifth birthday to Samuel and his desire to star as the first gay *Bachelor* before his thirtieth.

They had nothing in common, yet everything.

When they finished eating, she helped him clear the table and, despite his protests, clean the kitchen. He washed and she dried, and in no time they were down to the last plate. Lucas handed it to her, then leaned one hip against the counter, watching her as she dried it.

"I have an answer for you," he said.

Paige folded the dish towel and placed it on the rack. "An answer for what?"

"Do you fold dirty clothes too?" he teased.

She stuck her tongue out at him. "Very funny," she said. "And that was a question, not an answer."

"My *answer*," he clarified, "is to a question you asked me last night."

Paige flicked through her memories but couldn't recall a question he had left unanswered. "When we were playing Twenty Questions?"

He nodded. "You asked what I would take if the house was on fire."

"And you said nothing. So technically you *did* answer." *Jeez, Parker, do you have to be right about everything?* "Unless... Has your answer changed?"

"No. But I want to explain it. I wouldn't take anything because none of it matters. People matter."

"Well, you're right, but you're sort of missing the point of why I ask. I'm trying to reduce the things people—"

He silenced her protests by pressing a finger against her lips. "What if you had nothing, Paige. Would your life still have meaning?" He brushed a stray lock of hair behind her ear and let his fingers trail along her cheek. When he spoke again, his voice was low and husky. "Seems to me you don't need all of your stuff perfectly organized. What you need is one special person to share the mess of life."

He stepped closer. Close enough for her to smell the woodsy scent of his soap, to see his eyes darken, and to hear his breath quicken. His gaze dropped to her mouth, setting a flurry of butter-flies loose deep down in her belly, and then he dipped his head, pausing just before his lips touched hers.

And then...

...the shrill sound of a phone rang right next to their heads. Paige jumped back. What the hell? Honestly, who even had a landline anymore?

Lucas reached for the phone mounted to the kitchen wall. "Hello," he said, never taking his eyes off Paige. "Okay. Sure. Thanks. I'll let her know."

Let her know? Was he talking about her? Probably, seeing as how it was unlikely a four-year-old had friends calling the house. But who even knew she was there?

"That was the harbormaster," Lucas said as he hung up the phone. "The storm clouds are clearing, and the ferry should be up and running by morning. He figured you'd want to know ASAP. Said you were anxious to get off the island."

She was. At least she had been. But that was then, and this was...what exactly? Paige didn't have the answer to her own question. All she knew was that the news she'd been waiting for hadn't brought the happiness she'd expected. In fact, it was quite possibly the worst news she'd had all week.

Paige stared up at him, searching his expression for any clue to what he might be thinking. A moment ago, she knew exactly what he wanted, but that moment was broken. In its place was nothing but an awkward silence.

Lucas put his hands on his hips. "So, I guess you'll be heading out in the morning."

I don't have to, she wanted to say. But she didn't. She didn't tell him that she wanted to stay for the rest of the week, or that she wanted to finish their game of Twenty Questions, or that she wanted him to take her in his arms and kiss her like nothing could touch them.

"Guess so."

He hesitated for a moment, then gave a tight nod. "Right, then," he said. "Better get some sleep. The sun will be up before we know it."

Paige couldn't speak. Instead she merely watched as Lucas turned toward the stairs and headed up to bed.

CHAPTER 12

PAIGE KEPT HER EYES CLOSED, trying her best to ignore the sunlight streaming in through the window. She wasn't ready to wake up. Not when her dreams brought images of Lucas, bathed in the soft glow of the fireplace. Like they had been the day before, his eyes were lit by the reflection of the flickering flames, but in this version, he wasn't wearing a supersoft black sweater. No, Paige's subconscious preferred him just as she'd first met him, bare-chested and wearing only a pair of faded jeans and a few days' worth of stubble. She had wondered how it would feel beneath her fingertips, against her cheek, or even between her thighs. But unlike in real life, where her fantasies remained on the pages of romance novels, dream-state Paige was brazen, bold, and wanton. She reached out, her fingers tracing the outline of his jaw. His gaze darkened as he leaned closer, so close she could feel his warm breath against her cheek like a ray of sunlight on a cold winter's day. Her lips parted in anticipation…

Wait.

A ray of sunlight?

What the...

Her eyes opened, and as they did, her sexy carpenter vanished like a genie being sucked back into his bottle. She groaned, as much from the bright sunshine as the evaporation of another near-kiss.

Paige's hands flew to her face, shielding her eyes as she rubbed away the last remnants of sleep. She didn't want to wake up. She wanted to stay in a dream world where cloudless skies and ferry boats didn't mean the end of something that had barely begun.

Leave it to her to find herself plopped into a Hallmark movie where the storm clears too early.

No sense putting off the inevitable, she thought.

Paige rolled over...

...to find a small child beside her bed.

"Uh, hello tiny human."

The little girl giggled as though someone had tickled her toes. "Hello, large human."

Large, eh? Paige had always heard that kids were brutally honest. Then again, maybe she meant as compared to her size, not to humans in general.

"And who might you be?" Paige assumed she was Lucas's daughter, but still, introductions were in order.

"I'm Maddie."

Paige held out her hand—did you shake hands with a child?— but it didn't matter because without hesitation Maddie placed her small hand in Paige's.

"Why are we holding hands?" she asked.

"We're shaking hands," Paige corrected. She gripped the

child's hand and gave it a quick shake. "It's what people do when they introduce themselves. I'm—"

But Maddie didn't bother waiting to hear the large human's name. Instead she bent down to get something off the floor. "Do you want to see what I've got in this box?" It didn't seem as though Paige had much choice in the matter, since the shoebox in question was now resting on the mattress beside her. Not that she would have said no. The little girl's eyes sparkled with such excitement, Paige found herself more than a little intrigued.

Maddie carefully removed the lid. When she did, she let out a small squeal, which was nothing compared to the shriek that came out of Paige's mouth as she peered over the edge of the cardboard to find a large, lumpy toad.

Paige bolted upright, pulling the duvet with her. "Maybe we should keep the cover on that box."

The little girl looked up at her, confused. "But you can't pet him if the box is closed. Roger wants to say hello."

Paige frowned. "Roger?"

"The toad, silly."

Of course. "How about we save that introduction for after breakfast?"

Maddie shrugged. "Okay." Once the lid was securely back in place—and Paige's heart rate had slowed to a mere sprint—she asked, "Are you my dad's girlfriend?"

"Girlfriend?" And there went the heart rate again. "Oh, no, no, no. I'm here on vacation."

Maddie cocked her head to the side the same way her dad had a habit of doing, and a tousle of curls fell across her eyes. She blew them out of the way with a breath that sounded more like a raspberry. "In the winter?"

What was the expression? Out of the mouths of babes.

"It seemed like a good time to enjoy peace and quiet."

"My dad says I'm Captain Quiet Buster." She giggled. "He calls me Miss Chatterbox because I'm always talking. Said I came out that way." She set the shoebox back on the floor. "Sorry if the rain ruined your vacation."

"It didn't ruin it," Paige said, and in that moment, she realized she was right. The rain might have changed the course of her holiday, but for the better. Plus... "The rain brought puppies to stay," she pointed out. "Have you seen them?"

Maddie nodded, and her curls bounced up and down. "They are sooo cute! I wanted to hold them, but my dad said I should wait to see if the vet says it's okay. He's coming out later today."

"He is?" Paige squinted at the bright sun coming through the window. "So the ferries are running then?" Part of her had hoped the harbormaster's call had been premature and they'd have at least one more day.

Maddie nodded.

"Well, if the ferries are running, I guess that means I can head home," she said, more to herself than to her small visitor.

The little girl's eyes grew so wide she looked like one of the Precious Moments dolls Paige's mom used to buy for her when she was little. Even as a child, Paige had despised a cluttered bedroom, and knickknacks were public enemy number one.

"You can't leave! My dad says the puppies printed on you."

Printed? Did she mean imprinted?

Lucas appeared in the doorway. "There you are."

"I wanted to introduce the pretty lady to Kermit," she said, pointing to the box on the floor.

Paige narrowed her eyes. "I thought you said his name was Roger."

Maddie nodded. "Oh, right."

Lucas's gaze shifted to the box, then back to Paige. "Sorry," he mouthed.

Paige smiled. "It's fine." And it was. Assuming Roger/Kermit couldn't knock the lid off of his box.

Their eyes locked, and for a moment, they weren't innkeeper and guest standing in a room with a pint-sized human and a quart-sized amphibian. They were just a man and a woman with some seriously unfinished business of the kissing variety. The connection was there. She hadn't imagined it. But why hadn't he said something last night? Why did he turn away?

Why didn't you speak up? The Lizzie McGuire cartoon version of Sammy began a lecture that would no doubt have come and gone all day, but Paige snuffed him out. She knew she'd messed up when she left so much unsaid. She didn't need an imaginary version of her assistant pointing out the obvious.

"Sure you don't want to hold him?" Maddie asked, bringing her right back to reality. Paige looked at the small girl. If it weren't for the sincerity in her eyes, Paige would've thought she was joking.

"I'm good, thanks."

"Ms. Parker is a guest, Maddie. Who did not leave a wake-up call."

"What's a wake-up call?"

Lucas scooped his daughter into his arms. "That would be you." Watching the two of them, Paige was struck by how much Maddie resembled both of her parents. She definitely had her father's hazel eyes and slightly crooked smile, but her hair was a mane of dark-brown curls like her mom's.

"Well, we've never had a guest before." Maddie's lower lip jutted out in a tiny pout. "How was I supposed to know?"

Lucas tickled his daughter, and just like that, her pout dissolved into a fit of giggles.

"Out, missy," he said as he set her feet back on the hardwood floor. "And take your new friend with you."

"But I wasn't done talking to Ms. Parker."

"You can call me Paige."

Maddie cocked her head to one side. "Like a book?"

Paige smiled. "Sort of."

Maddie picked the shoebox up off the floor. "What kind of book? A funny one or a scary one? Oooh! Is it a book with kissing?"

Lucas's brows shot up. "Kissing?" he asked, more than a little bit appalled. "What would you know about that?"

Maddie rolled her eyes. "I'm not a baby, Daddy. I know about lots of things."

"Is that so? Well, we can talk more about that downstairs." He placed his hands on Maddie's shoulders, guiding her to the door as he shot a comically exasperated look at Paige. "Five one day, fifteen the next."

Paige had to stifle a laugh. Poor guy had no idea what he was in for over the next few years. If he thought toads and talk of kissing were bad, wait until he had to deal with training bras and texting.

Lucas was about to pull the door closed behind them when Maddie poked her head around the frame. "Will you stay and help us take care of the puppies?"

Paige's eyes darted to Lucas, and when he looked at her, an almost shy smile crept over his face. "You *are* their sensei."

"Well, it's settled then." Paige surprised herself by agreeing without so much as a moment's hesitation, but by the time she was halfway down the stairs, she had already started to wonder if she'd made the right decision. Last night she and Lucas had shared a moment. Granted, it was a moment that amounted to nothing but a whole lot of frustration, but it *was* still a moment. They hadn't had a chance to talk about it, let alone revisit the idea—something she wasn't even a little bit ashamed to admit was extremely high on her personal to-do list.

But what if he wasn't that into her once the moment had passed? Then again, it sort of seemed like they'd had another moment in the bedroom. And he did have a supercute smile on his face when he seconded Maddie's request that she stay. He was seconding it, wasn't he? What else could he have meant when he said she was the puppies' sensei? *Gah!* Why did romance have to be so confusing? If only she had a few minutes to sit down with a memo pad so she could properly dissect the last twenty-four hours. Right, she thought, because that's exactly what any normal woman would do after a man almost kissed her—make a flipping Venn diagram about how into her he may or may not be.

"You must be Paige," a woman said as Paige made her way into the kitchen. "I'm Sophie, Luc's sister." The smile on her face led Paige to wonder if she knew about the previous night's near-kiss situation because her enthusiasm seemed a bit over the top to be just about having a paying customer. Then again, Paige *was* paying double.

"Nice to meet you, Sophie. Lucas has told me so much about you."

Sophie's brows shot up. "Don't believe any of it. Well, unless it's about how fabulous I am, because that is one hundred percent true." She laughed. "But if he tells you the story about the time we ran away, just know that he was the one who packed Mr. Pickles, not me."

Lucas cut his sister a look that was impossible to miss even from across the kitchen. "More like how you're the world's most unscrupulous landlord."

"Yeah, about that, I'm sorry. Don't know what possessed me. All in the name of family, I guess." Sophie winced. "Hope you won't hold it against Luc. He honestly had nothing to do with it."

Paige's gaze shifted to the stove, where Lucas was pouring pancake batter onto a hot griddle. Maddie was perched on the island across from him, swinging her feet as she called out the shapes she wanted him to make with the batter. "All will be forgiven if you make me one of those snowman pancakes," she said.

He looked at her and smiled. "Deal," he said. "But we'll have to skip shaking on it." He winked, then raised the spatula he held in one hand and the mixing bowl that was in the other. "My hands are a bit full."

Sophie looked back and forth between her brother and Paige. Yeah, she knew. Or at least she suspected.

"I thought you shook hands when you said hello," Maddie said.

"And sometimes when you close a deal," Paige replied.

Sophie's attention was focused on Lucas, which meant there was no way she'd missed the toe-curling glance he shot Paige between batches. "Sorry I had to bring Maddie back early," she said. "But the fire alarm at the store has been going off again. The plumber could only meet with me this morning, and if the dang thing malfunctions and the store floods…" She winced. "Let's just say Blazing Books would be toast. I can come back to get her in about an hour."

"No worries." Paige said. "Can't have Maddie missing out on time with the puppies. Plus, now that the rain has stopped, I need a tour guide. Think you could show me all the coolest places on the beach, Maddie?" For the life of her, she had no idea what made her ask. Normally she wanted to be as far away from children as possible. But something about this little girl's total openness and sincerity made Paige want to be close to her. As long as her toad wasn't in her lap.

"Sure," Maddie said as she decorated her snowman with chocolate chips.

"I mean as long as that's okay with your dad?" Paige looked over her shoulder. Lucas had stopped making pancakes and was watching her. Judging from the look on his face, he was most definitely on board with the idea. And this time, no Venn diagram was needed.

CHAPTER 13

LUCAS DID EVERYTHING HE COULD to avoid being alone with his sister, but she cornered him in the kitchen when Paige and Maddie went to the door to greet the vet. Sophie Croft might be his annoying little sister, but she was also smart as a whip. There was no way she'd missed the looks he and Paige had exchanged. There was also no way she was going to let it slide.

"What was *that*?" she demanded the minute they were alone.

Lucas looked down the empty hall. "What?" It was a lame response, but if he was lucky, it might buy him enough time. All he needed was for Paige to come back to the kitchen…

"Don't play dumb with me, Lucas Cornelius Croft."

"You know that's not my middle name."

"Today it is."

He eased toward the door, but she stuck her foot on the counter of the island to form a barricade with her leg. She was flexible, he'd give her that. "Those gymnastics lessons really paid off, I see."

"Yeah, I figured someday it would get me to the Olympics, but detaining my stubborn brother will have to suffice."

He chuckled. "Do you really think I can't get past you?" She talked a big game, but he had about sixty pounds on her. If he wanted to, he could open the freezer door and put her on ice. Literally.

"Lucas," Paige called from the living room.

"Sorry, Soph. I'd love to stay and chat, but you have a plumber to meet and I have a vet in my living room."

"Fine, but for the record, I'm totally on board with whatever this is." She narrowed her eyes. "Just don't do anything to mess it up."

Now that was a promise he couldn't make. No matter how hard he tried, messing things up with Paige Parker seemed to be second nature for him. They'd already had two do-overs, and if that wasn't bad enough, when everything was finally going right, he'd somehow managed to blow that too.

Stay. That's all he would have had to say, and last night would have had a completely different ending. But no, he just stood there like some kind of idiot. *Guess you'll be leaving in the morning.* Was it pride, fear, maybe a little of both? Whatever the reason, he'd put everything on her, and when she hesitated—probably shocked that one minute he was about to kiss her and the next he was assuming she's about to leave—he sulked off like a toddler. Scratch that, toddlers at least tell you why they're sulking. He just stormed off to bed.

Then came Maddie to the rescue. Leave it to his sweet, unassuming daughter to clear things up with one heartfelt request. It wasn't the first time he could have stood to learn a lesson or two from his daughter, and it probably wouldn't be the last. But for now at least, Paige Parker was staying for the rest of the week. Even he could set things right in that amount of time.

He stood beside the sofa, watching the scene unfolding in his living room. Paige and Maddie sat side by side on the couch, dutifully supervising, although it was hard to say which one of them was in charge. In the end, his money was on Maddie. Each time the vet began an examination of one of the pups, Maddie would introduce the dog by name, then turn to Paige and ask her to explain why she'd chosen it for that particular puppy. At first Paige seemed a bit embarrassed by the whole thing—was that a blush he she saw on her cheeks?—but she was a good sport, and by the time they were done, even the doctor was cracking Ninja Turtle analogies.

"Does this mean the puppies are going to be okay?" Maddie asked after Lucas showed the vet to the door.

"That's exactly what it means," he told her.

"And does that mean I can hold them now?" She looked up at him from beneath impossibly long lashes. "Pretty pleeease?"

"Yes," Lucas said. "As long as you sit on the couch and are very gentle."

Maddie scurried onto the couch and patted her lap. "I'm ready."

One by one, Paige handed her each of the puppies for a cuddle and a kiss.

"Why don't we let these guys have a little rest with their momma," Lucas suggested when she was done. "This has been a lot of activity for them in one morning."

"It's okay," Maddie said. "I promised Paige I would show her my favorite places on the beach."

"That's right," Lucas said, pretending that he'd forgotten. "Where do you think we should start?"

Maddie narrowed her eyes. "She didn't ask you, Daddy."

Ouch, blocked by his own kiddo.

"Think we could let him join us?" Paige asked. Her question was spoken in a whisper, but loud enough for him to hear.

Maddie twisted her mouth while she considered her answer. Paige watched her with a warm smile on her face. "Yes," his daughter finally said. "We need someone to carry the bucket."

"The bucket?" Paige asked.

"For the seashells, silly." Maddie slid off the couch and scampered toward the kitchen.

"Looks like we're headed to the beach," Lucas said as they followed her. "Thanks for scoring me an invite."

Paige laughed. "Anytime."

By the time they reached Maddie, she was standing by the door with a bucket in one hand and one of her favorite toys in the other. "Floppy wants to come," she said. "Stanley and Stinky are going to stay here and watch the puppies."

"Nice of them to offer their services," Lucas said with a straight face. "You and Paige can head on out. I'm just going to pack a few things in my backpack, and I'll be right there."

Maddie reached for Paige's hand. "Come on, I'll show you where the baby turtles hatched last summer."

"Turtles hatch in the summer?" Paige asked. "Not in February?" Lucas knew full well she was taking a swipe at him for yet another unfulfilled promise made when she booked the room. But the smile she flashed him as she looked back over her shoulder told him that Paige Parker could care less about the amenities. She was exactly where she wanted to be.

His daughter, on the other hand, sure was in a rush to get away from him. Little twerp never even looked back. She did, however, give him one more chore to do before joining them.

"Don't forget the kite, Daddy."

Lucas smiled to himself. Second fiddle, huh? Yeah, he could live with that.

....

Paige and Maddie walked hand in hand across the wooden planks that formed a path through the tall grass until they reached a sandy stretch of beach. Maddie showed her where the turtle eggs had been and explained how some people from the mainland had come out to set up "yellow tape" and took turns sleeping in beach chairs until the babies hatched. She was talking a mile a minute, with more enthusiasm than even Sammy on his best day, but best Paige could tell, when the babies hatched, everyone huddled around to keep other animals from eating them before they made it to the water.

When Maddie was done, she took a deep breath and stared out at the water. Her hair danced in the wind, but other than that, she was perfectly still. For all of two minutes.

"Paige is a funny name," she said out of the blue.

"Well, it's not spelled the same as the page in a book," Paige explained.

"My mom named me after a book too," Maddie said, seeming to completely miss Paige's point. "A girl in a book," she qualified. "Not the paper part." She began skipping down the sand.

Paige walked faster to keep up. "Which book is that?" She suspected she already knew the answer, but she wanted to hear Maddie tell the story. Because what had appeared at first to be a nonsensical transition now seemed like a necessary conversation.

"Madeline." Maddie stopped skipping and stood perfectly still as she recited the opening lines to Ludwig Bemelmans's classic tale. "'In an old house in Paris that was covered with vines, lived twelve little girls in two straight lines. The smallest one was Madeline.'"

When she was finished, she looked up at Paige. The expression on her face changed from one of bliss to concern in a matter of seconds. "If my dad goes to live with my mom in heaven, will I go to live in a house like Madeline did?"

Paige's heart ached. How scary it must be for this sweet child not only to lose one parent, but to worry about the fate of the other as well. And now there she was, looking to Paige for an answer she wasn't qualified to give. Paige wasn't family. She wasn't even a close family friend. She'd only met Maddie that morning, but that didn't do anything to lessen her desire to comfort the young girl.

"I'm sure not." She had no idea what Lucas's will stipulated for Maddie's care, but she felt quite certain that she would not go to an orphanage. At the very least, she had an aunt.

Maddie breathed an exaggerated sigh of relief. "Good, because I would hate to have to walk in two straight lines," she said before zigzagging through the sand toward a cluster of seagulls, her arms wide as though she herself were a bird.

Paige smiled to herself. There she'd been, worried about Maddie's fears about the future, when in reality the frown that had creased her tiny forehead was over something far simpler. Paige couldn't blame her really. The pictures of that spooky-looking nun marching those girls around Paris like little toy soldiers had always bothered her as well. In her opinion, the only thing worse was the creepy child collector in *Chitty Chitty Bang Bang*. Honestly, what were some adults thinking?

"Was she talking your ear off?" Lucas asked from behind her. Paige turned, and the sight of him nearly took her breath away. She couldn't explain it really. He was only wearing jeans and a quarter-zip fleece, but he looked like he'd just stepped out of a magazine ad for some overpriced men's cologne. The ocean breeze played with his hair, giving it that sexy, rumpled look she found so irresistible, and the way he looked at her, smoldering and yet shy all at once? Let's just say she was darn happy she agreed to stay.

"Penny for your thoughts?" he asked.

Maddie ran up, which was just as well because if Paige had told him her thoughts, she would have had to reveal that she'd been thinking about how it would feel to run her fingers through his unruly hair, or how badly she wanted to slide her hands under his fleece and feel the warmth of his skin against hers, or how she wanted him to kiss her until they were both breathless.

"Can we look for shells?" Maddie asked.

"Well, we need to collect *something* with that bucket. Should it be shells or crabs?"

"Oooh gross, why would we collect crabs?" she asked. It seemed crabs were bad but toads were good. Go figure.

"Then shells it is," Lucas said. He took Paige's hand as they fell in line behind the four-year-old leader of their expedition. Paige couldn't remember the last time a man held her hand. In fact, it had been so long, she was quite sure the last male to do so was merely a boy, and not a man at all. "This okay?" he whispered, nodding toward their joined hands.

Paige smiled. It was more than okay. It was perfect. And so was their day. The three of them spent hours walking along the beach, collecting seashells or using their feet to draw silly faces in the wet sand. Lucas and Maddie even had a game where they tried to spell out a word before the other one could guess what it was. Granted they were supershort words—*cat, bat, hat... Today's day at the beach was brought to you by the letters a and* t—but Paige was still impressed with how Lucas combined education with fun and games.

When Maddie finally grew tired, they found a place on the beach to spread out a blanket. Once they were settled, Maddie and Lucas unleashed the kite. It was in the shape of a giant panda bear, something Paige found both peculiar and fantastic. She watched as the bear bobbed around in the wind, much to Maddie's delight.

"Did you bring a snack?" Maddie asked. Now there was a girl after her own heart.

Lucas's expression went blank. "I thought you were going to bring the snacks."

Maddie's jaw dropped open. As it did, her father began to laugh. "Close your mouth, missy. A seagull might fly in."

Maddie giggled. "My mouth is not big enough for a seagull."

Lucas narrowed his eyes as he sized her up. "Hmm, you might be right." He tied the kite to a piece of driftwood, then reached into his backpack and pulled out a banana. "Is it big enough for a banana?"

"Maybe," Maddie said. "But it could definitely fit a cookie."

Paige fought to keep a straight face.

"Sorry," Lucas said. "I'm fresh out of cookies."

Maddie looked to Paige. "Do you have any cookies?"

Paige reached into her coat pocket and pulled out a tin of breath mints. She always carried them with her in case of an emergency. Like if she'd just finished a garlic-heavy meal and a client had a crisis that required face-to-face intervention. Or the scenario Sammy preferred: she was trapped in the elevator of their building with the hot guy from the twenty-third floor. A crisis that in her assistant's opinion would require a different kind of face-to-face action. "Only these."

Maddie cocked her head to one side as she tried to sound out the word. "Aaaalllltoids."

Mental note, almost-five-year-olds can read. At least this one could, and not just words that ended in *at*. *Right*, she thought, *no spelling dirty words in front of the kiddo.*

"What's an Altoid?" Maddie asked.

"A grown-up candy," her dad answered.

"Can I have one?"

"Are you a grown-up?" he teased.

"Almost." Maddie made the declaration with total sincerity. Paige tried to remember being four years old. Had she thought turning five was a major milestone as well? All at once, she remembered being at the store and telling her mother that turning five meant she was old enough to get her ears pierced. Of course her mother had disagreed, telling Paige that pierced ears were for adults, not children. But still, maybe she could relate to a kid after all.

"I don't think you will like them," Lucas said. "They're kind of hot."

"What if I eat the banana?" Maddie flashed her father a smile sweeter than any cookie. "Then can I try one?"

Paige had to hand it to her, the girl was good. Between her adorable face and her precocious charm, there was probably nothing she couldn't negotiate. Then again, her father wasn't a very difficult mark. He was clearly wrapped around his daughter's tiny finger.

"Deal," he said. Not the toughest negotiator, Paige thought. But extra points for letting her learn from what would no doubt be a mistake.

Maddie stepped forward and extended her hand. Lucas tried to hand her the banana, but she shook her head. "No silly, I want to shake on it."

"Shake on it?"

"Yes, that's how you close a deal."

Lucas glanced at Paige. "Wonder where she learned that?"

She tried to twist the smile from her lips, but it was no use. This kid was a hoot.

Lucas grinned and shook his head. "I'm doomed," he said before taking his daughter's hand.

When enough banana had been consumed to fulfill her contractual obligation, Maddie held her hand out to Paige. "May I have my Altoid, please?" Hilarious and polite? Even better.

Paige opened the lid of the small red-and-white tin. Lucas was right about one thing; while small, the cinnamon-flavored mints were intense. As she held out the metal box, she couldn't help but wonder how the transaction was going to end.

Maddie stood on her tiptoes for a better view of the coveted mints. She pressed her lips together while her eyes roamed over what felt like every single piece and, after what seemed like an eternity, carefully selected one from the top of the pile.

Paige and Lucas watched as she placed the mint on her tongue.

One.

Two.

Three seconds.

Maddie's brows shot up and her eyes grew wide, but she said nothing. Instead she began to chew. Fast. And then she swallowed. Hard.

"Well?" Lucas asked, knowing damn well that he'd just watched his kiddo swallow a fiery mint rather than her pride.

"It was good," she said.

"Want another one?" he asked. Holy hell, the way these two matched wits now, the teenage years were certainly going to be interesting.

"I don't want to take all of Paige's candy," Maddie said. She was trying her best to play it cool, but the deep breaths she was taking through her mouth were a dead giveaway.

"How about some water?" Lucas asked.

Maddie smiled, although Paige wasn't sure if it was because of her victory or thirst. "Yes, please." She drank nearly half the contents of her Dora the Explorer water bottle, then wiped her mouth on her sleeve and yawned.

"Time for a nap?" Lucas asked.

Maddie looked horrified. "I'm almost five, Daddy. Only babies take naps."

He nodded. "What about a piggyback ride? Do big girls accept those?"

She giggled as Lucas swung her onto his back. When she was settled, the three of them began making their way back to the inn. They had just started up the wooden-plank walkway when Lucas whispered, "This one thinks she doesn't need naps anymore but…"

He turned so Paige could see Maddie's face. She was sound asleep, with her cheek pressed against her father's shoulder. "Let me run put her down." He disappeared up the stairs, and when he returned, he was just finishing a phone call.

"That was my sister," he said, shoving his phone into the pocket of his jeans. "She'll be by to grab Maddie in about an hour."

"She doesn't have to leave on my account. I mean, you haven't gotten to spend much time with her the last few days." Paige was still getting to know Lucas, but one thing was already abundantly clear. His daughter was his world. She felt guilty that her presence had kept them apart the last few nights. Then again, maybe he didn't want his daughter spending so much time around a relative stranger. "Unless you don't want me…"

"Oh, but I do," he said. The rough timbre of his voice seemed to vibrate right through her. Paige's brain short-circuited, and for a few beats she completely lost her train of thought. "I meant if you don't want me to spend that much time around your daughter. It's not like you really know that much about me. I could be a crazy person." She was certainly acting like one. How was it that she could be so completely calm and put together at the office, then so completely awkward around Lucas?

He stepped closer and wrapped his arms around her waist. It was all Paige could do to keep from leaning into his embrace. Instead, she brought her hand to rest on his chest. The contact was meant to be simple. Yet feeling the solid contour of his chest, the rise and fall of each breath, the rapid beat of his heart, suddenly felt anything but simple. It felt intimate and immediate. It felt real.

"Maddie had a great time today." He dropped his lips to her ear. "So did I." She felt his warm breath against her skin, and her knees nearly buckled. "And I was hoping tonight we could pick up where we left off last night."

"Oh?" she said. Her voice sounded all breathy, as though the air in the kitchen was suddenly too thick. Then his hips brushed against hers, and she felt for herself just how ready he was to pick up where they left off. "Oh," she said with much more enthusiasm.

Paige wondered if everything had to wait until later that night. Was it okay to kiss while his daughter was upstairs napping? She had no idea what the protocol was for making out with a single dad. All she knew was that if he didn't kiss her soon, she might spontaneously combust.

She looked up at him, and for several long moments, they said nothing. The air between them seemed charged with awareness and need, but they'd been there before, twice in fact, and the moment had always come and gone.

Not this time.

Lucas leaned forward ever so slightly and touched his lips to hers. It was soft and gentle, yet sent a spark rushing through her like a live wire. She thought that might be it, just a quick peck, a placeholder and promise of what was yet to come. But then he reached up, cupping her jaw and deepening the kiss. Her fingers slid into his hair, and her lips parted, inviting him in. He took full advantage, and suddenly she was hot everywhere, yet shivering at the same time. A delicious ache built inside her, and without thinking, her body went lax against his, and for a few brief moments she forgot about everything except how badly she wanted to have this man over her, behind her, inside her...

Lucas groaned ever so softly, then broke their kiss but not their contact. For several sweet seconds, his forehead rested against hers while their collective breathing slowed. When he finally pulled back, an adorably cocky grin curved his mouth. "Did that convince you?"

Paige wobbled ever so slightly. She would have loved to have a sexy comeback for him, but at the moment, it was taking everything she had just to remain upright, let alone form a coherent if not somewhat witty response. But then her brain jump-started and the synapses began to fire. "How about a compromise?" she said.

"If your compromise involves my balls being as blue as they were last night..."

She laughed. "No, not at all."

He dropped his lips to her neck.

"I was going to suggest maybe a compromise for the evening."

"I'm listening," he said. Except he wasn't just listening, he was distracting. And the trail of soft kisses he was leaving on Paige's neck were making it very hard for her to keep track of what she was saying.

She gave him a gentle shove. "I can't focus when you do that."

"Sorry, sorry," he said. But the boyish grin on his face told

Paige he was anything but sorry. Horny maybe, but definitely not sorry.

"Why don't you spend some time with your daughter while I cook dinner for the three of us, and then she can go spend the night with her aunt."

"Agreed. But with one caveat."

"So now this is a negotiation?"

He gave her a look that very clearly accused the pot of calling the kettle black. "I will spend time with Maddie *and* you. I'll run to the store to get what we need, and then we can all three cook dinner." He moved closer, and his hands found their way back to her waist before sliding over the swell of her hips. "Then we can have some grown-up time."

Grown-up time. Paige liked the sound of that. Forget getting her ears pierced, she thought just before Lucas kissed her again, *this* was definitely the best perk of being an adult.

CHAPTER 14

LUCAS COULDN'T REMEMBER THE LAST time he felt so alive. He was wired. He was amped. He was horny as hell.

And it was all because of his unexpected houseguest.

Just the thought of her had him adjusting his jeans. He couldn't help but wonder what it was about this woman that got under his skin—in more ways than one. She certainly wasn't his usual type, from what he could remember of his type anyway. It had been so long since he'd been single, he wasn't even sure what his type was anymore. Maybe it had changed in the last decade. He certainly had.

As clichéd as it might sound, having a child had changed him. He wasn't interested in "chasing tail," as his friend Tom so eloquently put it. But he wasn't really interested in anything serious either. It wouldn't be fair to introduce another woman into Maddie's life. What if it didn't work out? A breakup wouldn't only involve two people anymore, and his daughter had lost enough. Which was why Lucas had sworn off the idea of women altogether, at least for the time being.

Then Paige Parker walked into his life. More like barged into it, seeing as how she'd just walked into his home that first morning like she owned the place. Although to be fair, at that point she practically did, seeing as how she was the only thing standing between him and the county tax assessor. She'd been demanding and abrasive and so uptight he could practically hear her grinding her teeth from across the room. But she was also one of the most beautiful women he'd ever seen. Even when she'd come back that first night, soaking wet and mad as hell, all he could think about was how much he wanted to kiss her.

And now he finally had.

He'd only meant for it to be a simple gesture. A quick peck to tide them over until later that night. But then she'd looked up at him with those big green eyes and her teeth nipped her lower lip and damn if he wasn't a total goner. It had taken every ounce of self-control not to press her up against the refrigerator. Or even better, lay her out on the counter so he could take his time exploring every luscious inch of her. The thought alone had an audible groan vibrating in the back of his throat.

Get a grip, he thought. There were still—Lucas glanced at his phone—at least four more hours until he'd have the chance to kiss her again. If he kept on the way he was, he'd end up jumping her like some overzealous teen the minute they were alone. Probably last that long too. He needed a distraction. So instead of indulging his fantasies, Lucas turned his attention to the aftermath of the storm.

He assessed the damage as he made his way through town. The awning on the post office had a rather large tear, and the Kitchen

Spoon had lost the trellis they'd installed on their patio. There were a few downed trees and washed-out roads, but all in all the little island seemed to have weathered the nor'easter quite well.

So well, in fact, that it seemed nearly half the town's population had decided it was time to venture out to the grocery store. At least it was restocked.

Lucas dialed his sister with one hand while reaching for a grocery basket with the other. If there was one surefire way to avoid small talk at the market, it was to be otherwise occupied. He knew talking on the phone as he worked his way up and down the aisles made him a bit of a douchebag, but it was an effective deterrent. And in this case, necessary. He needed to catch Sophie before she left.

"I was just about to head out," she said when she answered.

Lucas tucked the phone between his shoulder and his ear and reached for a bundle of broccoli. "Don't."

He turned to find a well-meaning neighbor headed his way with that look that told him she was gearing up for a chat. But as she rounded the grapefruits, she realized Lucas was on the phone. "Oh, sorry," she mouthed as she backed away. Worked every time. Lucas gave her a friendly nod, then started toward the tomatoes.

"Wait, so now you *don't* want me to come get Maddie? I'm confused. I thought things were going well between you and Paige."

"They are," he said without thinking. Damn Sophie for getting him to admit there was anything between them, let alone that it was going well. "I mean, she's enjoying her stay. Probably give us a good review too."

"Drop the act, Luc. It was obvious you have a thing for... What did you call her? Ah yeah, the pain-in-the-ass city lady."

He added three Roma tomatoes to his basket. For a moment, he considered changing the topic, but for some reason, he dropped his guard. "I like her, Soph."

"Whoa. Okay. I mean, I suspected after the way the two of you were all googly eyes this morning but..."

"But what, you didn't think I'd admit it?"

Sophie snorted. "Not without some mild torture."

"Very funny." Lucas tossed a box of pasta into the basket and then stopped midstride. He hesitated a second before turning on his heel and heading to the rear of the store.

"How do you feel about that?" Sophie asked.

He could have really blown her mind and told her he was about to buy condoms, but instead all he said was, "Let me call you right back."

"What? Don't think you're going to avoid—"

Lucas ended the call just as he reached the display. Damn, were there always so many options? He scanned the descriptions, then grabbed the closest pack. His heart was racing so fast, he could feel it thumping against his chest. One more memory from the high-school highlight reel.

He tucked the box of condoms under the pasta and made his way back down the aisle. As he did, he realized that after the condoms came the pregnancy-test display and after that, shelves of diapers. The product placement was either one hell of a coincidence or someone in the store had a sick sense of humor.

When he reached the checkout, Mr. Jenkins, the store's owner, opened a new lane and waved him over. Thank God. He was far better off having Mr. Jenkins ring him up than, say, Mrs. McKenzie. She would no doubt have spread the word about the condoms the moment he left the store. Then again, maybe that would have gotten the die-hard matchmakers off his back. Certainly would have given them something to talk about over at the coffee shop.

"Morning, Mr. Jenkins," Lucas said as the older gentleman began scanning the items. He didn't react at all when he scanned the condoms. Lucas exhaled in relief. Maybe he would be able to keep his personal life private. At least for now.

"I can do that, Mr. J," Lucas told him as the grocer began to bag the items. But it was no use. Mr. Jenkins was old school. To him, grocery stores were not places with self-checkouts, and that included the bagging portion of the transaction.

"Full service, Mr. Croft." He flashed a kind smile. "In my grandfather's shop, I used to carry the bags to the car. I'd do that now." He laughed. "If you had one."

"Thank you." Lucas gathered his bags and headed for the door. He'd barely dialed when he heard his sister's voice coming through the phone.

"Did you honestly hang up on me just when you got to the good part?"

Lucas couldn't help but smile. Even after all these years, he still got a ridiculous amount of satisfaction from yanking his little sister's chain. "Sorry, just wanted to get away from prying ears."

Sophie laughed. It was a genuine, full-throated sound. "Might need to leave the island for that."

She had a point, but there was no time for that.

"So…?" she prompted.

"I think I'm ready." He knew he didn't have to say more than that. Because even though they were four seemingly benign words, his sister knew they packed one hell of a punch.

"You know how I feel on the subject." Not only had Sophie been a constant source of support after losing Jenny, but she had also been the first one to start telling him that it was time to move on. Scratch that, she was the first one he actually listened to. No one else knew him or his pain the way she did. So when Sophie told him six months ago that it was time, he'd considered it. Hadn't done anything about it, but he'd heard her out and given it some thought, which was a hell of a lot more than he could say for anyone else. "It's time, Lucas." Her voice grew softer. "You know Jenny wouldn't want you to live like a hermit your whole life."

That he did know. They'd even talked about it. The day they signed their life insurance policies, Jenny had made him promise that if something ever happened to her, he would move on. He'd brushed it off at the time, telling her it was ridiculous even to talk about. They were young and healthy. Nothing was going to happen to either one of them. The insurance policies were just that, insurance. A safety net that in having it, would somehow ward off the chance of ever needing it. But that wasn't the case, and in her own way, Jenny had prepared him for the transition he now faced.

Lucas paused in the middle of the sidewalk, and for a moment, he considered telling Sophie about the daffodils. If there was anyone in his life who would believe that Paige's love of the simple flower was not merely a coincidence, but rather a sign, it was his sister. Except Lucas wasn't entirely sure he believed it himself.

Although even he had to admit that the blooms sprouting a few weeks ahead of schedule had thrown him a bit. Still, saying it out loud would no doubt sound absolutely ridiculous. Which was why in the end, he decided to play it safe.

"Look, I'm not saying it's going to turn into something." If he knew anything about his sister, it was that she would take that little sliver of hope and run with it. "We're just going to—"

"Netflix and chill?"

"Aren't you a bit old to use that expression?"

She laughed. "Aren't you a bit old to know what it means?"

"Touché."

"So, what are the plans?"

"Nothing special. We're going to make dinner with Maddie, so if you wouldn't mind coming to get her after..." An idea hit him. "Sorry, Soph, gotta run."

"Again? I feel like I'm watching one of Aunt Betty's soap operas. 'Tune in tomorrow for the next episode of *How the Island Turns*.'"

"Hilarious," he said, not thinking she was half as amusing as she thought she was. "Come by around seven. Later, Smalls." A slow grin formed on his lips as he made a turn on the cobblestone street, and by the time he'd reached the door of Sweet Inspirations, it was a full-on smile.

The shop was even more crowded than usual, likely due to the fact that it was the first day folks could actually be out and about. Nearly all of the iron scroll tables were occupied by the town's Gray-Haired Gang, as Lucas liked to call them. A pack of women who spent their days gardening and gossiping. Today it seemed their agenda involved drinking tea, playing cards, and chatting. Lots and lots of chatting. But it all came to an abrupt halt when the bell chimed on the front door.

A dozen gray heads turned as one to see who had arrived. When they saw who it was, a dozen jaws went slack. Lucas had no idea what their deal was. He was out and about in town nearly every day. Hell, he even got Maddie's birthday cakes here each year. Yet for some reason, the group in the bakery looked as though they'd seen a ghost.

"Mr. Croft," the owner said as she stood up from a seat at one of the tables. "How lovely to see you."

"Thank you, Mrs. Shaw." Twelve sets of eyes followed him as Lucas made his way to the counter. "Sorry to interrupt."

"Oh dear, never a bother." She bustled around the tables to meet him at the cash register. "What can I get you?" she asked. But before Lucas could respond, she was making suggestions. "Do you need some Danishes, or maybe a few desserts for your guest?"

Looked like Sophie was right about the news spreading.

"Glad to hear you're back in business," a woman said from somewhere on the left.

"Let me know if you need a painter. My grandson is starting a business here in the spring," said one in the back.

Lucas turned to the group and flashed them a patient smile. "Thank you for the support, ladies. But I'm just fine." He'd said those words probably a thousand times over the last two years, but this time it was different. This time he actually meant them.

CHAPTER 15

PAIGE WAS ALONE IN A house with a child. And four puppies.

How the hell did *that* happen?

A normal person would have taken a moment to process even half of the feelings she was having about the change in direction her vacation had taken, but Paige never claimed to be normal. So instead she stood in the kitchen listening for sounds of distress from either the bedroom upstairs or the living room. Didn't they have monitors or something for this kind of thing? It was like she was one of those guards at Buckingham Palace. All she needed was a bearskin hat.

Then her phone vibrated in her pocket, and she jumped. Between the cell outage and the fact that she suspected Sammy had forwarded her calls as part of her work hiatus/exile, the device had been uncharacteristically quiet.

Speak of the devil, Paige thought as she looked at the screen.

"Hey there!" she said. She was actually surprised at how much she'd missed hearing his voice. At least the one that wasn't chirping in her head like a snarky subconscious.

But when he spoke, Paige didn't hear his normal voice, but rather one so deep it sounded like it came from his toes. "And on the fifth day of vacation, God said, 'Let there be cellular service.'"

Paige laughed. "I seriously doubt God had anything to do with it." More likely the crews working tirelessly to repair the towers on the mainland.

"Never know," Sammy said. "He works in mysterious ways."

"Because if there is a God," she said, "and that's a *big* if, his first order of business after the storm that *he* created would be to restore cell service."

"Maybe it was so I could bring you spiritual guidance," he said. "Now tell me everything that has happened."

"So that you can dispense spiritual guidance?"

He laughed. "No, because I'm bored and I'm hoping you've got some spicy stories to keep me awake."

Paige looked at her watch. Four thirty. Not exactly quitting time. "Aren't you still at work?"

"Yes, which is why I am B-O-R-E-D." He sighed. "Been getting everything done before lunch. Amazing how productive I am without the Boss Lady interrupting me all day."

"Sounds like she's a real shrew."

"Totally," Sammy said. "That's why I'm hoping she's been getting some on her vacation."

Paige's momentary silence spoke volumes.

Sammy gasped. "You got down and dirty with the sexy innkeeper?" He lowered his voice as though someone might hear. "Did he look like Ryan Reynolds everywhere, or just the face?"

"No. I don't know. Maybe?" She sputtered.

"So you haven't seen him naked?"

"I saw him without a shirt on the first day I arrived, and at least from the waist up, Mr. Reynolds has nothing on Lucas."

"But I thought you said you were getting some. Tell me you did not do it with the lights off!"

"I didn't do anything." She waited a beat, then added, "Yet."

"Ooooh!"

"Settle down," she said. "Jeez Louise, it's not that big a deal. And it's not even a yes, it's a maybe."

"Boss Lady, you getting laid by a new man happens about as often as the Vatican gets a new pope. Should I send up the smoke signal? I'm sure there's something around here I can toss into the fireplace."

"Those are gas logs. Do not put paper in there."

"Luuucas," Sammy said his name as though he was tasting a fine wine. "I like how it rolls off the tongue. Speaking of rolling tongues—"

"Samuel!" Paige whisper-shouted into the phone.

"What's with the whisper? Oh! Is he there? Should we FaceTime? Let's FaceTime."

"No, we should not FaceTime. And no, he isn't here. He went to the grocery store."

"Wait, back up. Did you say maybe?"

"Yes." she paused. "I think we are but…it's complicated."

Sammy laughed. "Aren't they all?"

"No, this one is extra-complicated. He was married."

He tsked. "*Was* being the operative word. That bitch is gone."

"Sammy," Paige grew serious. "She died."

"Oh, shit." Sammy's tone was somber. "Sorry. Didn't mean it that way." He took a deep breath. "How long?"

"Two years."

"People move on, Paige. You don't have to feel guilty about that." Up until that moment, Paige hadn't quite been able to work out the mix of emotions she felt whenever she thought about being with Lucas. Sure, there was the obvious attraction. Even the first day she met him, she'd wanted to push him up against the refrigerator and climb him like a tree. And sure, there was the obvious trepidation about getting involved with someone else after the way she and her ex had gone down in flames. But there was something else. Something she couldn't quite put her finger on.

Until now.

She knew it was ridiculous. Lucas was a young man. His wife had been gone for two years. He was entitled to move on. None of which made her feel any less guilty. But for what exactly? For wanting this woman's husband? For being alive when Jenny wasn't? Paige hadn't even known either of them then. She had no reason to feel guilty. But there was something else swirling around in the pit of her belly.

Fear.

"I just don't know if he's ready."

"That's for him to decide. You have to take him at his word."

At his word. Like when her ex used the words "Will you marry me"? Or how about when he said "I love you"?

"I know that's hard for you," Sammy said. "But it's time, Paige. Well past it, if you ask me." He always read her like an open book. For a while, she thought she must have given clues with her body language or facial expressions, but apparently his skills extended to phone calls as well.

"That's not all."

"What, has he decided to switch teams?" Sammy teased, clearly trying to lighten the mood. "Because if so, I'm on the next flight."

"He has a four-year-old daughter." She paused before dropping the bomb she knew would send her assistant over the edge. "Who I'm currently babysitting."

Sammy erupted in a fit of laughter. "Good one."

"I'm not joking."

"You? Babysitting?" The laughter started again. "Then what are you doing talking to me? Shouldn't you be playing Barbies or something?"

"She's sleeping."

"Ah, that explains it."

"You don't have to sound so smug. I'll have you know I actually get along quite well with her."

"Have you bonded over your mutual love of chocolate?"

"Not yet," Paige said. "I can't explain it really. She's just a lot more curious and insightful than I expected a kid her age to be. Don't get me wrong; if dessert is on the line, she works every angle with her dad." Something Paige could totally relate to. "And she drags this ragtag team of stuffed animals with her all over the house." A level of clutter Paige could do without. "But her outlook on life is just so...refreshing."

"Is that the tick-tock of a biological clock I hear?"

Paige snorted. "Absolutely not." If she were being honest, she would have admitted that earlier, when she was watching

Lucas with his young daughter, she found herself starting to think maybe she could have room in her life, not to mention her heart, for a child. But the moment the idea crept into her mind, she swatted it away. What in the world had she been thinking? She'd opted for a cat because dogs were too much responsibility. What would she do with a baby...leave a litter box in its nursery? Although to be fair, the puppies in the living room were starting to do a number on her resolve as well. Paige shoved the thoughts aside, deciding this was just the type of crazy thing that happened when a person had too much downtime. She'd return to normal once she was back in Chicago. "My life is perfect just the way it is," she said, more to herself than her friend. Problem was, even to her own ears, she didn't sound very convincing.

Paige heard a yelp from the living room. "Gotta run, Sammy. Something is up with one of the puppies."

"Puppies?" His voice was so high she was surprised anyone but a dog could hear.

"Yeah, Lucas and I rescued them from a storm drain. Long story."

"Call me back then because *this* I have to hear."

Except she didn't call him back because by the time she got the pups settled, Lucas had returned with the groceries. He'd no sooner walked into the room when Maddie appeared at the bottom of the stairs, crying because she'd been put to bed without Stanley—was that the avocado or the bear?—and Samantha began barking by the back door.

"I swear everything was under control until a minute ago," Paige said over the din. She had been totally killing the whole babysitting thing. As long as all the babies she was sitting were asleep. Talk about striking out at your first at-bat.

But Lucas took it in stride. "Why don't you go let Momma out, and I'll see if I can find Stanley." He turned to Maddie. "Did you see if maybe he had just fallen off the bed?" Paige heard him ask as she left the kitchen.

Once the dogs and the child were settled, the three humans in the household began to make dinner. Lucas tossed the salad while Paige made the pasta sauce, with Maddie in charge of dumping ingredients into the bowl. She was also chief food taster, a title that was bestowed upon her with an official ceremony that involved her standing on a chair wearing an apron and trying not to giggle while her dad knighted her with a wooden spoon.

They sat in the dining room with Maddie at the head of the table, which seemed only fitting seeing as she was the only one in the room who had received a royal accolade. "That was yummy," she said after she took her last bite of pasta. Judging by the amount of sauce on her face, Paige wasn't entirely sure any had made in into her mouth. Still, it was sweet of her to say, and Paige found herself more than a little gratified by Maddie's seal of approval.

"Thank you," Paige said. "My mom taught me how to make that. I would have made a crème brûlée for dessert, but I forgot to pack my torch." She smiled at her own joke. "What's your favorite flavor of crème brûlée, Maddie?"

"Crème bru what?" she asked.

"It's a dessert," Lucas said. "Kind of like pudding but with a sugar shell on top."

Maddie nodded as though she understood the intricacies of

burnt sugar. "I've never had a lady cook for me," she said matter-of-factly. "Just a daddy."

"What about your aunt?" Paige asked. "Doesn't she cook for you?"

"Aunt Sophia gets me lots of meals in white containers," Maddie replied, and the three of them shared a laugh.

"Did someone say my name?" Sophie said as she came through the front door.

"Maddie was just telling us how you keep her alive with takeout containers," Lucas said.

"Hey, we can't all be Martha Stewart." Her eyes widened at the sight of the pasta primavera. "But it looks like someone here is." She grabbed a plate out of the cabinet behind her and began loading it down with fettuccine.

Lucas stared at her nonplussed. "No, please, help yourself."

Sophie stuck her tongue out at her brother before shoveling a forkful of pasta into her mouth. "This is good," she said, echoing her niece between bites.

"Her mommy taught her how to make it," Maddie said. She smiled at Paige as if they were conspirators in some secret club. Paige was cool with that. As long as the club didn't involve toads. "What else did she teach you how to make?"

Assuming "how to make a vodka martini" probably wasn't the answer she should give to a four-year-old, Paige offered the only other recipe of her mom's she knew by heart. "Oatmeal chocolate-chip cookies."

Maddie bounced in her chair. "Oooh, can we make them now? Pleeease?"

"Afraid not," Lucas said before Paige could reply. "You and Aunt Soph need to put a move on if you want to watch an episode of *Ryan's World* before bed."

Maddie held up three tiny fingers. "This many."

"One," Lucas said. It was a valiant attempt to hold his ground, but even Paige knew he was fighting a losing battle. Lucas was a bit of a pushover when it came to his daughter. After being away from her for three nights, the poor guy didn't stand a chance.

"Okay, two," Maddie countered. The satisfied grin on her face gave Paige the impression that had been her goal all along.

"What is it with the women in my life and negotiations?"

For a moment, Paige wondered if she was included in that group, but then Lucas glanced at her and winked. It was a small gesture that not only answered her unspoken question, but set off a flurry of butterflies in her belly.

"Fine," he conceded. "Two. Then right to bed."

"But I'm not sleepy," Maddie said on a yawn. What was it about kids and sleep? From what she'd learned from her friends who were parents, being stubborn about going to bed was a universal trait, something Paige couldn't quite understand. What's not to love about climbing into bed after a long day and snuggling deep beneath the covers? Were kids really that worried they were missing out on something important while they slept? Did they think the adults only imposed an earlier bedtime for pip-squeaks so that they could have an all-you-can-eat ice cream buffet without interruption? Or maybe they thought all the adults played with their toys after they went to bed. After eight o'clock, it was Barbie and Lego time for the over-thirty age group. Not a bad idea, Paige thought. Throw in a few themed cocktails, and you'd have quite the retro happy hour.

"Alright, munchkin," Sophie said. "Time for you and me to hit the road."

"Let me grab Kermit," Maddie said as she slid off her chair. She returned a moment later with the shoebox in hand.

"I'll walk you out," Lucas said. He began to follow his sister and daughter to the door, then looked back to where Paige had started stacking dishes. "Leave those," he said. "I'll do them in the morning."

Leave dishes until the next day? Was he crazy? Paige was about to launch into the million reasons why she could never do that, but then Lucas's expression darkened as his eyes raked over her in a heated glance that took her breath away. Nothing went unnoticed—from the warm blush that rushed across her cheeks, to the stray curl she tucked behind her ear, to the way her sweater pulled across her breasts, and the way her jeans hugged her curves.

His voice was rough when he spoke, revealing the effect his once-over had had on him as well. "Wait for me."

As if there was anything else she would rather do.

CHAPTER 16

LUCAS WALKED SOPHIE AND MADDIE out to the sidewalk. He would have offered to help his daughter with her helmet, but he'd learned his lesson on that months ago. Apparently big girls didn't need to have their helmet straps fastened by their dad. Something told him that information was just the tip of the iceberg.

"Thanks for taking her tonight," he said to Sophie.

"Are you kidding? Me and the Peanut are going to have loads of fun." She secured her own helmet, then leaned closer so that only he could hear. "Something tells me her dad will too."

Lucas shook his head. He'd definitely created a monster by confiding in his sister that he felt ready to move on. She had only been mildly annoying before, but armed with this new information, she'd be downright intolerable. "We're just going to watch a movie," he said in an attempt to downplay the situation. *Yeah, fat chance of that.*

"Are you going to Netflix and chill?" Maddie asked. Lucas and his sister turned as one to see his daughter perched upon her hot-pink bicycle. Lucas had wanted to get her one that resembled a mountain bike, but she had insisted on the sparkly pink one, complete with a white basket on the front and metallic silver and pink streamers dangling from the handlebars.

"Where did she learn that?" he asked his sister.

"Don't look at me?" she practically squeaked. The wide-eyed innocent look might have worked for Maddie, but on Sophie it fell a bit short.

Since he was absolutely sure his daughter was oblivious to the euphemism, Lucas let it go. "Call me if there are any problems."

"We'll be fine." Sophie said as she kicked one leg over the seat of her bike. "But I expect a full report tomorrow."

"Yeah, that's not happening," he deadpanned. Clearly a few boundaries had to be redefined.

Sophie shot him a knowing smile, and then they were off. Lucas stood on the sidewalk, watching his daughter pedaling alongside her aunt until they'd turned the corner. He looked back at the house. Inside, a beautiful woman was waiting for him. But as he walked up the stone path, he grew increasingly aware of how anxious he was. He'd never been nervous before. Well, except maybe before his first time. In some ways, that's exactly how he felt. Paige more than made him feel alive again; with her everything felt brand-new.

He drew a deep breath. *Stop being such a wuss*, he told himself. The "It's just like riding a bike" expression popped into his mind, and while he would normally have laughed off something like that, the truth was, he wanted their night to be perfect. Not so much for him—because let's face it, sex was great for a guy no matter how it happened: slow, fast, rough, tender—but for her.

On the surface, Paige Parker had been easy to read. A tough-as-nails ballbuster who not only wanted everything her way, but usually got it. Over the last few days, though, her protective layers had started to peel away. She'd surprised him in a hundred different ways, and yet a part of her was still guarded. If only he could get her to open up a bit, to lower her defenses and let him in.

Lucas opened the front door to find Paige standing in the hallway in front of the large oak-and-glass curio.

She smiled when she saw him. "That's quite a seashell collection you have."

"Probably ought to pack some of them up." Lucas knew Paige well enough now to realize just how crazy it must have made her to see all those beachcombing souvenirs so haphazardly displayed. Hell, he was surprised she hadn't rearranged them the way she had parts of his kitchen. Then again, perhaps she felt as though that was one area that was off-limits. Organizing souvenirs from time he spent with his late wife was hardly the same as lining up mugs or sorting his pantry by food group. He was fairly sure he'd heard her shuffling things around on the porch the other night as well. But the items in this case were different. They were a personal time capsule. And while he wasn't about to bury them in the yard, it was time most of them found their way to the attic. "There's a lot in that case that should be packed away."

Her expression softened. "If you're talking about the picture"—she nodded toward the cabinet—"I disagree."

Lucas followed her gaze to find that the framed photo of him and Jenny standing in front of their newly acquired inn was no longer tucked behind driftwood. Paige had moved it front and center. "You do?" How could someone who was interested in him be okay with a picture of his late wife staring at her every time she walked through the door.

Paige nodded. "That photo marks the establishment of this inn," she said. "And while I do think the display could do with a bit of tidying…"

"Ever the organizer," he teased.

"Always," she said.

She stepped closer. "Lucas, I don't think you should try to hide away your memories." Something told him she wasn't only referring to the photo. "They are part of who you are, and maybe more importantly, they are part of Maddie." She reached out and placed her hand on his arm. "She needs to know about her mom. Don't ever feel like you have to change or apologize for that, for me or anyone else."

"She's starting to forget her," he said. It broke his heart when he would mention something about Jenny, something Maddie at one time could recall, and his daughter would draw a blank. In a way, it felt like losing her all over again, one piece at time.

"All the more reason to keep those memories alive."

"You're pretty amazing, do you know that?"

She flipped her hair over her shoulder. "So I've been told."

He chuckled. "Looks like I also need to add modesty to the list."

Paige drew back. "You're making a list?"

"A mental one," he said. "But yes."

"Of?"

"Interesting facts about Ms. Paige Parker."

She smiled. "Don't you mean Ms. Paige Parker, certified pain in the ass?"

Lucas cringed. Pain in the ass or not, he hadn't intended for her to hear that, even when all she was to him was a disgruntled guest. "You know about that, do you?"

Paige nodded. "Walls here aren't so thick."

"To be fair, we didn't exactly get off on the right foot."

She raised a brow. "And whose fault would that be?"

"You have a point."

"It wasn't all your fault," she conceded. "Maybe only eighty percent."

"You'll take the blame for twenty?" he asked. "That's mighty decent."

"Well, I'm not exactly low maintenance."

He couldn't believe she managed to say the words with a straight face. "That I know."

"So tell me, what else is on this list of yours?"

He had definitely piqued her curiosity, which brought him a surprising amount of satisfaction. But he wasn't about to put all his cards on the table. At least not yet. "I'm afraid that's classified information," he said.

"Think you've got me all figured out, huh?"

"Hardly. The list is very much a work in progress."

"Well, we never did finish that game of Twenty Questions. Maybe you'll find a few more items for the list then," she said.

"Ah, yes, and I still have all ten of mine."

"If I'm not mistaken, I have what...eight more to ask you?"

His head fell back on a laugh. "Nice try."

"What?" she asked, knowing damn well what.

"You're worse than Maddie, do you know that?" It was meant as a joke, but the similarities between this and the conversation he'd just had with his four-year-old daughter were hard to miss.

Paige stared at him, nonplussed. Lucas had to admit, she was good. Step one in any negotiation: Never back down on the first move.

"You have four questions left," he said.

"Five," she corrected. Guess there wasn't much point to standing your ground when you'd been busted. "One was up for debate, but the jury ruled in my favor."

He grinned. "How quickly her memory returns when it suits her."

"There's a lot you don't know about me," she said. "Competitiveness isn't only in my nature. It's in my blood."

"I'll add that to the list." Lucas grew more serious. "Tell me more."

She narrowed her eyes. "Are you officially using one of your questions?"

"If you insist."

"Well, I've already told you I'm wicked when it comes to rummy," she teased. "But I can be just as ruthless with a good old-fashioned game of Candy Land, so best to keep Maddie away from me as well."

He knew she was only playing, but as she said the words, Lucas realized just how far from the truth that was. Paige had only spent one afternoon with his daughter, but even after that short amount of time, the two of them had already made a connection.

A bit of an awkward one, no doubt—who shook hands with a four-year-old, let alone asked what kind of crème brûlée she preferred?—but still.

"I don't know about that. My daughter can be quite ruthless when it comes to Go Fish. Especially if we're betting with M&Ms."

Paige laughed. "I can respect a girl who goes for the jugular over chocolate."

"Speaking of chocolate," he said. "I have a surprise for you. Meet me in the living room."

CHAPTER 17

PAIGE PACED BACK AND FORTH in front of the fireplace so many times, even the dogs grew tired of watching her. As a rule, she hated surprises, even good ones. Just one more side effect of being a type A control freak, but knowing that about herself didn't make the waiting any easier.

Luckily, Lucas didn't keep her in suspense for too long. He joined her a few moments later, holding a pink bakery box in his hands.

"Is that…"

Lucas nodded. "I know the booking wasn't exactly as you imagined. Figured the least I could do was make good on the cake order." He lifted the cover of the cardboard box to reveal a round cake decorated with pink roses and the words *Happy Singles Day*.

"Hope you like chocolate cake with white butter cream," he said. "Inventory was a little light seeing as how they are just now back in business."

"It's my favorite," Paige said. "My mom used to make one for my birthday every year."

Lucas set the cake on the coffee table and pulled a fork out of the back pocket of his jeans. "Here you go," he said as he handed it to her.

Paige gaped at him. "You can't be serious? You want me to just dig in?"

"Why not?" He took a seat on the floor and waved his hand in the direction of the nine-inch cake.

"Aren't you going to have any?" Surely he wasn't expecting her to eat a giant cake all by herself.

Lucas flashed a boyish grin as he produced another fork from his pocket. "Absolutely, but ladies first. Plus, it is your cake, after all."

"Is it too much to hope that you're going to pull a knife and two plates out of that pocket?" The peanut butter on the banister was starting to make a lot more sense. If utensils were optional, it's amazing the whole place wasn't covered with remnants of food.

He laughed. "Live a little, Paige. Not everything has to be picture perfect. Sometimes you just need to eat a cake right out of the box."

That sounded great and all, but Paige wasn't convinced. "What if your sister wants some cake? And you know Maddie will. Are we just going to offer them a mangled mountain of crumbs?"

He reached for her hand and tugged her to the floor beside him. "If it will make you feel better, I promise to cut off the part where we ate before they come back. But for now"—he stuck the fork in the cake, breaking off a rather large chunk and holding it in front of her face—"taste."

Sensing her hesitation, he turned playful. "Come on. You have to try some," he said. "Least you can do after a shop full of the island's busiest bodies heard me ask for this inscription."

Paige reached for the fork, but Lucas shook his head. "Let me."

"I can feed myself," she started to protest. It was one of the stipulations she'd made for the wedding-that-never-happened. Under no circumstances was she going to allow herself to be fed cake in front of two hundred and fifty guests.

"That's not the point." His voice dropped. "Now, open for me."

Oh boy. Paige shifted in place. How in the world had he turned pigging out on cake like a couple of eight-year-olds into something so erotic? Forget the cake, she was ready for a different kind of dessert.

But since Lucas seemed determined not only for her to try the cake, but to feed it to her as well...

Still feeling slightly foolish, Paige opened her mouth and allowed him to feed her a bite of decadent chocolate cake. "Mmmm..." Her eyes drifted shut as she savored the mouthwatering bite. When she opened them, she found Lucas watching her with a penetrating stare.

She tucked a stray curl behind her ear. "Surely this is not that exciting?"

"More than you know," he said.

Holy guacamole, he was doing it again, saying seemingly innocent words in a way that shot through her like a jolt of electricity. Every inch of her sparked to life, even parts she thought had long gone dormant.

"Would you like another taste?"

"Yes, please." Her breathless tone revealed the effect he was having her.

He lifted the next forkful. Paige licked her lips and saw Lucas's eyes flare ever so slightly. Oh yeah, he wanted more than cake too. His jaw fell slack as he eased the bite into her mouth, never taking his attention off her lips as she slid the cake off the fork.

"So are you close with your mom?" he asked.

Paige choked on her cake. Talk about a libido buster. "What?" she tried to ask, but all she ended up doing was inhaling more cake crumbs.

"Shit. Hold on." Lucas disappeared into the kitchen and returned seconds later with a glass of water. "Sorry," he said as she downed three huge gulps.

"No, it's fine." she said. "I just wasn't expecting to be asked about my mom." Not when she thought Mr. Sex-on-a-Stick was seducing her with chocolate cake.

"You mentioned she used to bake a cake like this for your birthday, so it got me thinking that might be a good place to start."

"Start?" Holy hell, if this was his idea of foreplay…

"My ten questions." He cocked his head to one side. "What did you think I meant?"

That you were starting the seduction of Paige Parker. Talk about getting their wires crossed. "Nothing." She gulped down more of the water. "But for the choking, I'm docking you two."

Lucas laughed. "Fair enough," he conceded. "But you still have to answer the question."

"I'm not quite sure how to answer that." It was the truth.

Paige and her mother had a complex relationship, to say the least. It was going to be hard to put it into words.

"Paige Parker at a loss for what to say?"

She kicked him with her toe. "You don't have to look so shocked."

"Tell you what, you can think it over while I build us a fire."

Paige sat on the rug considering her answer while Lucas stacked several birch logs on the iron grate. "My mom and I are close," she finally said. "But only on the surface."

"Aren't those opposites?" he asked. "How can you be close, superficially?"

"We talk all the time, but never about anything important." She drew her knees up and leaned back against the couch. "My mom is complicated. She was a 1950s housewife living in the 1990s. For a solid twenty years, her entire existence revolved around me, my dad, and my brother."

Lucas lit the kindling, then closed the screen. "Was that a bad thing?"

"Not for us."

"For your mom?" he asked as he came to sit beside her.

"My mom was…" She corrected herself. "*Is* brilliant. Smartest one in our family, if you ask me. And I don't just mean with books. The woman can watch a YouTube video and teach herself to do anything. Hang a ceiling fan, install a new faucet, repair the garage door. You name it, she's done it. All while tutoring my brother, making home-cooked meals, and managing the family finances. She even did the taxes." The latter was something Paige never quite understood, seeing as how her dad was a CPA.

Paige stared into the brick fireplace as the white bark began to crackle. "She says she has no regrets, but sometimes I'd catch her looking at the framed law degree she'd hung in the living room." Paige blinked back the tears that always threatened when she thought of her mother living a life filled with what-ifs.

"I think she underestimated the personal price she would pay when she agreed with my father's plan for her to stay home with the kids. Which is why I try not to tell her anything negative. I want her to feel like the choice she made was worth it, you know?" She tried to laugh, but the sound she made was laced with far too much unease to appear lighthearted. "It's also why I've promised myself that I will never rearrange my life for a man."

The flames shot higher as the wood caught. "Is that why you're celebrating Singles Day?"

Paige rolled her eyes. "It's not like I'm a man-hater or against relationships as a whole. But I hadn't taken time off since I started my business, and then I saw this stupid quiz about finding your perfect vacation. I guess it made sense. At the time."

"No," he clarified. "Is that why you're still single?"

Paige looked down at the woven rug. A strand of wool had come loose from the weave. Just like her story, she knew that pulling that first string would unravel the whole thing. And yet she tugged. "I almost wasn't."

Lucas waited patiently for her to say more. Or maybe for her to change the subject, which she almost did. Talking about an ex can be even more of a mood buster than talking about your mother. But something about this man made her want to share the bits of herself she thought she'd locked away for good.

"I was engaged," she said.

"When was this?"

"Oh, a long time ago," she replied without even doing the math. But as she thought about it, she realized that it actually had been a long time ago. Nearly five years. "I met Bobby just after I finished grad school. On paper he was perfect. Straitlaced and mature. An accountant even."

"Like your dad?"

"Yeah." Paige nodded. "He was only three years older than I was, but he'd already accomplished so much. He'd graduated from college at nineteen, had his masters by twenty and had traveled the world twice over by the time I met him. He was..." She fumbled to find the right words.

"The perfect man to bring home to your parents?"

Paige hadn't realized it at the time, but even at twenty-five, she'd still been seeking their approval. "They loved him," she said. "And so did I back then. So much so that I shifted my life plans around him. Everything from where he wanted to live to the types of vacations we took."

"Sounds like you were doing exactly—"

"What my mom did?"

He nodded.

"It's funny, because when we're young, all we really have to base things on are our parents." She considered that, then added, "And even when that starts to change, well, it's not like our friends have all the answers either."

"How so?"

"I've watched it happen time and time again: smart, successful women making sacrifices for the men they love. Sometimes it's small stuff like going to the restaurants he likes, but then it morphs into taking vacations to the places he wants to see, planning the weekend around his friends and what he wants to do, or changing jobs because he got a better one in a new city."

"Are we still talking about friends?"

"Not entirely," she confessed. "I didn't realize it was happening, and looking back, I can't even pinpoint when it started. But yeah, I was headed straight down the same path my mom had taken." The realization brought a bittersweet relief. "So in the end, maybe my ex did me a favor by being such an asshole."

"What did he do? If you don't mind me asking."

As a rule, Paige hated talking about the past. But when it came to her ex, she avoided the subject like the plague. No looking back and all that crap. But Lucas had bared his soul to her when he'd told her about losing his wife. He'd shared the details of his broken heart. Least she could do was tell him about her own journey.

"Things were going great, too great I guess, and I let myself get comfortable."

"Comfortable?"

"Yeah, you know, the point where you're happy and you stop worrying that the happiness will end and you let yourself relax and enjoy it. Then fate comes along and punches you in the gut." As she said the words, she realized that Lucas knew about that all too well. And what happened to him was far worse than her loss. "I'm sorry, I feel like a jerk complaining to you when—"

He cut her off with a shake of his head. "No two people have the same story, Paige. You can't compare one person's pain to another's. We all feel what is happening in our own lives just as deeply." He smiled. "It's not a competition."

She took a deep breath. "We'd finally set a date," she said. "I'd just gotten a promotion, and he'd made partner at his firm. We were well on our way to having everything we'd ever wanted."

"And then?"

"And then I came home from a business trip to find him breaking in the bed my parents had given us as an early wedding present."

"You actually caught him in the act?"

"Oh yeah, I had a bedside view, so to speak. Guess I should be grateful. I mean, I didn't have to snoop around like some suspicious girlfriend. I lived in ignorant bliss until the moment I flung open the door to see my boss riding my fiancé like a bronco at the state fair." She had only told the story to a handful of people, but when she did, she always used that analogy. Because that's exactly what she'd looked like, one arm in the air, her head thrown back, and her ass bouncing up and down.

It took a minute for the information dump to sink in, but when it did, Lucas's eyes grew wide. "Wait, did you say your *boss*?"

Paige nodded, then explained how she lost her fiancé and her job all in one afternoon. As she did, that familiar lump formed in her throat. Even after all this time, the sense of betrayal could bubble to the surface at a moment's notice. "Jeez," she said, willing herself not to cry. "It was three years ago." She rolled her eyes at herself. "Think I'd be over it by now." Defense mechanism two hundred and twelve: self-deprecating humor. But Lucas wasn't buying it. He didn't laugh along with her. Instead he took her hand.

"I'm so sorry, Paige."

"Don't be." She shrugged. "That afternoon changed my life for the better as far as I'm concerned. I was spared being saddled with a lying cheat." She winced. "Okay, maybe not the best choice of words, given the whole bronco thing," she said, hoping once again to shift the conversation with a laugh. No such luck.

"Anyway," she said on a drawn-out exhale, "that's what pushed me to start my own business. Opening Chaos Control was the single best decision I've ever made. Maybe I should send the two of them a thank-you note." The suggestion didn't even earn her a small grin.

"Chaos Control?" he asked.

She nodded. "My company. I had considered Get your Shit Together, but it looked a little long on the front door."

Still no laugh? This guy was a tough nut to crack. That, or he just wasn't going to let her use humor to hide her feelings. Her money was on the latter.

She looked down at the rug, only to realize she'd twisted the strand of wool into a knot. Lucas lifted her chin to meet his gaze. Instinctively, she wanted to look away, but for some reason she couldn't. She was fully dressed, and yet she'd never felt more exposed in her entire life. It was as though he could see right through her, past the tough exterior to the woman who deep down had always wanted more, but was too proud or scared to admit it. Not anymore. Her protective shell wasn't just cracking, it was shattering into a million pieces.

"Look, it sucked," she finally admitted. "It sucked more than anything I've ever experienced in my life. I threw all his clothes into the street. I bought refrigerated cookie dough and ate it right out of the plastic tube. I did all the clichés that women in movies do, but what I didn't do was cry." Her voice cracked. "I didn't cry because the man who said he wanted to spend his life with me thought it was fine to stick his dick in another woman. I didn't cry because my boss, someone who claimed to be my friend, who was planning my freaking bridal shower, thought it was fine to screw my fiancé, and I didn't cry because I knew that no matter how many damn Hallmark movies I watched, I was never going to believe in happy endings ever again."

Lucas looked at her with a sincerity unlike any she'd ever felt before. "Don't you get lonely?" he asked as his thumb stroked the back of her hand. The contact was minimal, but the connection was strong.

"I could ask you the same thing."

"Maddie doesn't allow much time for loneliness." His mouth quirked into half a smile. "Or anything else for that matter."

"And besides, I'm not alone. I have Mr. Rochester. And Sammy, my assistant. And I have friends. Not that I spend much time with them," she conceded. "But that's only because I work so many long hours."

"You need more than your work and your assistant," he said. "Don't you want someone to come home to?"

That was the whole point. She didn't want any one person to mean that much. Paige's throat tightened, causing her words to come out in a hoarse whisper. "It's easier this way." She swallowed, then spoke her truth. "Safer."

"Not every man is a pig, Paige." He waited a beat, then asked, "What, no cracks about the mess in my house?"

Paige had spent the entire conversation walking the fine line between laughter and tears, but his smile and lighthearted words tipped the scales. "I wasn't going to say a word," she said, matching his grin with one of her own.

Lucas grew serious again. "What I meant is not every man is a weasel who is going to betray you." He reached up and stroked her cheek with his fingertips. It was the simplest gesture, barely anything at all, and yet every inch of her awoke from his touch. "And believe it or not, not every man would expect you to sacrifice who you are simply because you love him."

She looked at him, and for the first time, she realized that it wasn't only grief that was holding him back. Paige wasn't the only one who'd been too scared to try again.

"And not every woman will leave you either, Lucas."

"Maybe we both need to let our guard down just a little."

He leaned forward and touched his lips against hers. Paige wanted to reach for him, to pull him closer, while at the same time still wanting to push him away. That was the safe thing to do, to end this before it began, before he had a chance to break her fragile heart. But Lucas didn't go anywhere. He stayed right where he was, his hand cupping her jaw as he teased her with featherlight kisses until her breathing turned shallow and her skin grew hot. Too hot. Like every inch of her was on fire and relief could only be found in his touch.

"Are you okay?" he asked when she shivered beneath his hand.

"I feel…so vulnerable."

His lips brushed hers yet again, but he said nothing. Instead he waited for her to find the words in her own time.

"It's scary." Such a simple statement, and yet so hard to admit.

"It doesn't have to be," he said.

"But what if—"

"What if it's fabulous?"

"That would make it even worse."

"It's a chance I'm willing to take," he said. And so was she. Because instead of pushing Lucas away, Paige reached for him, her hand on the back of his neck as she drew him closer. But it wasn't enough. She needed to feel his touch on her skin and the weight of his body on hers, moving together until they were lost to everything but each other.

Lowering them to the rug, Lucas rolled her beneath him, pressing against her soft flesh right where she needed it most. "I want you, Paige." He reared back to look at her, his voice tight with a barely leashed restraint. "But only if you're sure."

Paige placed her hand on his chest and felt his heart pounding beneath her palm. She stared up at him, his eyes glittering in the warm glow of the fire, and all of the doubts and fears of the last three years vanished.

"I'm sure," she whispered in reply. With Lucas there was no promise of a future—no next year, next month, or even next week. There was only the here and now with a man who not only understood her but cherished her, even if only for one night.

CHAPTER 18

A SMILE SPREAD ACROSS PAIGE'S face as the first hint of consciousness seeped into her mind. Without opening her eyes, she slid her hand across the cool sheets to find...

Nothing.

Her eyes popped open. Lucas was nowhere to be found.

She sat up in bed and the sheet pooled in her lap. Last night had been... Paige searched for the right word. Every adjective that came to mind sounded so clichéd—amazing, magical, life-affirming—yet that's exactly how it felt. They'd spent hours lost in each other, and when they'd finally collapsed against the mattress, Lucas hadn't run off. He'd stayed right where he was, holding her in his arms until they both fell asleep. It had felt natural. It had felt right. And not one ounce of her was afraid he would wake in the morning and catch sight of something that would send him running for his life.

So where was he now?

She looked through the large bay window. The sun was much higher than it was when she usually woke. Maybe Lucas wasn't the type to sleep in, even if they had been up until nearly dawn. A sense of unease filled her belly as another thought crept, unwelcome, into her mind. What if the sunrise had brought a sobering regret? What if he wasn't as ready to move on as he thought? Then again, maybe he just needed some time to process. This was all new to him. Not that Paige had any idea what "this" was exactly. It didn't feel like a one-night stand. A vacation fling maybe? But weren't they too old for that?

She hashed over the options as she got dressed, but ultimately Paige decided not to analyze the situation to death and instead just try to enjoy it for what it was. Whatever that might be. She hadn't come to the island to fall for a hotter-than-hell innkeeper. And despite her assistant's hopes to the contrary, she hadn't even come looking for a fling. This trip was about celebrating her single life. Whatever she'd found with Lucas, she hadn't been looking for it. And yet there she was. Which was why she decided that, for once in her life, she just needed to go with the flow.

By the time she reached the stairs, she was nearly convinced. That is, until she made it to the kitchen to find Lucas sitting at the island, hunched over his laptop with a distraught look on his face. Then every fear and insecurity came rushing back to her, along with the reminder of why she'd given up men in the first place.

Don't assume the worst, she chanted to herself. Whatever had him so stressed out might have absolutely nothing to do with her or the night they'd just spent together. She was debating whether or not to ask, when he looked up from the screen.

"Hey," he said.

"Hey." Well, that wasn't awkward at all.

"Sorry you woke up alone. I couldn't sleep, and once I'm up..."

"No, I totally get it." Her teeth sank into her bottom lip.

Mind your own business, she heard Sammy McGuire say.

But Lucas looked so distraught...

"Everything alright?" The moment the words left her mouth, she regretted asking them. *Don't chase bad news*, her grandmother always used to say. But instead of listening to her, or the cartoon version of her assistant, Paige had charged full speed ahead toward an answer she was, in all likelihood, not going to like.

"What? Oh yeah, fine," he said, his focus returning to whatever was on his laptop screen. "Just have a lot on my mind." An uncomfortable moment passed before he added, "Give me a second, and I'll get breakfast started."

Paige shoved her hands into the pockets of her sweatshirt. She'd opted for casual, dressing in a pair of yoga pants and her favorite Northwestern hoodie, but now she wanted nothing more than to be wearing her power suit and her favorite pair of impractical heels. She felt like she could conquer the world in that outfit. It was what she wore to her most important meetings. Her battle armor, so to speak. And in that moment, she could have really used a steel barrier between Lucas Croft and her fragile heart.

"You know what, I think I'll take a rain check on breakfast, if that's all right?"

Lucas's eyes shot up to meet hers. "Are you sure?"

"Yeah." She checked her wrist for a watch she wasn't wearing. "It's nearly lunchtime anyway. Plus, I really wanted to get out for..." What? She panicked, and the next words to come out of her mouth were possibly the most untrue she'd ever spoken. "...a run."

"You're going out for a run?" he repeated. "I didn't realize you liked to jog."

"Oh yeah, absolutely." Not. "I love a good hard run. Haven't been out on the pavement..." EVER. "...in a week. You know, with the storm and all." She eased her way toward the back door. "And it will give me a chance to see a bit of the island."

With that, she was out the door. What the hell had she been thinking? A run? For starters, she was wearing Keds. With no socks. But what was worse, she didn't have on the industrial-strength bra she wore to the gym. And there she only read a book on a recumbent bike or watched Netflix on the elliptical. She didn't actually *run*.

Paige looked down at her bosom. *Hang on, girls.*

Deciding that a beach run was not for beginners, she opted for the sidewalk. She made a valiant effort, keeping her strides long and her head up, until she was out of view of the inn. Then she slowed to a shuffle while supporting her boobs with her hands. Even that didn't last long. Just as well. The folks she passed as she jogged were giving her and her "hand"-made support bra more than a few odd looks. She could just imagine the island gossip. *Did you see that woman from Chicago fondling herself while she ran through town?*

Paige stopped, bending at the waist as she tried to catch her breath. When she straightened, she realized she was right in front of the fire station. Convenient, she thought. At least the paramedics wouldn't have far to go. But then she wiped the sweat from her eyes and, on closer inspection, realized the stone and brick building wasn't a fire station at all, but rather a bookstore. In a fire station.

Blazing Books.

Sophie.

Paige rounded the corner in search of the front of the shop. The sign in the window read OPEN, so she pushed on the bright-red door. Inside was no ordinary bookstore. The character of the old firehouse remained, everything from the exposed brick walls to the high arched windows. There was even an old fire truck, or at least the front end, in the far corner.

A bell chimed as the door closed behind her, and a moment later, a woman slid down a brass pole in the middle of the store. She hit the floor with practiced ease and turned to greet her customer. When she realized who it was, Sophie's face lit up.

"Hey, Paige!" she said. "Glad you decided to come by." There was really no decision involved. She was more or less on the lam. But either way, she was glad her aimless run had brought her to Sophie's door.

A small head poked out from behind the fire engine. "Is that my daddy's Paige?" Maddie asked.

Paige had spent the last three years establishing her independence. She was her own woman, not an accessory for a man. Which was why she was so surprised when the use of the possessive adjective sent an unfamiliar warmth spiraling through her body. But she wasn't Lucas's Paige; she wasn't Lucas's anything. The warm sensation finally settled in her chest, where it turned into a far-more-familiar burn.

Maddie didn't wait for an answer. Instead she skipped straight toward Paige. When she reached her, she threw her arms around her in a bear-cub hug.

"Did you come to visit Floppy, Stanley, and Stinky?" she asked with complete sincerity.

"Actually, I was just out for a jog, and then I saw the bookstore, so I thought I would come in and say hello."

Sophie's eyes drifted to Paige's shoes. She didn't say anything, but Paige knew she'd been busted.

"We're having a tea party in the fire truck. Want some?" Maddie asked.

Paige looked to Sophie for guidance. Her questioning look was met with a smile and a nod.

"If you're sure you have enough," Paige said.

Maddie giggled. "It's pretend tea, silly. There's always enough." She took Paige's hand and led her to the rear of the truck. Only a partial frame remained, and that had been converted into an adorable playhouse. Inside were piles of pillows and a pint-size table and chair set. Maddie's favorite toys occupied all but one chair, which left Paige to find a spot on the pillows. Just as well. Something told her the small wooden chairs wouldn't hold a full-size human.

To Paige's relief, Sophie joined them. Not that she minded being alone with Maddie, but she had no idea what the proper etiquette was for drinking invisible tea and eating imaginary cake. In the end, it turned out she didn't need a guide. Maddie took care of that all on her own, giving instructions as she directed the tea party from beginning to end. Reminded Paige of herself at that age. Always in charge.

When they were done, Sophie turned her attention to her niece. "Maddie, why don't you go find a book to take home with you while I give Paige a tour of the store."

She waited until the little girl had gathered her toys and scampered off between the rows of books before addressing the elephant in the room. "Out for a jog in those shoes?" At least she hadn't mentioned the bra situation. "Is everything okay?"

"I just...needed some air."

Sophie's eyes narrowed. "What did my butthead brother do now?"

"Nothing."

His sister wasn't buying it. "You're not a very good liar."

"It's...complicated." Jeez, she sounded like a Facebook status.

"Always is with him." Sophie laughed. "I love my brother, but he's a bit much sometimes. Always getting in his own head." She folded her legs in front of her like a pretzel. Clearly she wasn't as adverse to yoga as Paige was. "I keep telling him he needs to relax more and think less."

"He's been through a lot," Paige said.

"He told you?"

Paige nodded. Sophie seemed a little surprised, but in a good way. Her entire body relaxed as though she'd been holding in a breath.

"Maybe he's not as ready to move on as he thought he was," Paige offered. "Last night was perfect but—"

"Today he's acting moody and withdrawn?"

"A bit, yeah." She didn't want to criticize him to his sister, but fact was the change in him had been anything but little. Somewhere between falling asleep and making coffee, Lucas Croft had done a complete one-eighty.

"I wouldn't be so quick to assume his mood has anything to do with you," Sophie said, as though reading Paige's mind. She looked over to where her niece was now reading a story to a very well-worn bunny. "Lucas has a lot on his plate right now with trying to restart the business."

Paige knew from the first day's eavesdropping that it was more than that. From what she'd heard, Lucas was in danger of losing the place. But that had been the case all along. What she saw this morning was something different. Something worse. "I don't think that's what was bothering him."

"Did you ask him?"

Paige looked down at the teacup she still held clenched in her hand. Hearing Sophie ask something so obviously simple made her suddenly feel very foolish for hauling ass out of the house. "No."

"I'll let you in on a little secret, Paige," she said, dropping her voice to a whisper. "My brother is crazy about you."

Paige looked up. "What?"

Sophie grinned. "You heard me. I saw how he was with you. Can't even remember the last time he had such a dopey look on his face." She stood and pulled Paige to her feet. "Why don't you jog back to the house and ask him what's up?" She looped her arm through Paige's as they walked arm in arm toward the door. "Just don't tell him about the dopey-face part."

Paige met Sophie's grin with one of her own. "Your secret is safe with me."

CHAPTER 19

IF PAIGE THOUGHT ABOUT IT too long, she'd chicken out.

She'd been standing on the sidewalk in front of the Copper Lantern Inn for at least five minutes, debating how best to broach the subject with Lucas. Sophie had made it seem so easy that Paige had left the bookstore in total confidence. But the closer she got to the inn, the more her courage waned, until she found herself standing in front of the picket gate overthinking her next move.

This never happened at work. She had no problem charging into a meeting with her hand extended and her head held high. But this was different. It wasn't a project or a new client on the line. It was her heart.

Suck it up, Parker, she thought. It certainly wasn't going to make things any better if he saw her outside pacing like a loon.

Lucas was still in the kitchen, sitting at the island, right where Paige had left him. There was a fresh carafe of coffee on the counter, so at least he'd moved at some point. But that was the only evidence that he'd taken his eyes off the computer at all.

"How was your run?" he asked when she walked into the room. He didn't look up. Not a good sign.

Paige drew a blank. "My run? Oh yeah, my run. Good."

He finally looked at her. His eyes were glassy, probably from staring at the screen for no telling how long, and his hair looked as though he'd run his hands through it a few dozen times. "I made coffee while you were out."

"Thanks." Paige didn't really even want coffee—her morning outing had provided enough of a jolt to her system—but pouring a cup was a good excuse to avoid the conversation. At least for a few more minutes.

She stalled, stirring the cup of coffee far longer than necessary considering she hadn't even added anything to it. Time to put on her big-girl panties.

"Hey," she said, finally turning around to face him. "I know this is all new to you. If you're upset about last night, if it's too much too soon, we can take a step back. I didn't come here looking for... And well, you've got a lot on your plate."

"Oh God no," Lucas said. "Is that what you thought?"

"I wasn't really sure what to think. I mean, I thought everything was great last night." She shot him a knowing look. "Really great." Really great three times over, thank you very much. Actually, thank *him* very much. "But then this morning, I woke up and you weren't there, and you'd seemed totally fine last night, but then I came down, and you were sitting here all tense and you looked so upset." Paige paused to take a breath. Even she knew she was rambling. "I just assumed it was because—"

He closed the gap between them in two easy strides, swallowing her protests with a kiss. Instinctively her arms snaked around his neck, and then he shifted, pressing against her in a way that had her moaning into his mouth. Her reaction was met by one of his own. A low groan rumbled in his chest as Lucas's hands gripped her waist, lifting her so that she sat perched atop the butcher-block counter. She spread her legs, inviting him in, and Lucas took full advantage, seating himself against her warmth and rocking against her in a rhythm that left them both breathless when he finally reared back to look at her.

"Does that answer your question?"

"Technically, I hadn't asked a question." Gah! She really had to do something about her need to always be right.

Lucas merely smiled and shook his head. "You're a little crazy, do you know that?"

She winced. "Sorry."

"Don't be," he said, "I happen to like your kind of crazy."

"You do?" No one liked her crazy. Not even her.

Lucas didn't answer. Not with words anyway. Instead he kissed her again, and for once in her life, Paige Parker lost the urge to win a debate.

But that did nothing to erase her concern for the man currently wedged between her thighs. "So, if it's not us," she began when they finally came up for air. "Look, I don't want to pry, so feel free to tell me it's none of my business, but...are you sure everything's okay? The look on your face when I walked in the room this morning..."

Lucas reached for his laptop and spun it around so it was facing them. "I got an email from Maddie's grandfather," he said.

230 ANN MARIE WALKER

Paige already knew that Lucas and Sophie's parents had been killed by a drunk driver, which meant he had to be talking about Jenny's dad.

"Go ahead." Lucas nodded toward the screen. "Read it."

Paige slid off the counter, sat down on one of the stools, and read the email, twice. Lucas stood behind her, his entire frame vibrating with tension. She could feel it rolling off him in waves. What Paige couldn't figure out was why. The email seemed pretty straightforward. John and Jane Randolph would be arriving Sunday to visit their granddaughter. With the exception of the fact that Mr. Randolph mentioned how worried his wife had been about "Madeline's safety" during the recent storm, the whole thing read more like business correspondence than a message between family members. Although technically, was Lucas even related to them anymore? The email certainly didn't give that vibe. Even the closing was just his professional signature block: John James Randolph, CEO Randolph Industries.

She turned on her stool and looked up at him. "They're coming to visit?" Was that really such terrible news? Then again, Paige had no idea what sort of relationship Lucas had had with his former in-laws. Even if they'd been on the best of terms when Jenny was alive, their new dynamic might be complicated water to navigate. Still, was a simple visit from Maddie's grandparents, no matter how the three of them got along, really what had put Lucas in such a state?

Lucas gave a tight nod. "Jane's freaked out from the storm."

That wasn't exactly what it had said. "He said she was worried. I'm sure it's just normal grandma stuff."

"You don't know John Randolph. A quick pop over on the weekend would be one thing. But a spur-of-the-moment trip that requires him to be out of the office during the week?" He shook his head. "Jane had to have been near hysterical to prompt that."

"Okay, well, Maddie is fine. So are you, for that matter, and once they see that the house is still standing," she said in an attempt to bring a little levity to the conversation, "I'm sure every-thing will be okay." Paige had meant the words to bring Lucas a modicum of reassurance, but she had the distinct impression she'd only made things worse.

Lucas walked over to the window. His stance was rigid as he stared through the glass. "Jenny's death hit her parents really hard. She was their only child. When she died…" He turned to face Paige. His eyes were red and glassy, but Paige knew in her heart that the unshed tears in Lucas's eyes weren't for his late wife. He'd spoken about her before, and it had never looked like this. The pain he felt now was about something else, something even worse than losing his wife. "They wanted to take Maddie."

All the air sucked out of Paige's lungs, leaving her unable to reply. Even if she could speak, what would she say to a man who had lost his wife only to find out her family wanted to take his daughter? On instinct, she went to him, wrapping her arms around him and holding him tight. "I'm so sorry," she whispered.

Lucas welcomed her embrace but for long moments didn't speak. When he did, his voice was hoarse. "They've wanted custody ever since Jenny died. They didn't think I was capable of raising her on my own."

"*What?*" Paige reared back to look at him. "I know I haven't spent that much time around the two of you, but enough to know you're doing a great job with her."

"Thank you, but I may have biased the jury a bit." He gave a half-hearted smile. "Let's just say that the Randolphs still think of me as the guy who wasn't good enough for their daughter."

"That's ridiculous. Maddie is a pretty amazing kid. Do they think that just happened by accident?"

"They also don't think the island is a good place to raise her."

"But wasn't that what their daughter wanted? It's not like you moved here on your own."

"Believe me, they didn't like the idea back then either. There just wasn't much they could do about it." The tension in his shoulder eased, but to Paige it felt more like resignation than relief. "And that was when this place was in good shape. I'm afraid once they see what it looks like now, they're going to insist she come to live with them in Nashville."

She glanced around the kitchen. It wasn't really *that* bad. There might be stacks of paper everywhere, a bunch of mismatched plastic containers piled on the counter by the refrigerator, and more reusable grocery bags than a person could use in a lifetime scattered about, but... She narrowed her eyes. Was that an empty milk carton on the floor in the corner? Okay, maybe it *was* that bad. But it wasn't a lost cause. Underneath the mess was a pretty spectacular kitchen. In fact, the entire house was only a week away from being picture-perfect. At least that's what she would have told Lucas if he were one of her clients.

If he were one of her clients...

Paige looked Lucas in the eyes. "Then fix it up so they have nothing to complain about."

His head fell back on a laugh. "Yeah, right, I'll just wave my magic wand. Or wait, maybe those elves from the book Maddie loves will show up while we are sleeping."

"I'm being serious, Lucas."

He grew quiet. "I know you are," he said. His hand cupped her face, and then his gaze softened. "And it's unbelievably sweet, but this place will take a hell of a lot more than a quick cleanup."

"You're right about that." She was vibrating with so much energy, she practically bounced on her toes. "It will take a professional to whip this place into shape. Lucky for you that you happen to know one."

A frown momentarily creased Lucas's brow until realization dawned. "You?"

She stepped back, straightened, and gave him a dramatic salute. "Head elf reporting for duty."

He shook his head. "No way."

"Why not? You need the help of a professional organizer, and you just so happen to be sleeping with one." Paige regretted the last part as soon as the words left her mouth. She'd started the morning with a whole lot of uncertainty about whether Lucas regretted sleeping with her. And while he'd done a damn good job of reassuring her that wasn't the case, they'd never finished the conversation, which meant Paige still wasn't sure if their sex life was past or present tense.

"I already crossed one line by sleeping with a guest, Paige. I'm certainly not going to take advantage of you professionally too."

234 ANN MARIE WALKER

"You're not taking advantage," she said. "You didn't even ask. I offered."

"Still no."

"Lucas, this is what I do for a living, yes, but I also get a great deal of satisfaction from helping people bring order to their lives." In Paige's opinion, a cluttered house meant a cluttered mind, or at least a mind under duress. One of the perks of her job was seeing the improvement not only to her client's surroundings, but to their state of mind as well. "Nothing would make me happier than to help you and Maddie stay together." She didn't say it out loud, but she also hoped to bring Lucas a bit of peace. Many of Paige's clients ended up in need of her services by letting things get out of hand following a tragedy or loss. She found they often turned a corner after getting things back on track. "Besides," she cringed as she admitted, "Technically, I've already started."

One corner of his mouth quirked up. "Yeah, been meaning to talk to you about that." So he *had* noticed. "Who puts spices in alphabetical order?"

"It just makes good sense." Realizing he was teasing, she blushed. "Sorry, occupational hazard."

His lack of further protest told her he was considering her offer, which meant she needed to keep talking.

"And I wouldn't be doing it alone. We'd need all hands on deck—you, Sophie, even Maddie—if we stand a chance of getting it done in"—she glanced over his shoulder to the clock on the stove—"forty-eight hours." Holy hell, she was good, but even she wasn't sure she could pull off that miracle. Of course that didn't mean she wasn't going to try.

"This is crazy." Lucas might have thought she'd lost her mind, but he was smiling as he said it.

Paige's brain was already racing through the next steps. "We'll need Ziploc bags, colored markers, and as many of those plastic storage boxes as you can find. Is there a hardware store on the island? Cleaning supplies, of course—nothing says perfection quite like the smell of pine-scented cleaner—and a dumpster, if time allows; otherwise, lots of garbage bags."

She hadn't even realized that she'd begun to pace the length of the kitchen until Lucas reached out, hooking his arm around her waist as she passed by.

"Come here," he said, pulling her flush against him. "It's incredibly sweet that you want to help me, but to be honest, I'm barely keeping this place going right now. And even that's only because of my sister's con job. No way I would let you contribute anything else without paying you, and as much as I hate to admit it, I seriously doubt I can afford you."

"Hmm," she hummed. "Plus, at this time of year, I usually charge double the going rate." She winked. "Lucky for you, I have a special friends discount."

He narrowed his eyes. "Do you mean a special discount for friends, or a discount for special friends?"

She laughed. "Now who's talking crazy?"

"Must be contagious."

Her smile twisted as she pretended to consider her answer. "I'd say you'd qualify for a very-special-friends-with-benefits discount."

"I like the sound of that." He bent his head for a kiss, but Paige pulled back.

"I wasn't finished."

"Oh, sorry." He straightened. "Continue." But he wasn't sorry, and he didn't let her continue. At least not without distraction. She no sooner began to speak than his lips found their way to her neck.

"One last thing. You can't get mad at me when I play tough."

She felt his grin. "Did you say you'd like it a little rough?"

Paige ignored his blatant attempts to distract her. "I'm serious. I usually like to play nice and let my clients do the first wave of sorting before I lower the boom. Seeing as we've got less than forty-eight…"

He sucked on that sensitive spot just below her ear, and her mind went blank. Damn, the man was good with his mouth.

"You were saying," he murmured against her skin.

Must. Focus. Paige pushed against his chest. "We'll never get everything done if you keep this up."

"Sorry, sorry," he said, trying his best to sound contrite.

Paige crossed her arms over her chest.

"What?" he asked. She didn't need to answer. "Fine. I'll be good. But only until ten."

"What happens at ten?"

"We're getting naked."

Oh.

"What can I say?" he said. "You're sexy as hell when you go all cleaning commando."

Words uttered by no man ever.

"Do we have a deal?" he asked.

She could barely manage a nod.

"Good, now I'll make omelets while you make the list."

"What list?"

He looked at her and smiled. "My guess is that everything in Paige Parker's world starts with a list. Come on," he said, taking her hand, "I've got a whole box of notebooks in the garage."

Three orgasms, a hot breakfast, and a box of notebooks? Pigsty or not, Lucas Croft might actually be the perfect man.

CHAPTER 20

LUCAS FELT AS THOUGH THE storm was back. But instead of a nor'easter, this time it was a full-blown hurricane. Hurricane Paige, to be exact. The woman was certainly a force of nature.

Step one had been the surface stuff. Lucas was in charge of that, which mostly involved clearing away trash and recycling. The trash hadn't been so bad, but the recycling was another story. He had no idea how it had happened really, but somehow he'd filled a considerable portion of the house with stacks of what had at one time been important papers, junk mail, old magazines— when was the last time he even read a magazine?—and Amazon boxes. Lots and lots of Amazon boxes.

Paige had been in charge of what Lucas teasingly referred to as "making a bigger mess." Basically she dragged everything out of the cabinets and closets, leaving them all in a huge pile in the middle of each room. Next came the sorting. Everything had to go in one of three piles: toss, donate, or keep. The tossers went to the dumpsters down by the docks. and the donations were bagged and tagged and stored in the garage until a charity pickup could be arranged. It was all easy enough. The keepers, on the other hand, were a bit more difficult.

After the first wave, Paige had surveyed the pile and sized up the available storage space before insisting that a second, harsher wave take place. Lucas finally understood what she meant when she said he couldn't get mad at her for being tough. Although even that had been an understatement. The woman showed no mercy. Not even for the Star Trek glassware he'd dutifully collected each week from the local Burger King back when he was in high school.

"How long have you had these?" she'd asked.

"About fifteen years."

"And in that time, have you ever used them?" She'd raised what could only be interpreted as a judgmental brow. "Or have they just sat on the top shelf collecting dust?"

"They could be collectors' items," he'd offered as a defense. If he'd answered her question and told her he'd never once even looked for them, let alone drank out of them, Captain Kirk would surely have been sent to join the other donations. "What if these glasses are like on that antique show where people find out their junk is worth a million dollars?" Granted, a million dollars was a bit of a stretch even for the Spock glass, but still. They had to be worth something after all these years of being moved to and from various dorm rooms and apartments.

Paige had rolled her eyes, but hadn't said a word. Instead she dug out her phone and after some faster-than-the-speed-of-light thumb action, held up the screen for Lucas to see. "There are currently one hundred and seventy-five sets for sale on eBay, ranging from ninety-nine cents to twelve bucks. But those have to still be in the box."

Which was how the crew of the Starship Enterprise ended up in the garage.

It was like that in every room. Sophie helped and so did Maddie, although she had pretty much insisted that all of her toys were "keepers," something that, much to Lucas's amazement, she somehow got away with. Seemed even the cleaning commando was no match for his young daughter, a fact Lucas found endlessly entertaining.

Once they'd whittled each room down to only the items that made the final cut, the real work began. In the world of professional organization, nothing could go back in a cabinet or closet without first being bagged or boxed and then tagged. Lucas had no idea where Paige had found a label maker on the island. For all he knew, she traveled with one, something that wouldn't have surprised him in the least. The woman was out of control. So much so that he half expected to end the night with a label on his manhood. Then again, turnabout would be fair play, and just the thought of exploring and playfully labeling every inch of her had him moving the boxes at a faster pace. The sooner they were done, the sooner she was all his. At least until six, which was the start time she'd negotiated in exchange for clocking out no later than ten.

They'd started with the kitchen, working their way through the main floor on the first day before moving upstairs on the second, until there was only one room left.

The master bedroom.

Going through the bedroom he'd shared with Jenny was something that was long overdue. He'd left their room exactly as it had been the day she died. But if he was serious about moving on with his life, he knew he had to face that dust-covered bedroom.

Paige had walked with him to the door. "Are you sure?" she'd asked. It was the only time in the nearly forty-eight hours of whip cracking that he'd seen a chink in her commando armor. He knew if he asked her to, they would have skipped that room entirely. But it was time. Lucas knew it, but more than that, he was at peace with it.

"Yes, but if it's alright, I think I'd like to do this room on my own."

"Absolutely," she'd replied. Then she'd smiled at him and squeezed his hand, a small gesture that perfectly conveyed the concern and understanding he saw reflected in her eyes. Surprisingly, it didn't take him as long as he thought it would to go through the room. Clothes were donated, furniture was dusted, and everything else was boxed up to share with Maddie one day. When he was finished, he followed the sound of the Jonas Brothers only to find Paige and Sophie in Maddie's room. He'd watched from the door as the three of them danced around the room with Maddie's favorite toys, before being dragged into the mayhem. Lucas didn't consider himself much of a dancer, but he was fairly confident his moves were better than Stinky's, and either way, his humiliation was a small price to pay for the smile it put on his daughter's face. The look Paige had given him was pretty fantastic as well, although in a completely different way.

Impromptu dance parties aside, restoring the house to its

former splendor was a lot of hard work, but in the end they'd somehow managed to turn the Copper Lantern Inn back into a rental property worthy of its website. Paige insisted the job was far from over—according to her, boxes stuffed under the bed were a no-no—but even she had to admit the place looked pretty great.

Only problem was, it took every bit of the time Paige had left on the island. Lucas could have thought of at least a hundred different ways he would rather have spent that time, and pretty much all of them started with getting her naked.

They'd followed his "no work or clothing after ten" rule both nights, although Paige had tried her best to convince him to work overtime the first night. He'd turned those protests into sighs and moans that made him grateful his daughter had gone home with her aunt, a fact that had the added benefit of allowing him to maintain the no-clothes rule until well after dawn.

The days were long and the nights were short, and before he knew it, Paige was leaving.

On her last day, they'd overslept, which not only ruined his plans to bring her breakfast in bed, but made the entire morning a confusing rush. They'd scrambled to get ready, her throwing things haphazardly into her suitcase and him running from room to room making the beds. If there'd been time, he would have cracked a joke about how they'd somehow swapped personalities, but they were at T-minus twenty minutes before the ferry was due to dock.

When Lucas finally came downstairs, he checked the clock. Five minutes to spare. Paige was already waiting by the door, her suitcase at her feet and Leonardo in her arms. He reached out to stroke the pup. "I half expected this little guy to be in your suitcase."

Paige laughed. The sound wrapped around his heart like a warm embrace. But then it struck him that, in all reality, he'd probably never hear it again, and just like that, the embrace turned into a choke hold.

"Believe me, I thought about it," she said. "But I think Mr. Rochester is quite set in his ways as an only child."

"Don't go yet," Maddie squealed as she ran down the hall toward them. "I have a present for you, Paige."

"You do?"

Maddie's curls bounced as she gave an exaggerated nod. She brought her hand from behind her back and held out the stuffed avocado that was one third of the merry band of misfits she dragged with her everywhere she went. Those toys were her prized possessions. And now she was giving one to Paige.

Paige blinked. "You want me to have Stanley?" She looked about as shocked as Lucas was that Maddie was willing to part with him.

Maddie nodded again.

"Are you sure?" Paige asked.

"Yes. I want you to have something to help you remember us. And Stanley has always wanted to travel the world," she said as if avocados collected passport stamps. "He can start with Chicago."

"Thank you, Maddie. I'm honored to be Stanley's traveling companion." She took the stuffed avocado from Maddie, trading her for Leonardo. "Promise you'll take good care of him?"

Lucas wasn't entirely sure if Paige was referring to him or the dog.

"Deal." Maddie held out her hand for Paige to shake on it.

Lucas smiled to himself because while the handshaking thing was probably going to get real old, real fast, it was obvious that Maddie had taken to the woman who had turned his life upside down. Literally and figuratively. And while he hated to admit it, it was just what he needed.

"Only if you promise to come back and visit," Maddie added before letting go of Paige's hand. "Maybe next week?"

Paige's smile faltered. "I'd love to, kiddo, but Chicago is a long way from here..."

Maddie opened her mouth, but her protest was cut off by a knock at the door.

Paige's gaze darted to Lucas. "Looks like my ride is here."

"Are you sure you won't let me take you to the ferry?"

"And miss the chance to ride in Gus's sidecar again?" Paige shook her head. "No way."

She had insisted Lucas wait at the house for his former in-laws to arrive. He hadn't liked the idea last night, and he liked it even less now that she was ready to leave. He knew she was right, that a goodbye on the docks would have been awkward if they'd run into Jenny's parents—and even if they didn't, the mere sight of him embracing "the jogger," as Sophie informed him she'd been dubbed by the busybodies, would have stirred up enough gossip to keep the island humming for weeks.

But now that it was time for her to leave, he felt like a real horse's ass for not taking her to the ferry himself.

Paige swung the door open. "Hey, Gus, thanks so much for giving me a ride."

He tipped his cap. "Not a problem, ma'am. Gives me an

excuse get the old heart pumping." Lucas knew it also gave him an excuse to take a break from his wife's "honey do" list and, since he was there anyway, cast a few lines down at the dock.

"Good to see you, Lucas," Gus said as he shook his hand. He tipped his hat to Maddie as well. "You too, Miss Maddie." He smiled at her. "Lordy, how you've grown."

Maddie stood up a little straighter. "I'm five."

Not for two weeks, but who was he to stop her from rounding up?

Gus nodded to the puppy in Maddie's arms. "And who might that be?"

"This is Leo." She kissed the small pup on the head. "His real name is Leonardo. He's a mutant."

"Ninja Turtle." Paige tried to explain but the reference was lost on the older gentleman.

"Appreciate you helping out, Gus," Lucas said. "Have some folks arriving soon, so I really need to—"

"Don't mention it. Glad to see you're back in business." Gus picked up Paige's suitcase. "Meet you out at the sidewalk," he told her before ducking out the door.

"Well, I guess I better get going," Paige said. She looked at Lucas, and though no words were spoken, the silence was deafening. But what should he say to the woman who had awoken his heart? Thank you? Nice meeting you? See you around? At the very least, he should have kissed her goodbye.

But he didn't have a chance.

Without another word, Paige picked up her bag and turned toward the door. When she did, Maddie set the puppy on the floor and threw her arms around Paige's waist, perfectly capturing everything Lucas had wanted to say.

She hugged his daughter, then pushed through the screen door. Her movements were hurried, though not fast enough to hide the tear that slid down her cheek.

CHAPTER 21

PAIGE NEVER THOUGHT SHE'D RIDE in a bicycle sidecar once in her life, let alone twice, yet there she was, leaving the island in the same manner in which she'd arrived.

Lucas had wanted to walk her back to the harbor, but she'd declined his offer. Not that she didn't want to spend her last hour on the island with him, but because she knew saying goodbye to him and Maddie was going to be difficult. Last thing she wanted was to get emotional in front of the harbormaster. Bad enough she'd flashed him her panties the day she'd arrived. And Lucas surely didn't need to be the target of any more island gossip. Paige could hardly imagine the tongue wagging that would have gone on if any of the locals had seen Mr. Too-Hot-for-His-Own-Good smooching the City Lady at the docks. Which was why a quick goodbye at the house was exactly what they needed.

It was a perfect plan. If only she'd stuck to it. But then Maddie hugged her and Lucas looked at her with those eyes and, dammit, she was a goner. She'd actually started to cry, and Paige Parker *never* cried. Not over sappy commercials, not when she broke her arm, and certainly not over handsome innkeepers who somehow made her frozen heart begin to thaw.

At least not in front of him.

The burning sensation she'd felt creeping over her face had no doubt given him a hint, but at least he hadn't seen the tear that had slipped down her cheek. She'd wanted nothing more than to drop her bag and throw her arms around his neck. But to what end? So she could stay a few more days, a week maybe? And then what? Her life was in Chicago and his was here, with his daughter and sister. What was she supposed to do, start a long-distance relationship with a man who she'd only known for a week?

Her chest tightened as she let herself imagine a life that included Lucas Croft. Because no matter how much they might want it, a relationship between the two of them wasn't sustainable. Sure they'd have a few months of happiness, maybe even a year. But then the trips would become less frequent and the distance would widen until all that was left was resentment over the fact that neither one of them was really living in their own reality, but rather squeezing an entire relationship into long weekends peppered between heart-wrenching gaps. It was better for everyone to make a clean break now. Better to have a manageable amount of sadness in the moment than to suffer a debilitating loss somewhere in the not-so-distant future.

"Thanks, Gus," she said as he unloaded her bags. "Really appreciate the ride."

He squinted in the midday sun. "My pleasure. Much nicer day this time at least."

Paige closed her eyes and tilted her face toward the warm

rays. If the sun had been shining when she arrived, would she have taken that ferry back to the mainland and never gotten past Lucas's prickly shell? Had fate used a fast-moving storm to bring the two of them together? Her stomach rolled as though she'd already stepped onto the waiting ferry. She had to stop torturing herself. Thinking about the what-ifs was a waste of time and emotion, something she'd learned a long time ago. This vulnerable version of Paige Parker needed to be stuffed back into a closet, labeled box or not.

Her phone vibrated in her pocket.

Flight on time. Car service ordered, Sammy's text read.

Business as usual had already begun. But then tiny bubbles filled the screen as he typed. Should I bring wine or vodka when I come over?

Paige didn't have to think twice about her answer. Vodka, definitely vodka. For a moment, she considered telling him to skip the Grey Goose and head straight to the whiskey aisle, but tomorrow was Monday, and it was never a good idea to start the week hungover. In fact, she would normally have declined all offers of alcohol on a Sunday night, but Paige already knew she was going to need something to numb the emotions that kept popping up, no matter how hard she tried to bat them away.

One night. She'd give herself one night to wallow, and then she'd put Lucas Croft in the past. It might not have been where he belonged, but it was for the best. Maybe if she told herself that often enough, she might actually start to believe it.

"Ferry's here," Gus said from behind her. "Should be ready for you as soon as they finish unloading."

She turned toward the dock, where a small crew was unloading crates from the stern of the vessel. Then the door at the bow opened and a couple emerged. Paige knew at once that they were Lucas's in-laws. The silver-haired man was nicely dressed in a pair of tan pants and a sport coat, but it was the woman who really caught Paige's eye. She wore a two-piece sweater dress, St. John Knits, if Paige wasn't mistaken, and a pair of what her mother would call "sensible heels." Her platinum-blond hair was swept into a perfectly coiffed twist, her makeup was refined yet noticeable, and her neck and ears were adorned with pearls Paige would bet her condo were real.

The woman smiled and shook the captain's hand, thanking him for such a smooth journey. Paige wasn't sure what she'd been expecting—a cross between Cruella de Vil and the witch from "Hansel and Gretel" perhaps—but this woman certainly wasn't it. Neither of them was. The couple in front of her were a far cry from some evil villains. In fact, they seemed quite nice. So why in the world would they want to take Maddie away from her father? Paige could only assume their motives were based on the emotions they felt over losing their own daughter.

Paige never considered herself to be a very religious person, but as she boarded the ferry, she said a silent prayer in the hope that Maddie's grandparents would see what a wonderful life she had with Lucas and realize that the important thing was the love they shared, not whether or not there was peanut butter on the banister.

CHAPTER 22

ONE MONTH LATER

LUCAS STRAPPED THE LEATHER TOOL belt around his waist and tightened the buckle. The inside of the house had never looked better, but on the outside, there was still so much to do. The bulk of it would have to wait until the weather warmed up, but a few items, like the broken front step, were a welcome distraction from the feeling that had gnawed in his gut ever since Paige Parker had left the island.

He hated himself for letting her walk out the door. He didn't even kiss her goodbye, and, damn, he'd wanted to. He'd wanted to take her in his arms and kiss her until her fingers found their way into his hair and her body went lax against his. But more than that, he wanted her to stay. He almost asked her to. But her life was in Chicago and his was with Maddie, and what would he be asking her exactly—to stay with him on a sleepy little island that only came to life four or five months a year? And as what, his girlfriend? They'd barely known each other a week. Besides, she'd

254 ANN MARIE WALKER

made it very clear that she was never going to rearrange her life for a man. Any man.

He pried the loose board free and tossed it aside before placing the new one on the tread. It was too cold to paint it to match the others, so for the time being, the treated wood would have to remain as it was. Paige would hate it. The thought of her matchy-matchy OCD having to walk up mismatched stairs brought only a fleeting smile to his face. Because the truth was Paige would never see the mismatched stairs. She wouldn't see that Maddie was keeping her room clean "just like Miss Paige did it" or that she'd lost her first tooth. She'd never know how surprised Jenny's parents had been when they saw the inn. Or how impressed they were with the way Maddie looked after the puppies. She'd never know the difference she'd made in their lives. Or the place she'd taken in his heart.

He'd thought about calling to tell her all that and more, even going so far as to google her name. He told himself it was just so he could find her office number, but truth was he spent more time than he should have scrolling through the images that popped up on the screen. Most were of Paige at industry events or charity functions. She looked formal and stiff in nine out of ten, but there was one photo, taken of her and a man who, based on her description, had to be the infamous Sammy. They were seated behind a stodgy-looking speaker who was no doubt boring as hell because in the photo Sammy was leaning over whispering in Paige's ear and she was smiling. And not a forced smile for a posed picture, but a genuine, warm smile that brought back memories of the Paige he knew. His Paige.

In the end, though, he hadn't called, for all the same reasons he hadn't asked her to stay.

Lucas placed a nail on the wood and swung his hammer. Hard.

Again.

Then again.

He kept hammering nails until the stairs were fixed. If only everything in life were that simple. No matter how hard he tried, he just couldn't get Paige Parker out of his thoughts.

When he was finished, he took a bandanna out of the back pocket of his jeans and wiped the sweat from his brow. He'd been keeping himself busy since the day she left, but sometimes, when he stopped moving, his thoughts drifted to what might have been.

Paige had been in his life for a such a short time, but that didn't stop him from picturing her with him for the long haul. Only problem was, when his mind indulged in the fantasy, it was never in his life. No island, no inn, no beach. The backdrop for the bittersweet scenes were always blank.

Because they aren't real, he thought.

His gut twisted. He had to stop indulging in a fantasy that had zero chance of coming true.

"Whatcha doing?" a sweet voice asked from behind him. Lucas turned to find his favorite distraction standing on the porch holding Floppy under one arm and Stinky under the other. Correction: holding Raymond under the other. Now that the teddy bear had gone for a spin in the washing machine, Lucas was forbidden to call him by his nickname. It was a hard habit to break, seeing as how he'd been Stinky for so long, but Paige had somehow convinced Maddie to let her wash him, which was almost as shocking as the fact that Stanley now lived in Chicago. Lucas never thought he'd find himself in a situation to be jealous of a toy vegetable, but when he thought of the little green bastard possibly sleeping in Paige's bed—something he was embarrassed to admit crossed his mind almost every night—he couldn't help but be envious.

"Hey, Peanut," he said. To his surprise, Maddie didn't correct him. Perhaps now that she was a mature woman of the ripe old age of five, childhood nicknames didn't bother her anymore. "I was just fixing the front steps."

She walked to the top of the stairs to inspect his work. "Looks good, but they don't match."

Lucas chuckled. Maddie might look just like her mother, but she and Paige certainly shared more than a few personality traits. "I can't paint it until it gets a little warmer."

Maddie nodded. "Does that mean you're done?"

Much to her delight, Lucas twirled his hammer like a gunslinger from the Old West, then holstered it in his tool belt. "That's exactly what it means."

She hopped down the stairs and sat on the newly replaced tread. Lucas joined her. He watched as she arranged her two furry friends between them. When she was done, she rested her crossed arms on her knees and stared off into the distance. He wasn't sure what she was looking at, but he was happy just to sit with his daughter, listening to the distant sound of the surf.

They stayed like that for several minutes. When Maddie finally spoke, it wasn't about the seagulls that had raided the trash can across the street, the gecko that had scampered across her foot, or any of the dozen or so other sights that would normally have sparked a running chatter.

"I know why you're sad, Daddy," she said matter-of-factly.

Lucas stilled. Whatever he'd felt over the last two years, he'd tried his best to never let Maddie see his emotions. "You do?"

She nodded. "You've been printed."

"I've been what?"

"Remember when you told me about how the puppies had printed on their Aunt Paige?"

"Oh, you mean imprinted?"

She nodded again. "Well, I think you did too."

"You think the puppies imprinted on me?" The conversation finally made sense. The puppies were eight weeks old, which meant they had started moving to their new homes. Even though they were all remaining on the island, Lucas knew Maddie was sad to see them leave the inn. It was only natural she'd assume he felt the same way.

"No, silly," she said. And then his sweet five-year-old daughter rolled her eyes. At him. He was in for it when she actually *was* a teenager. He was about to tell her that eye-rolling was not acceptable behavior when she finished her explanation. "I think you imprinted on Paige."

That one he didn't see coming. "Is that so?"

"Yes, and I know what it means now because I asked Aunt Sophie." Maddie squinted up at him against the morning sun. "She said it means you think of someone as family and you love them with all your heart."

Lucas pulled Maddie into his lap. "You're my family," he said, kissing the top of her head.

"I know that," she said. He couldn't see her face, but Lucas would have bet all the tax money that she'd just given him another eye roll. He definitely needed to nip that in the bud sooner rather than later, but for now he was happy just to hold her in his arms. Ever since her birthday, Maddie had been telling him all the things she was "too old for." He knew that snuggling with Dad would eventually join the list, so for now he was going to enjoy each and every one. "But families can be more than two people." She reared back to look at him. "It's okay to love both of us."

There'd been countless times over the last five years that Lucas had been amazed by his daughter. Her inquisitive nature, her love for all animals no matter how slimy, and her emotional maturity were just the tip of the iceberg. But this topped them all. "How did you get so smart?"

"Aunt Sophie says I inherited that from her," she answered with total sincerity.

"Is that so?" He began to tickle her until she was a wiggling ball of giggles. "Up for an adventure?" he asked as he set her on her feet. "Tide's out, so I bet we can find all sorts of treasures."

Her eyes lit up, and just like that, she was five again. "I'll get my bucket." Maddie scampered up the steps and, as she reached the door, looked back at him over her shoulder. The expression on her face damn near took his breath away. She was the spitting image of her mother.

"Come on, slowpoke."

Lucas stood, and as he did, a sense of calm settled over him that he hadn't felt since Jenny's death. His wife might be gone, but she would never be forgotten. She would live on in the stories he would share with Maddie, but more than that, his daughter would see her mother's face every time she looked in the mirror. He shook his head as a wistful smile formed on his lips. She was so like her—not just in her looks, but in the way she thought about the world. Leave it to a five-year-old to point out the one thing Lucas couldn't grasp. Because she was right; nothing, not the passing of time or the presence of another woman, would eclipse Jenny, but there was also room in his heart for more than one love.

He walked through the house, taking stock of the past while thinking about the future. The daydreams that had tormented him over the last month were blank because they represented a story that had yet to be written.

He dropped his tool belt on the island, then grabbed coats for himself and Maddie before making his way across the back porch. When he reached the screen door, he saw her, sitting a few yards away in a patch of sand, sifting clumps and putting her discoveries into the plastic bucket she took with her whenever they went exploring. She was happy here, but he knew his daughter. She would be happy anywhere, as long as they were together.

Lucas stepped outside and drew a deep breath of salty air as he stared out across the tall grass to where the waves broke in a hypnotic rhythm. In his heart he knew the truth. The castle by the sea wasn't his life anymore.

Maddie looked up and a smile lit her face. "Ready, Daddy?"

"Just about. I need to call Aunt Sophie first." He pulled out his cell phone and hit the number he'd dialed so many times before. Only this time, he did it with a resolve he hadn't felt in years.

She answered on the first ring. "Miss me already?"

"Actually, I have a favor to ask."

"Name it."

"Swing buy after work and I'll explain." It was a two-minute phone call, seemingly insignificant. But in reality, Lucas knew it was the start of the next chapter of his life.

CHAPTER 23

PAIGE COULD FEEL SAMMY WATCHING her. He was supposed to be preparing the contracts for a deal she'd just closed with a large estate-sale company, but she could feel his eyes on her like a laser beam. That's what she got for leaving the door to her office open.

"Might as well come in," she said without looking up from her laptop.

There was a rustle in the reception area, followed by the pitter-patter of Gucci sneakers. Paige had first thought the shoes were a little casual for the office, but Sammy argued that the gold bumble-bees embossed on the fabric definitely gave them an elegant vibe. When she hadn't been entirely convinced, he pointed out that they cost six times what she'd paid for her stilettos. Fair point. Besides, when he paired them with his favorite slim-cut Tom Ford suit, he looked more like he worked for a company that designed cutting-edge fashion, not one that got rid of outdated clothing.

"Thought you'd never ask," he said as he plopped into the chair across from her.

"Technically, I didn't." She looked up from her laptop and smirked.

"But you were thinking it."

She laughed. "Now you read minds?"

"When it comes to you, Boss Lady? Most definitely."

"Then you should have known that I was thinking you should be working on the paperwork for Home Liquidators."

"Done."

"What about the designs for the Fahey addition? The master closet needs—"

"Done."

"And the—"

"Done, done, and done." He crossed his legs. "It's all done."

Paige opened her mouth, then closed it without saying a word. She joked that she had to limit her compliments lest he get an even bigger head, but the fact was, her assistant was far too talented to simply be her assistant. Not anymore at least. Paige had hired him right out of college. At the time, the job had suited him, but now he was more than ready to spread his wings. If she was honest, he'd been more than ready for a while. And if she was *really* honest, she'd admit that she was too selfish, or maybe too scared, to lose him. Paige was a one-woman company. She didn't have any way to promote him to a better job. Moving up meant moving on. Unless…

An idea flickered to life in Paige's mind, but Sammy interrupted her train of thought before the spark could catch.

"Want me to tell you what you're thinking right now?" he asked. "Aside from how devastatingly handsome I look."

Paige leaned back in her chair and crossed her arms. This ought to be good. "Do tell."

Sammy narrowed his eyes as though decoding a puzzle. "You're thinking that you'd like an Asian sesame salad for lunch."

"That's not mind reading. It's a lucky guess. I order that salad at least twice a week."

He held up one finger. "I wasn't finished. You'll want the dressing on the side—even though we both know you'll end up dumping the whole thing in the bowl—and have them leave off the wonton strips, but then you'll bitch about not having them the entire time you're eating."

He was right, of course, but she didn't have to admit it. "What else?"

"That you need to remember to pick up cat food on the way home."

"Oh, please." She snorted. "You read that reminder on my phone."

"And that you need to call your mother."

"It's her birthday tomorrow," she countered. It was looking like Sammy's special skill wasn't quite so special after all. But he wasn't deterred.

"And that despite the fact that you have thrown yourself into your work, there's nothing you'd rather do than fly back to Love Island and into the arms of the sexy innkeeper."

Game over. "Now that you mention it, that salad sounds pretty good. Would you mind placing the order for delivery? I'm going to work from my desk."

"It's only 9:45." He didn't even bother looking at his watch. Smug bastard.

"I skipped breakfast." She opened her email, staring blindly at the list of unread messages.

"Fine," he said.

That was easy, Paige thought. *Too easy.*

"I think I'm going to order a salad today too. But which one?" He tapped his fingers on the arm of his chair. Sammy never needed time deciding what to order. He had his standing favorites for every restaurant in the Loop. "Maybe the warm quinoa salad?" he asked of no one in particular. "Oh, I know! I'll get the Southwest. Hold the tortilla strips but extra..." He paused, then lowered his voice for dramatic effect. "...avocado."

Paige knew what he was up to, but she fell for it anyway. As if on instinct, her gaze shifted to the stuffed avocado that now graced the corner of her Norwegian sofa. Of course Sammy had noticed the unusual addition the moment it appeared. Hard to miss really. When he'd walked into the room that first morning back, he'd immediately started singing a song she recognized from a childhood spent watching *Sesame Street*. "*One of these things is not like the others.*"

Part of her still couldn't believe Maddie had insisted she take one of her favorite toys. Paige had held it on her lap during the flight back to Chicago—a fact that drew some interesting expressions from the other passengers seated in the first-class cabin—and Stanley had been her daily companion ever since. It had been a month, and yet the sight of the little green blob never failed to make her smile. Of course, with that came the sense of loss that always crept in once she opened that door. Which was why, after spilling her guts the first day she was back, Paige told Sammy that the subject of Lucas was officially off-limits. That went for the avocado as well.

"Don't," she warned.

"Don't get the salad?"

"Don't bring up Stanley," she said, referring to the toy by the name Maddie had given him. "And don't play dumb. It's beneath you." Samuel Lee was far too clever to play such an obvious game. She knew it, and so did he.

Sammy's shoulders sagged on an exaggerated exhale. "Fine. But I'm still getting the salad." He picked a piece of lint off his sleeve, then circled back for one more try. This time he pulled out the big gun: total sincerity. The mischievous twinkle was gone from his eyes, and the sarcasm that normally laced his voice was nowhere to be found. "I've known you what, three years?"

It was a rhetorical question. If pressed, he could probably pinpoint when they first met down to the hour.

"And in that time, I've seen you go from a brokenhearted, insecure woman who had to pull herself up by the bra straps"—he waved his hand toward her—"to this confident, take-no-prisoners badass."

It was obvious he was on a roll.

"But through all the highs and lows, I have never seen you smile the way you do when you look at that silly vegetable. Not even when we closed the Sullivan deal. And since I have never in my life seen you eat an avocado, I can only assume that the look on your face has nothing to do with Stanley and everything to do with Lucas and Maddie."

No nicknames. No smirks. Not even a Ryan Reynolds

reference. This version of Sammy was disarming and genuine and, much to her dismay, far more effective.

"Sammy, I—"

He held up his hand. "You don't have to say anything. I just want you to think about this: being in love isn't a weakness."

The words hit her like a physical blow. Not only because of their truth, but because they echoed the words Lucas had spoken to her that night at the inn. *Maybe what you need is to let your guard down.*

Paige swallowed the lump that had formed in her throat. "Thank you, Sammy," she said. Her sincerity matched his, but they both knew that this momentary departure from their norm had to end. A beat of unspoken affection passed between them before Paige set them back on course. "Now get out of my office so I can get some work done."

He feigned offense and was no doubt about to hit her with some pithy reply when his phone vibrated in his hand. He glanced at the screen, frowning momentarily before breaking into a smile Paige would have thought reserved only for Johnny Weir or Elton John.

"What is it?"

As he looked up from the screen, his expression returned to the Sammy scowl. "Nothing. Just the lobby." He was already in motion. "There's a package downstairs they need me to sign for." And with that he was gone, leaving Paige alone in her office with nothing but Stanley and her thoughts, which often proved to be a dangerous combination.

Paige turned her attention to her laptop. She needed to get back to work. Diving into projects was the only thing that kept her from indulging in fantasies that had no chance of coming true. Of course that didn't stop her from wanting to see Lucas again. In the first few days after she was back, it was all she could do to keep from calling him. But to what end? Sure, she wanted to know how things had gone with his in-laws, but if they'd gone poorly, there wasn't a damn thing she could do about it. Not knowing was better than feeling completely helpless. And aside from that, what would they even talk about? The weather? If he'd kept the inn's listing online?

Right, like she hadn't checked.

Paige knew damn well the listing was still online because in one of her weaker moments she'd looked it up, which resulted in a ridiculous amount of time spent scrolling through the pictures on the inn's website. There weren't any of Lucas—and the weirdo wasn't on any social media platforms, which would have really allowed her inner stalker to have a field day—but it didn't matter because every photo from the inn brought her memories to life. Walking the beach with Maddie, talking in front of the fire, saying goodbye on the stone porch. Eventually she'd stopped looking because it was just too painful. Even the photo of the kitchen got to her, conjuring an image of Lucas on the first day they met, bare-chested and crabby, that would start her on a roller-coaster journey down memory lane that ultimately resulted in a date with both Ben and Jerry.

The phone on her desk buzzed, startling her. "Your new client is here for your ten o'clock," Sammy said over the intercom.

Paige drew a blank. Her ten o'clock? And what new client? She didn't remember Sammy saying anything about a new client, much less an appointment. She clicked the calendar app on her computer. No new client meeting. Nothing until the conference call at three.

Her pulse raced. She had no idea what the meeting was about, and she certainly hadn't prepared a presentation. What was wrong with her? She'd been this way all month, focused one minute, distracted the next. It had been that way ever since she came back from vacation.

Paige took a deep breath. She could do this. She'd probably met with over a thousand clients since opening her business. What was one more?

One more with no notes, no PowerPoint, no clue.

Her stomach rolled.

Sometimes you just have to eat cake out of the box.

She stood, looked out the window at the Chicago skyline, and took another deep breath. Then she turned, ready to greet her new client with a warm smile and a steady hand—and came to an abrupt halt. Her smile slipped and her hand fell.

Lucas.

He stood in the doorway, more like filled it, watching her with an expression she couldn't quite decipher. His hair was as unruly as ever, enticing her to run her fingers through it, and the stubble on his jaw was just the right amount to burn so good against her skin. He was wearing jeans, as always, and her favorite hunter-green sweater, the one that turned his hazel eyes the same color. The one he'd worn the first night he'd kissed her.

"What are you doing here?" The moment the words left her mouth, she regretted them. *What are you doing here?* No hello, what a surprise, or nice to see you? But when she left the island, Paige had resigned herself to the fact that she'd never see him again. Now he was there. In Chicago. In her office.

"He has an appointment," Sammy said. He peeked around Lucas like some sort of cuckoo clock. "Perhaps you should say hello and invite him in?"

It took a moment for his words to register. "Of course." She moved toward Lucas, trying to wipe her palm discreetly on her skirt, and held out her hand. They were at the point in a meeting where she would normally introduce herself, but she and Lucas were already well acquainted. Intimately, as a matter of fact. So why the hell was she using a handshake to greet the man who mere weeks ago had turned her inside out?

Lucas looked down at her hand, then smiled as he met her gaze. It was an expression she'd come to know well during her time at the inn, half shy and unassuming and half panty-melting smolder. He stepped forward and took her hand in his, sending a familiar yet forgotten jolt of electricity through her. It was the spark that woke not only her desire, but her heart.

Paige blinked, then pulled her hand away more abruptly than she'd intended.

"I'll just leave you two to…" Sammy pulled the door shut. She had forgotten he was still in the room. Hell, she barely knew her own name at that point. Being this close to Lucas again—his touch on her skin, the familiar scent of his soap, the knowing look in his eyes—was overwhelming to more than just her senses. Every fiber in her being was aching to go to him, to press her body against his and kiss him until they were both breathless.

Over the past few weeks, she'd started to wonder if maybe he hadn't actually been as gorgeous as she remembered. If perhaps her emotions had helped her memory paint a picture of Lucas Croft that was more fantasy than reality. And if she were ever to see him again, if she'd realize that what she'd felt for him couldn't exist outside the vacuum of the storm-engulfed inn. But that wasn't the case, at least not for her. Every image came flooding back in vivid color, from the moment she stood in his kitchen, a sopping-wet mess who wanted nothing more than to wring his neck, to the moment she'd said goodbye on his front porch, an emotional mess who wanted nothing more than to stay.

But she hadn't stayed. And he hadn't asked her to. They hadn't even shared a last kiss goodbye. So why was he in her office?

"What are you doing here?" she asked again. Her tone was softer, but the confusion remained the same.

Lucas looked at the floor, her desk, the view, as though he was searching for the answer. Surely he knew it was the first question she'd ask? If he hadn't known the answer when he left the island, seemed like the trip from North Carolina would have afforded him enough time to come up with one. And yet there he stood, searching for the words.

His gaze finally landed on her couch. Something flickered in his eyes the moment he spotted Stanley. Then his body relaxed, and the smile she'd come to crave spread across his face.

"I realized I never thanked you for whipping my place into shape," he said. His eyes were focused on her, and only her. "Maddie's grandparents were impressed." He raised his brows. "And that's a tall order."

"So they dropped the whole custody thing?"

As he nodded, Paige exhaled a breath she hadn't even realized she'd been holding. "That's fantastic news." She knew she had to be grinning like a fool, but she couldn't help it. "I'm so pleased for you both." A charged beat passed between them. "How is Maddie?"

"She's great. Still a chatterbox and still pushing the limits at bedtime." He chuckled. "Oh, and Sophie got her a pair of hot-pink Converse for her birthday which are now the only shoes she'll wear."

"I missed her birthday?" It was a ridiculous question. Of course Paige had missed Maddie's birthday. She'd left the island knowing she was going to miss everything. Sort of par for the course with their whole "so long, see you never" goodbye. "Did she have a party?" she asked in an effort to steer away from her previous question.

"Oh yeah," he said. "Five little girls and enough candy to warrant an emergency trip to the dentist."

"Sounds perfect." She assumed Sammy was eavesdropping and was more than a bit surprised he didn't blow his cover with a laugh over that one. A party with five kids hyped up on sugar was not something Paige would have ever considered "perfect," and yet that's the first word that had come to mind. "And the puppies?"

"We found homes for all of them, except Leo. He's staying with us."

"You kept him?" Leo had been the pup that took to Paige the fastest. Whenever she was nearby, he'd wriggle over until she picked him up and cuddled him. He'd been Maddie's favorite too.

"Maddie wanted to keep all of them, but we compromised by keeping one and promising to visit the others."

"Sounds like a good plan."

"And Sophie adopted their mother," he added.

"That's great, really great." Two greats and a good. Some conversationalist she was turning out to be.

An awkward silence fell over the room. "Why are you really here, Lucas?" Paige finally asked. "Surely you didn't come all this way just to thank me."

Lucas shoved his hands into the front pockets of his jeans. "Actually, I'm here looking at schools."

"Schools?" Of all the answers he could have given her, *that* was one she never saw coming.

He nodded. "One of the Randolphs' main concerns has always been that the island was too small an environment for raising a child, much less a teenager. And they have a point. It seemed like a good idea when we first moved there, but the schools only go to sixth grade so…"

"So you'd be moving eventually."

"Exactly. I figure it would be better to make the change now, with her starting kindergarten in the fall, instead of switching schools later."

"Makes sense." Actually, none of this made sense. Leaving the island was one thing, but moving over eight hundred miles was another. Surely there were plenty of good schools a hell of a lot closer than Chicago. Unless…

No, she wouldn't even let herself go there. Not until he came right out and said it. "Why Chicago?" she asked.

"I hear there's a lot of construction work, especially out in the suburbs. And the schools are rated some of the best in the country." His gaze softened. "Plus, there's this woman who lives in Chicago."

Paige's pulse hammered in her ears.

"I haven't known her for very long, so I thought I would be okay just going our separate ways. But the thing is, I realized that I've fallen in love with her. And even though on paper we don't make any sense—and believe me, I'd bet my life she's made a pro/con list—there's just something about her, and I can't live the rest of my life wondering what if."

Paige blinked, partly to convince herself he was really standing in her office and that she hadn't cracked her head on the desk and was imagining the whole thing, and partly to hold back the tears that pricked her eyes. What was it about this guy? Twenty years without shedding a single tear and now she was a flipping faucet.

"I love you, Paige," Lucas said, repeating the words he'd casually slipped into his explanation. "I love that you show up with designer luggage but will ruin a cashmere sweater because a dog that most people would be afraid of has somehow told you that she needs help. I love that you think everything needs not only to be in a box, but with a label, but will hurl yourself into sewage to save a litter of puppies. I love that you are this tough business-woman but are so warm and caring with my daughter. And I love that you think it's normal to spend an entire night analyzing the personalities of four puppies so you can match each with the proper Ninja Turtle name. Hell, I love that you even know who the Ninja Turtles are."

A single tear rolled down her cheek. "I love you too, Lucas."

They moved at the same time, coming together in a blur of hands and lips and pent-up lust. She didn't think it was possible to miss something so much when she'd barely had it at all, but in that moment, Paige felt as though she'd been denied not just his touch, but the very air she needed to breathe.

She wrapped her arms around his neck and raked her fingers through his hair, holding him close as they lost themselves in a searing kiss.

"I've missed you," he rasped. His lips moved ever so softly across her cheek, kissing away her tears.

Her knees buckled as his mouth found the sensitive spot just below her ear. Lucas's arm tightened around her waist, holding her close.

"I thought I was a pain in the ass," she somehow managed to say.

"You are." She nearly gave him a shove for that one, but then she felt him smile against her skin. "But you're also one of the kindest, most amazing people I've ever met." He reared back and smiled. "And I don't care where I live, as long as it's close to you."

"You would really move to Chicago?"

"Of course." He smiled. "Where is it written that the woman has to be the one to change her life?"

Of all the things he'd blurted out since he'd walked into her office, that one might have meant the most. She didn't think it was possible to love him more, but she did. "What about the inn?"

"I was thinking about letting Sophie take over. She's much better at that sort of thing anyway."

She studied his face, and while what she saw was sincere resolve, she still had to ask. "Wouldn't you miss it?"

"Owning an inn was a dream Jenny and I had." He tucked a strand of hair behind her ear. "I think we should have our own dreams, plan our own future."

"Well, it just so happens I do have my own dream."

His muscles tensed beneath her hands. "Oh?"

She nodded. "I'm thinking of expanding my business."

Lucas cleared his throat. "That's great."

"Sammy proved he is more than capable of running the office on his own. I was thinking of promoting him to partner so I can focus on the expansion."

A loud thud came from behind the door. Hopefully Sammy hadn't passed out, but it would serve him right for listening.

"Have any place in mind?" His eyes were lit with a nervous anticipation.

"I'm thinking of starting a location down south on this charming little island off the coast of the Carolinas."

The wide grin that spread across his face was rivaled only by her own. "Think the folks down there could use your services, huh?"

"Absolutely. People have a hard enough time keeping their main home organized. A vacation home can be even worse. They turn it into a catch-all storage unit of sorts. Plus, there is a ferry— granted it's somewhat unreliable—that will allow me to service clients on the mainland as well."

Lucas grew serious again. "But your life is here."

"True. Which is why I was thinking about only going down in the summer."

"So you'd spend, say, the school year in Chicago, then head to the beach?"

She nodded. "For the busy season."

"Sounds like you've figured it all out." He glanced over her shoulder at her desk. "And without a notepad."

"Not quite everything," she said. "Going down for peak season might make it difficult to find a place to stay. Busy three months, from what I hear."

"Well, it just so happens I know this great little bed-and-breakfast. They're pretty booked up, but I know the owner, so I might be able to get you a room."

Paige raised a brow. "For double?" she asked. "Or would I qualify for a friends-with-benefits discount?"

Lucas grinned. "I was thinking something more along the lines of a family rate."

He kissed her again, then stepped back and extended his hand. "So do we have a deal?"

She wasn't sure if he was being playful or just teasing her, but either way, the expression on his face was a look that was totally working for him. "Deal."

A loud clap came from the reception area. Looked like Sammy had gotten his way after all. Paige had come back to Chicago with one hell of a vacation story. Except this wasn't an island fantasy. It was real.

Paige gave Lucas her hand, but rather than shaking, he brought it to his lips. He pressed a gentle kiss to her knuckles, then with a sharp tug pulled her flush against the hard planes of his body.

He cupped her chin, tilting her face to his. But instead of

kissing her, he hovered just out of reach, studying her as though he were committing every detail to memory. When he finally pressed his lips against hers, he did it slowly, deliberately, taking just a taste before coming back for more. Paige's skin tightened and her body swayed as though he were kissing her for the very first time. And then his hand came to rest on the small of her back, and she melted against him on a stuttering sigh.

"What do we do now?" she whispered against his lips.

"Everything."

They may have only gotten started, but something told her it was going to be a long and wonderful ride.

EPILOGUE

PAIGE STARED AT THE WHITE plastic stick. Two pink lines. She squeezed her eyes shut, then looked at it again. Still two lines.

"You know that holding your dress while you pee is one of my official duties," Sammy said through the bathroom door. He'd taken his role as man of honor quite seriously, but feeling slighted by missing out on a chance to gather yards of white fabric in his arms while his Bestie Boss Lady made a most unladylike trip to the bathroom was a bit much, even for him.

"I don't need you leaning over me while I'm on the toilet," Paige replied. *And certainly not while I pee on a pregnancy test*, she thought. Most women would simply have waited until after the ceremony—or better yet, have realized that they were six days late *before* the morning of their wedding. But not Paige. No, she had to have that epiphany as they were driving to the church. Although to be fair, with the crazy schedule she'd been keeping over the last few weeks—planning a wedding while at the same time running her business in Chicago and finalizing the grand opening of the new location in North Carolina, not to mention dealing with her mother!—it wasn't like she'd had time to study her calendar.

She'd feigned a need for breath mints, demanding the limo driver pull over so she could run into the drugstore for candy that only she was qualified to select. Sammy accused her of taking her control-freak tendencies to the next level, but other than that, he wasn't too fazed. The cashier, on the other hand, definitely knew what was up. Because while her dress was tucked safely in a garment bag as they drove to the church, Paige's hair was already swept up into an intricate twist, and her makeup was as glamorous as any cover girl's.

The real giveaway, though, was the rhinestone tiara. It wasn't exactly Paige's style, but Maddie had accompanied the bridal entourage to the dress shop and had insisted that a crown was necessary to ensure a "fairy-tale princess wedding." Who was Paige to argue with that logic? Besides, the smile on her soon-to-be stepdaughter's face was worth enduring the shock on the face of the store clerk. Paige couldn't really blame her. The intricate crown she wore could only mean one of two things: either Paige was a homecoming queen or a bride, and since she was well past the age of the former, it was safe to say the clerk assumed the latter, which would explain the smirk that curved her lips as she pushed the buttons on the cash register. Guess it wasn't every day she sold a pregnancy test to a bride.

Speaking of pregnancy tests, what the heck was she supposed to do with this one now? The trash can in the bride's room bathroom was a small wicker job with no lid. Not ideal for hiding evidence. *Because most brides don't realize they're knocked up thirty minutes before go time*, she thought. Smuggling the darn thing into the bathroom had been tricky enough. She'd wanted to get to it the moment they'd reached the church. Sure would have made taking aim a lot easier if she'd done it before she was strapped into a silk gown with a gazillion pearl buttons. But her mother had been waiting as the car rolled up, and between her and Bridesmaid-zilla, this was the first chance she'd had.

Paige cracked the bathroom door open. For once she was glad to find Sammy hovering. "Can you pass me my phone?" she whispered.

His eyes grew wide. "Tell me you are not working in there! I mean, we all text on the toilet, but even now?"

"Just do it, please."

He sighed. "Fine."

"Is everything alright?" her mother asked from across the room.

"Yeah, I just want to go over my vows one more time."

Sammy passed her phone through the narrow opening. "What, did you write them in notes?"

He sounded mildly horrified, but Paige didn't bother to answer. Instead she merely snatched the phone out of his hands and pushed the door closed. The exasperated harrumph from the other side told her Sammy did not appreciate the move, but at the moment she had far more pressing concerns.

Can you get my mom out of here? she texted him. I need a few minutes alone.

Done, he replied, probably relieved to have something to do. A moment later, Paige heard the unmistakable sound of Samuel Lee

282 ANN MARIE WALKER

at his best. The man could herd anyone anywhere so smoothly that they were usually halfway out the door before they even realized they were in motion. When the coast was clear, Paige made her way out of the bathroom and into the small parlor in the back of the church. A mixture of excitement and nerves swirled in her belly. She was going to be a mother. *Holy moly.* She took a deep breath. Over the past year, she felt liked she'd really been killing the stepmom thing, but Maddie had come into her life as a fully functioning human, more or less. A baby was a whole new ball game. She started to wipe her palms on her dress, then stopped. At this rate, she was going to end up with sweat stains under her armpits. She didn't need them streaked down the front of her gown as well.

She needed to talk to Lucas. But the ceremony was going to start in—she glanced at the gilded clock that sat on a pedestal table alongside her bouquet of lilies—twenty minutes! And wasn't there some superstition about the bride and groom not seeing each other before the big entrance? Oh, who was she kidding? There was no way in hell she was going to be able to make it through the entire ceremony without telling him the news. Surely it was better to do it in the privacy of the bride's room, taboo or not, than risk giving poor old Father Murphy, not to mention her mother, a coronary by blurting it out in front of the entire congregation.

I need to see you, she texted him.

Please have your phone, please have your phone, she chanted to herself as she paced the rug. After what felt like an eternity, her phone vibrated in her hand.

The groom isn't supposed to see the bride before she walks down the aisle, his message said.

He's also not supposed to have sex with her before the wedding night, she replied.

Fair point. Tiny bubbles filled the bottom of the screen as he typed. Where are you?

Bride's room. Back of church on left.

How am I going to make it past Sammy? More bubbles. Or your mom?

Got rid of them.

A second later, her phone rang in her hands. "Is everything alright?" Lucas asked. "You're not having cold feet, are you?" The nervous edge to his voice caused a wave of warmth to rush over her, instantly calming her. Not because she wanted to cause him any unnecessary anxiety, but because it reminded her of the last time she'd heard him sound so adorably panicked. It was the night he had proposed...

They'd barely seen each other that week as he'd spent the bulk of it finishing up a major kitchen renovation. It was his fourth project since arriving in Chicago, and the list of jobs he had lined up for the rest of the year was nearly twice that long. After only six months, Lucas had earned himself a reputation for top-notch work, something that allowed him to charge top-notch prices. But it was also how he ended up spending five straight nights with his crew instead of his girlfriend.

He'd called her at lunchtime on that Friday. Well, not actually her, but rather Sammy. That really should have been her first clue that something was up. Sammy told her that Lucas had called to see if dinner at six would work with her schedule, and to ask him to give her directions to the "great new place" he'd found on the north side of the city.

At the time, Paige didn't really think much of it. Because while Lucas had never done something like that before, he'd often joked about cutting out the middle (wo)man and just making plans directly with her assistant. But when she arrived at the address Sammy had given her, she was more than a little suspicious. Because while it did look like a "great place," it didn't look at all like a restaurant. The address was for a three-story brownstone, and while it wasn't unheard of for that type of building to house a business or restaurant, this particular location was in a residential area. The quiet, tree-lined street wasn't at all the type of place where you would find anything but individually owned homes. There was even a playground at the end of the block.

Maybe he had it wrong. Sammy had been wearing many hats over the last month as he prepared to step into his new role as partner, so maybe he'd transposed the numbers. Paige double-checked the address in his text, then looked at the numbers etched into stone on the front of the house. Yep, right place. But not only was there no sign indicating this was a public establishment, there weren't many lights on either. In fact, aside from one fixture that lit the porch, the place looked completely dark.

She was about to call Lucas when he appeared at the front door. He was wearing a pair of dark jeans, a charcoal sweater, and the smile that never failed to make her pulse race a little faster.

Shy and sexy all at once, the look on his face was her kryptonite, capable of melting her heart and her panties at the same time.

"Welcome," he said, gesturing to the door that stood open behind him. "Come on in."

Confused, Paige made her way up the stone steps and into the entryway of an empty house. The carved wooden staircase looked to be over a hundred years old, as did the electrical system if the cloth-covered wires poking out from the ceiling were any indication. There were cobwebs in the corners of the vaulted fresco ceilings, and the baseboards that stretched along the hardwood floors had to be at least nine inches high. The house was equal parts spectacular and horrifying.

"What are we doing here, Lucas?"

He took her hand and guided her through leaded-glass pocket doors to what was surely the dining room. An entire wall was filled with a built-in buffet, complete with beveled glass doors and a marble serving top. But instead of a formal dining-room table, the room held nothing more than a square card table and two folding chairs. They were nothing special, but what was on top of them contained everything Paige never knew she wanted: a silver picture frame with a photo of her with Lucas and Maddie taken shortly after they'd moved to Chicago. Next to the frame was a pair of tapered candles and beyond that sat two place settings.

"We're eating here?" she asked.

He nodded. "And for many years to come if you say yes."

Say yes? The words had barely registered when Lucas dropped to one knee. He never took his eyes off hers as he reached into the front pocket of his jeans and pulled out a small leather box.

"Paige Parker, you turned my life upside down." He smiled her favorite crooked smile. "You brought light into my dark world, and love into my heart. For that I will forever be grateful, and if you'll let me, I'll spend the rest of my life showing you just how much I love you." Tears pricked Paige's eyes as she watched Lucas ease the box open. Inside sat an emerald-cut diamond on a simple platinum band. It was exquisite and simple and exactly what Paige would have selected. "Will you do me the honor of becoming my wife?"

His wife? Paige had given up on the notion of marriage nearly four years ago, and yet there she stood in a dilapidated brownstone gazing down at the man who had not only shown her how to love again, but how to let herself be loved.

Still, she hesitated.

Lucas's brows shot up. "Gotta admit, I was hoping for a more immediate response," he teased.

Of course she had wanted to blurt out *Yes, yes, a thousand times yes*. But...

"There's just one thing," she said.

His expression was one of utter amusement. "Are you really going to turn my proposal into a negotiation?"

She laughed. "No, but my answer does have one condition."

Lucas cocked his head to one side. "Which is?"

"Maddie's blessing."

A wide grin spread across his face. "Are you kidding? The first words out of her mouth were 'flower girl.' She's been tossing petals up and down the hallway all week."

"All week?" Paige's eyes grew wide. "How did you get her to keep quiet that long?"

"It just so happens that five-and-a-half-year-olds are capable of keeping a secret. Or so I've been told. Repeatedly." They shared a quiet laugh as he removed the ring from between the two rows of satin. "So, what do you say?" His playful tone switched to a heartfelt sincerity. "Will you marry me?"

She held out her hand. "Yes, of course I'll marry you."

He looked at her outstretched hand and smiled. "You're not expecting to shake on it, are you?"

Paige rolled her eyes. The man kneeling before her had not only captured her heart, but he made her laugh every damn day, which was almost better than the orgasms he gave her nearly as often. Almost. "No," she said, wiggling her ring finger. "I thought you'd like to do the honors."

Lucas took her hand and slid the ring on her finger. When he was done, she pulled him to his feet and stepped into his arms.

"Did you buy this house?" He'd wanted to start looking at houses the moment he and Maddie had arrived in the city, but Paige had convinced him to take things slow, although the irony of that wasn't lost on her even as she spoke the words. Nothing about her relationship with Lucas had been slow. But buying property just so you could be close to a woman you wanted to try dating seemed a bit extreme, even for them. In the end, she'd convinced him to rent a house in the school district he'd selected, but after six months he told her he was ready to lay down some roots.

"I did. Thought my fiancée would love it."

Paige reared back to look at him. "Pretty confident, huh?" she teased. There was a time when her control-freak tendencies would have gone into hyperdrive over such a major decision. But when

Paige was with Lucas, she not only didn't sweat the small stuff, but even larger decisions were far less daunting. Nothing seemed to matter nearly as much now that her heart was so full of love.

"About the house or the fiancée?"

"Both."

He shook his head. "Not confident. Hopeful."

"It looks—"

"Like it needs a lot of work? I know, but wait until you see the ideas I have for fixing it up." His almost childlike enthusiasm faded ever so slightly. "Of course, if you don't like it, I can just flip it."

Paige pressed her fingers to his lips. "I was going to say it looks perfect." Lucas lowered his head and kissed her with all the emotion of a man who'd found exactly what he needed.

A tap at the bride's room door pulled her from her sweet memories. She eased the door open. "Is the coast clear?"

Lucas nodded as he slipped into the room. The sight of him took her breath away. She loved her sexy innkeeper no matter what he was wearing, and particularly when he wore nothing at all. But Lucas Croft in a tuxedo was almost too much for her brain to handle.

From the look on his face, it was safe to say she was having the same effect on him. "Damn, Paige, you look…"

When she'd asked Lucas to come to the bride's room, she hadn't really considered the fact that his reaction to seeing her in her wedding dress for the first time would be private, and not down the length of a church aisle with two hundred sets of eyes watching them. But now that they were there, hidden away from the world, not to mention their wedding guests, Paige found herself grateful for this intimate moment. Not only because of the news she was about to share, but because of the opportunity it afforded them to bask in the emotions of the day before all the craziness began.

After several long beats, Lucas swallowed, then attempted to speak. But despite his efforts to clear his throat, his voice remained rough. "Would it be bad form for me to undress you right now?"

A rush of excitement raced across her skin, and for a moment she lost all sense of place and time. But then her gaze fell to the full-length mirror behind him, and all at once she remembered standing in front of it for what felt like an eternity as she was strapped into her dress like Scarlett O'Hara. "You wouldn't be asking that if you had any idea how long it took Sammy to fasten all these buttons."

Lucas drew closer and snaked his arms around her waist. "I look forward to unbuttoning them," he said as his fingers strummed the length of her back. "Slowly."

Buttons or not, the fire burning in his eyes was damn near enough to have her consummating the marriage right then and there. He lowered his head, but Paige pulled back just before his lips touched hers.

"Ah, ah, ah," she chastised, then smiled at his wounded expression, knowing full well it was an act. "You might have seen me, but no way are you getting that kiss. Not before the priest says so." Paige might not have been much of a traditionalist, but even she drew the line somewhere.

Lucas straightened. "Fine. But Father Murphy might not approve of the kiss I have in mind."

Sweet Jesus, the man could turn her to a puddle with just the promise of a kiss. No wonder she was a knocked-up bride.

"I need to tell you something," she said.

Lucas's smile faltered. "Is something wrong?"

"Well, that depends…"

"On?"

Paige looked up at him. She hadn't thought it was possible to love him more, but in that moment her heart was so full, she felt as though it might burst.

"Do you think Maddie will mind not being an only child?"

Lucas's brows knit together. Paige watched as the momentary confusion that lit his eyes changed to excitement as her words registered. "Are you…"

Not trusting the giant lump that had formed in her throat, she merely nodded. And grinned. Huge. No doubt she looked like a lunatic, but Paige couldn't help it. She didn't think she'd ever been this happy in her entire life.

"How?"

A laugh bubbled up from deep inside her. "How?" She laughed again. "You really need me to explain it?"

"Of course I know how, but I thought… I mean, we were careful, weren't we?"

His words were a running stream of consciousness that was bouncing in six different directions.

"We were," she said. "But these things don't always work and—"

"And it's amazing," he said, cutting her off. Lucas tightened his arms around her waist and lifted her clear off the floor.

"What are you doing?" she shrieked with laughter. But he

didn't stop. Instead he swung her around in a full circle before setting her back on her feet.

"So this is good news?"

"This is spectacular news. And this day has turned out to be even better than I could have ever imagined, because I'm not only getting to marry you today, but I get to do it knowing you're carrying our child." His eyes were glassy. "I love you, Paige."

"Stop, or you're going to make me cry." And Paige Parker was *not* going to cry. Not because she couldn't, or because she thought it made her look weak—she'd come to terms with that months ago—but because she was terrified of what Sammy would do to her for ruining her makeup.

There was a knock on the door. "Paige," Sophie said from the other side. "Maddie was wondering if you were ready for her." Poor thing had probably been pacing the back of the church with her basket of rose petals.

"Should we?" Lucas asked.

Paige nodded.

He opened the door to find his sister and Maddie, each wearing a lavender dress, along with Leo, who was sporting a rather fetching lavender bow tie.

Sophie's mouth popped open. "Lucas Lancaster Croft," she said as she smacked him on the shoulder.

"You know that's not my middle name."

"And you know you're not supposed to be in here. It's bad luck to see the bride before the ceremony."

"Hey, don't look at me," he said, nodding toward Paige. "Miss Bossy Pants insisted."

"Soon to be Mrs. Bossy Pants," Paige corrected.

Maddie looked up at her dad. "Does that mean that after the wedding I can start calling you Mr. Bossy Pants?"

He swung his daughter up into his arms. "It most certainly does not." He tickled her until she giggled, something she'd been trying her best to fight lately since she was a mature woman of almost six years old, but as usual, she lost the battle. "I think you should do the honors," he told Paige as he set Maddie back on her feet.

"Can you keep a secret?" Paige asked the little girl who had stolen her heart even faster than her father had.

Her expression turned serious. "Yes, I can. Five-and-a-half-year-olds are very good at keeping secrets, and I'm almost six."

"How would you feel about being a big sister?"

Maddie's eyes grew wide. "Are we going to have a baby?"

"Yes, we are," Paige replied.

Lucas watched as his daughter threw her arms around Paige's waist. "Is this okay," she asked, looking up at Paige. "I won't hurt the baby, will I?"

"It's fine," Paige said.

Lucas dipped his head closer, stopping just before his lips touched hers. "Is this okay?" he asked, echoing his daughter's question as he attempted yet again to break tradition.

But this time Paige didn't stop him. Tradition was overrated and life wasn't always exactly how it was supposed to be.

Sometimes it was even better.

ACKNOWLEDGMENTS

When I finished this book, it had been three years since I'd typed "The End" at the bottom of a page. Throughout that tumultuous time, the people in this community of readers and writers kept me going, even when they didn't know it, which makes these acknowledgments even more important than any that came before.

To my agent, Pamela Harty, you've believed in my writing from day one and waited patiently for me to return to my laptop. I value your advice and am grateful for your friendship.

To my editor, Deb Werksman, when we met at Spring Fling, we said we hoped to work together someday. Six years and many conferences later, here we are, and I can honestly say it was worth the wait. Your notes and suggestions made this book infinitely better! And to the marketing team at Sourcebooks, especially Stefani Sloma and Katie Stutz, thank you for all your support. I hope we are celebrating various hashtag holidays for many years to come, if for no other reason than to have coffee with Freddie!

To my fellow authors, you are always ready with a text, call, or tweet of encouragement, and I'm so proud to call you friends. Jennifer Probst, Helena Hunting, Nina Bocci, and Melonie Johnson, thank you for taking the time to read and blurb my work. Abbi Glines and Julie Ann Walker, you have kept me sane (sort of), and I don't know what I would have done without you. Loretta Nyhan and Ally Hayes, I can't tell you how much I appreciate your support and counsel. Andrew Shaffer, thank you for putting up with hundreds of stupid questions. I'd like to promise there won't be any more, but we both know that isn't true. Season Vining, Rachel Goodman, and Karen Carroll, I never could have navigated these winding roads without knowing you were there if I needed to whine...or wine, as the case may be. To Jana Aston and Jen Bailey, we might talk more than we write when we meet at Starbucks or Panera, but I wouldn't have it any other way.

To the readers and bloggers, thank you from the bottom of my heart. Your messages and reviews are what keep me typing. Whether it be lusting after Hudson Chase, laughing at Olivia and Cole, or swooning over Prince Henry, you've made my world of make believe all the more real. Hopefully, Lucas and Paige will join the ranks of your all-time faves.

To Mathew Ford, who gave me the most precious gift of all, time. Without your understanding and encouragement, this book would never have made it to the page.

And finally, to Jasen Phelps, who I didn't meet until a month after I turned in this book. I will never get over the coincidence of not one, but two of my characters having the same name as people in your life, but I will also never forget the look in your eyes when you told me that I shouldn't change a thing. Your dedication to your children, and to Jenny's memory, are truly an inspiration, and I thank you for your friendship, your quick smile, and your kind heart.

ABOUT THE AUTHOR

Ann Marie Walker is the author of eight novels, ranging from romantic suspense to romantic comedy. She's a fan of fancy cocktails, anything chocolate, and '80s rom-coms. Her super power is connecting any situation to an episode of *Friends*, and she thinks all coffee cups should be the size of a bowl. You can find her at AnnMarieWalker.com, where she would be happy to talk to you about alpha males, lemon drop martinis, or Chewbacca, the Morkie who is kind enough to let her sit on his couch. Ann Marie attended the University of Notre Dame and currently lives in Chicago.

ROMANTIC COMEDY AT SOURCEBOOKS CASABLANCA

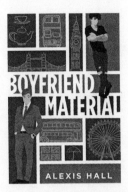

Boyfriend Material
Wanted: One (fake) boyfriend
Practically perfect in every way

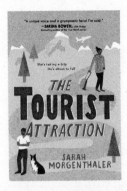

The Tourist Attraction
Welcome to Moose Springs, Alaska: a small town with a big heart, and the only world-class resort where black bears hang out to look at you!

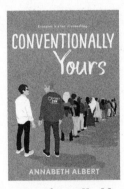

Conventionally Yours
Two infamous rivals.
One epic road trip.
Uncomfortably tight quarters
(why is there only one bed??!!)
And a journey neither
will ever forget.

Bad Bachelor
Everybody's talking about the hot new app reviewing New York's most eligible bachelors. But why focus on prince charming when you can read the latest dirt on NYC's most notorious bad boys?